Taming Dex

BOTTLES
69

TAMING DEX

69 BOTTLES #4

Zoey Derrick

Cover Design completed by Parajunkee and is copyrighted 2014 by Zoey Derrick. For more information on Parajunkee and to see her amazing work, please visit her page, www.parajunkee.net

Editing completed by Mandy Smith and Lorraine Montuori from RawBooks Editing - They've done an amazing job and I couldn't do this without them - if you need editing services - check them out: http://rawbooksonline.com

ISBN-13: 978-0996259835

The following is a work of fiction - all reference to persons, places or things is strictly coincidental. Some parts (though small)are based on fact or actual events that occurred for the author and are portrayed fictionally here.

Books by Zoey Derrick

Contemporary Romance/Contemporary Erotic Romance

Love's Wings Series:
Finding Love's Wings (Audio Coming Soon)
Chasing Love's Wings
—Box Set Now Available —

******

69 Bottles Series:
Bisexual, MMF Menage, Erotic Romance
Claiming Addison
Craving Talon
Redeeming Kyle
—3 Book Box Set Now Available —
Taming Dex
Devouring Raine - Coming July 2015
Defining Calvin Coming September 2015
Loving Eric Coming October 2015

******

One Week (Audio Coming Soon)

Paranormal Romance

Reason Series:
Give Me Reason (Audiobook available)
Give Me Hope (Audio Coming Soon)
Give Me Desire (Audio Coming Soon)
Give Me Love
— Box Set Now Available—

For the ultimate Zoey reading experience, here is a recommended reading order of stories (though not required). All books take place in the same "world".

Finding Love's Wings — 1 of 2
Chasing Love's Wings — 2 of 2
One Week — Standalone
Claiming Addison — 1 of 3
Craving Talon — 2 of 3
Redeeming Kyle — 3 of 3
Taming Dex — 1 of 2

About this world…

This world contains celebrities, rock stars, and the agents who represent them - a.k.a. Bold International, Inc.
You will find each of the characters beginning with Cami and Tristan in Finding Love's Wings will carry into the subsequent books.

For My Sweet Kelley -
My vocabulary is far to small to express the gratitude I feel towards you for being the Queen Assholian (said with the upmost love and gratitude)
and for putting up with me these last few weeks.
You're an angel! Thank you for helping me make Dex the man he is!

Please READ!!!

Have you read Claiming Addison, Craving Talon, and Redeeming Kyle?

NO? Then turn the page and enjoy Taming Dex! This books stands alone from the first three books in this series, so I truly hope you enjoy the story.

YES? Then a Disclaimer if you will.
When I wrote the first three books in this series, I had an idea of where I thought Dex would go, who he would end up with and what would happen along the way. As I started writing this story, I quickly learned that was not going to be the case.
You will notice a few discrepancies in the story - Like how Dex meets his girl, when he meets his girl and where he meets his girl. You will also notice some other subtle differences, though I tried my hardest to keep the conversations in tact as they were in Redeeming Kyle, however, some alterations had to be made.
The bottom line - THIS IS A GOOD THING!!
This also means that while you've read Redeeming Kyle, I'm pretty sure you were unable to predict all that happens in this story.
So sit back and enjoy the journey because it is one that I have truly enjoyed writing!

XX!

Zoey Derrick

Where it all begins...

"Get out," I whisper. All of my strength and any desire to fight are gone. Self-preservation takes over. Get him out of my apartment, then I can fall to pieces. "Damn you, Michael, get out," I growl.

"Let's talk about this."

I glare at him. "What. On. Earth. Is there to talk about?" I say in an exasperated huff.

"It just happened. Come on, baby."

"Fuck you! Get the fuck out of my house. I'm done. There is nothing to talk about and there is nothing to straighten out. If I was so important to you an hour ago, you wouldn't have been banging that skank in MY bed." I head straight for the bedroom door. It's the last place I want to be. It's where I saw his lily white ass bouncing up and down into her. "Leave. You're no longer welcome in my home."

I watch as he runs his hands through his too long hair. "Fine. Whatever."

With that, he leaves. Three years just went out the door...

chapter
1
raine

Six Months Later...

Knock, knock...

"Come in, Raine," the soft female voice says from behind the door.

"Thank you, ma'am." I push open the door.

"What can I do for you?" Trinity asks as she looks up from her computer monitor.

"There have been some developments with 69 Bottles. I wanted to run them by you before I called Cami."

Now I have Trinity's undivided attention. "All right. What do you have?"

I take a seat in one of the two chairs in front of her paper covered desk and press the button on my tablet, bringing it back to life. "Two things actually. First of all, Dex is making headlines with an incident that happened after the concert last night in Phoenix."

"That's Addison's area to deal with," she says without hesitation. I know this to be the case, but Trinity still needs to be aware.

'Yes ma'am, that was more a courtesy notification." She nods her understanding so I continue, "I've already attempted to make contact with Addison. I suspect however, that last night was a late night." Trinity nods again. "In fact, that's the primary reason why I'm here." I tap the play button on the video I'm saving to show Trinity and I place the tablet on her desk. The video plays for at least the fifteenth time since I found it an hour ago. I can hear Talon singing and the crowd going nuts. Then this beautiful, high octave rasp cuts across the sound. If you listen carefully you can hear the band slip just a bit.

"Well hell," Trinity exclaims as she watches the video. She doesn't say anything else until the video comes to an end. "Where was this taken?" she asks.

"Phoenix, last night."

"Cami would already know about the performance, she and Tristan were going."

"That solves that, but I wonder if she's aware that there are nearly two million views on that video."

I watch as shock and awe trade places on Trinity's face. "I haven't talked to her this morning. But let's go ahead and rectify that." She reaches for the receiver of her phone and presses two buttons and returns the phone to the cradle.

Vincent's distant voice rings through the room. "Yeah."

"Hey Vin, can you come to my office, please?"

"Yup." There is a click and then Trinity repeats the process, but dials a phone number and returns the phone back to its cradle.

The ringing sound pierces the quiet office just as the door behind me opens and in walks Vinnie. "What's up?" he asks and Trinity holds up her finger.

"I'll leave," I say.

Trinity shakes her head. Click. "Trinity, what's up?" Cami's voice comes over the speaker phone.

"Good morning. Listen, I know it's early, but Raine is here in my office with some rather interesting information. First of all, Dex is in the papers."

I hear Cami snort. "About time. But that's Addison's job."

"Right, we know," Trinity, says. "Just giving you a heads up on that, but there's more."

"Okay?" Cami responds hesitantly.

"Were you at the concert last night?" Trinity asks.

"I was."

"So you saw Addison's performance?" Trinity raises an eyebrow at me, I shrug. Cami and Tristan going to the concert is news to me. Though it's really their personal business.

"Yeah I did, was completely blown away by it. I'd planned to call you this morning to discuss what I saw and what to do next. I want to sign her."

"Well, I would fucking hope so," Trinity remarks, and the curse word is so out of character for her that I see Vinnie raise an eyebrow at her.

"Whoa Trin, that's unusual for you." Cami indirectly calls out our speculation.

"She is approaching two million video views." Trinity smiles at Vinnie who I can see is now a little more than intrigued. I grab my tablet off of Trinity's desk and hand it to him.

"No way? You're kidding right?" Cami says in disbelief.

"Two million two hundred thousand and counting," Vinnie says.

"Raine?"

"Yes, Cami."

"I can't come in, I'm in Phoenix. I'm going to need you to get a few things together for me. I will email you the list, all right?"

"Yes, Cami. Whatever you need."

"Trinity, Vin, I don't care what it is going to take, she's ours," Cami orders.

"You got it," Vinnie and Trinity say together.

"All right, let's get to work. Keep this between the three of you for right now. Trinity, use Raine for anything pertaining to this."

There's a knock on the door. "Come in," Trinity calls.

"I'm sorry to interrupt, but..." Becky, an admin, says as she walks in with a stack of phone messages in her hand. "These have all just come in over the last twenty minutes." Becky hands Trinity the stack of paper.

"Thank you, Becky," Trinity says and she dutifully leaves the room. I want to roll my eyes because now I know she is going to bug the shit out of me when I get back to my desk.

"Trinity, what's up?" Cami says through the phone.

"Who is taking point on Addison?" Trinity asks.

"We are. The three of us. I don't want someone else handling it, especially since she is already an employee."

"Okay, good because Becky just handed me at least twenty phone messages, press and labels, all wanting to know who the girl in the video is."

"Shit," Cami barks into the phone. "All right, damn it. Give me a little bit. Let me organize myself and figure out what to do next. I've got company coming into town this afternoon. Let me talk to Tristan and see if I can hop over there."

"Not necessary," Vinnie says. "We can handle the calls. We will deal with the press, no comment sounds good for now. As far as the labels are concerned, if they're this eager, they're not going anywhere."

"All right," Cami says through the phone. I feel like I'm getting whiplash with all the back and forth. I feel like an outsider.

"Cami, I can put together a press release," I interject without really thinking. "That way we can announce it as a whole. Step ahead of the masses before they overrun the building. I can also curb the labels with it."

"Excellent idea. Thank you, Raine. Go ahead and forward it to the three of us when it's done. In the meantime, keep screening the calls and taking messages. Don't let any of them through. We can't very well do anything without talking to Addison. Vinnie, let's discuss contract options in a little while. Let's figure out what we can do, what we can offer, etcetera, then go from there."

"Fair enough," Trinity says.

"All right, keep me posted, and Raine?"

"Yes ma'am?" I know Cami cringes but sometimes it is just far more appropriate.

"Good catch."

I smile. Both Trinity and Vincent smile too. "Thank you, Cami."

"Let's get to work," Cami says and disconnects the phone.

I spend a few minutes taking notes for Trinity and Vincent, like the dutiful assistant I am, before returning to my desk. "What is going on?" Becky asks as soon as I come to stand behind my desk.

I take a deep breath. "Nothing. How are the phones?"

"Insane." Becky lifts up another stack of messages.

I shake my head. "Okay, keep collecting them. Any messages outside of press or labels separate them from the stack and be sure to get those to Trinity as soon as possible. The rest can wait." I sit down and wiggle my computer mouse, waking my computer back up and get started on my press release.

More than an hour later and fifteen various emails between Trinity, Vincent, Cami and myself, I have finished the press release. I notice idly that there is an awful lot of information that I am being copied on, information that I normally see in Cami's email, never in mine. I can't help but wonder what that is all about. I shrug it off for the time being and send the press release to Cami for final approval before I head down to the cafeteria to grab some lunch.

chapter
2
dex

Meanwhile in Phoenix...

"Nope, I'm wide fucking awake," I bark as I walk into Talon's suite. I walk straight up to Addison. "Look Addison, I'm really fucking sorry about what I did last night. I promise it won't happen again." I can't feel the conviction of the words I've just said to her. I am so pissed off but I want to believe that this will not happen again, but reality is exactly that.

I watch as relief washes over her beautiful features. Talon is one lucky bastard. Those luscious lips are enough to make any man crazy. "Dex?"

"Yeah."

"Breathe. You were set up last night."

"Fuck me," I say. "How so?"

I watch her carefully, she looks like she's fighting a smile and it pisses me off. "Well, one of your little blonde bimbos was approached and offered five hundred dollars to seduce you, drug you, and then finally fuck you."

Why the fuck would someone pay to set my ass up? "Five hundred?" I ask, raising an eyebrow, desperately trying to cut the tension I am feeling. "That's the going rate for rock star sex these days?" I laugh. It's not funny, but I would have figured I was worth way more than that. I mean, hell, I can handle a whole gang of girls at once.

Addison laughs. "Well, see, the person doing the paying said that she needed proof or Blondie wasn't going to get paid. So I'm guessing sometime after you passed out Blondie did her job and sent out the pictures to her point of contact and that person then turned around and sold the story to news outlets across the country, or maybe it was just one, we're not sure yet. But anyway, they pocket the cash, scamming not only you, but Blondie as well. I'm guessing those pictures grossed, maybe fifty grand." Her eyes dart to where the bodyguards were standing when I came into the room, but I don't follow her gaze before she continues. "If the contact was smart, that is. Now here's the real kicker. The point of contact could have and probably should have used an anonymous email so that we couldn't trace the pictures. But the middle man wasn't that smart."

"Well, what the fuck?" I stutter. "I've never in my life…well, fuck. I don't even know…shit." Speechlessness is not something I'm used to, so I look away from Addison, toward the circle of men in black. Standing in the middle is, fuck, what's her name? Kate? Kyle's assistant. "What's she doin' here?"

Addison smirks. "Dex, meet the point of contact. Who I'm guessing is pretty pissed because she didn't get fifty g's for the pictures."

"Fucking hell," she spits out.

"So Kate, how much did you get for the pictures? You know, for curiosity's sake," I ask her. She doesn't answer me. I'm not sure I can blame her, but looking at her now, actually paying attention to her, she's oddly familiar and I don't know why. "I know you. How do I know you? Why did I never see it before?"

"Because you're too busy sticking your dick into some bitch's cunt," Kate snarls back at me and I see Addison take a step back. Kate has always been awkward when I've seen her. It's almost comical seeing her so pissed off. But I'm baffled by what has her so pissed off.

"Well now, aren't we feisty? So tell me, darlin', what exactly have I done to you to make you want to pull a stunt like this?" I ask her. I can tell that pulling information from her is going to be nearly impossible.

"No way, Dex, you didn't fuck her, did you?" Addison asks me.

"Hell if I know."

Kate starts bawling and everyone in the room freezes. "What on earth would make you want to do something like this, Kate?" Kyle starts walking toward her, but he stops a few feet in front of her. That's probably best because god only knows what she's capable of right now.

"He..." She cries louder. "He's responsible for my sister. He's the reason she tried to commit suicide. He's the reason she's gone crazy."

My mouth falls open. "What?"

"Stacy, do you remember her, asshole? Do you remember what you did to her? She was my sister and you fucking dumped her so that you could go off whoring around with whoever you wanted. It's all your fault," she sobs.

"She understood, she said she fucking understood. Now you show up here, trying to blackmail me, when she said she fucking understood." I can't help the rising irritation in my voice. Stacy and I made a mutual decision back then. What the fuck is this girl trying to do?

"She wasn't enough for you. She was never enough, you always wanted more than her, and yet she stood by you, was there for you every night, then you just dumped her like yesterday's garbage."

"How much, Kate? How much did you get for the pictures?" I ask her. I need to know, I need to start rectifying this situation. I feel slightly responsible, but in the same token, I don't.

"I needed money. I need money to pay for her hospital. I fucking need to save her," she wails.

"How much, Kate?" I say to her.

"Ten grand," Kate blurts.

"I didn't know, Kate. Honest to god, I didn't know." My voice is eerily soft.

"If you cared about her at all, you would have never left her like you did, you would have never put her in the position she's in."

"So you decide to use me to get money for her? Did it ever occur to you that I might actually help her?" Kate's eyes dart to mine, confused, shocked, I don't really give a fuck. I'm pissed off, yet overwhelmed by what she's done and the reason why...I don't even know what she's talking about, Stacy and I broke up a long time ago, and it wasn't like we were together, together.

"She doesn't need your fucking money, Dex. She needed you."

Addison steps in between Kate and I. "This is no longer my concern, or anyone else's for that matter. If you want to continue talking to Kate, that's your choice, and I highly recommend it. But at this point, I think you need to take it to a private location. Without the audience." Addison looks at Kate and then back to me before she leans in and whispers, "Keep one of the guys with you, for safety, they won't judge you. But you really should talk to her. Talk to her before this turns into something bigger than it needs to be. This is personal and private, try and keep it that way."

I nod and look at Kate. "Will you come with me? Talk to me some more?"

"I have nothing left to say," she says snottily.

Addison straightens her spine and approaches her. She's on the defensive. If I wasn't so fucking hung-over and twitchy, I might have gotten a semi watching her. "You wanted his attention, you got it."

"She was supposed to leave before sending me the pictures so this wouldn't have come out," Kate says to Addison. She's retreating, retracting and regretting her course of actions. I can't help but want to smile.

"Well, it did, and I'm sure I speak for Kyle and the label when I tell you that you're fired. This might be your last chance to talk to him. Give him details on your sister and her condition. Believe it or not, I really do believe he had no idea and that he wants to help. Let him talk to you." Addison's voice is soft, but I'm shocked over the fact that Addison fired her. That's really Kyle's area. But I shrug it off.

"Fuck you," Kate snarls at Addison. I notice Talon and Kyle both twitch in Addison's direction, ready to protect her at a moment's notice. Addison straightens a little further.

"Listen here, Kate, I am not your enemy. I feel sorry for your sister, honestly I do, but this is no way to help her. You've got ten grand now, but what about when you need more money, what next? Talk to him, work it out with him. Pinning this on him isn't fair."

She finally nods and I take that as my cue. I nod at Beck who precedes us from the room. Just before the door closes behind us I hear Addison telling someone, "Make sure she gets her stuff off the bus and out of her hotel room. Get her on a plane to wherever she needs to go and get her away from the band. We don't need another incident like this popping up, at least not like this."

chapter
3
dex

I usher Beck and Kate into my suite. It's still a mess from last night. I need to get the fuck out of here. I pray to god they got the coke out of here before now. Jesus, I don't need that temptation. It's bad enough I can feel that familiar ache burning in my veins. My desire for another line is growing stronger by the minute. I do not want to take it out on Kate, but unfortunately I'm wound tighter than a guitar string.

"All right Kate, you've got to understand something," I say as soon as Beck closes the door behind us.

"Does he have to be here?" She points at Beck.

"Yes, I don't trust you. You've already gone to a pretty big extreme with the stunt you pulled last night. He's here for my protection and yours," I tell her, my voice grows higher with anxiety. "Look Kate, I don't owe Stacy anything. I'm sorry she's sick, but fuck, Kate, it's been three years."

She sits down on the couch. "That's how long she's been in there."

I shrug. "Look Kate, I'm sorry for what Stacy is going through, but you know as much as anyone what kind of life this is. You know as well as I do that Stacy wasn't cut out for the road life. She wanted things that I don't. She deserves things that I can't give her," I tell her as I cross my arms and lean against the wall. Stacy and I were never really together. I could never bring myself to fuck her like all the other girls, but that was because within a few hours of meeting me, she was all 'I love you, Dex'. Okay fine, it wasn't that dramatic, but it was pretty fucking close. I tried for weeks to get it through her head that I wasn't interested like that. She wanted so much more than I was willing to give her.

She doesn't say anything, but I can see the fight leaving her body. "Look Kate, I will help for a little while because I don't need further blackmail from you."

"Look, I'm sorry. I didn't know what else to do."

"You could have talked to me, Kate," I tell her. I step away from the wall, walking closer to her. "You could have told me who you are. We would have discussed this. But instead you feed me the two things I can't resist. Women and coke. Fuck, Kate. I've been sober for more than four years. I fight my addiction every day, and I sure as hell fight it every night." I watch as the reality of what I'm telling her sets in. "Do you have any idea what that's like? Fighting addiction?" She shakes her head. "It's not easy."

"It was just one time."

"It only takes one time." I sit down on the couch opposite her. I put my hands in my hair and my elbows on my knees. I can't remember doing the coke. I can't remember the high. I can't remember anything about last night.

"Dex, I'm sorry."

"Which part?" I grumble.

"The coke."

"So that makes blackmailing me okay?" I ask deadpan.

"No. I… I didn't know what else to do."

"She's not my responsibility. I think you're holding the wrong person accountable for Stacy's choices," I tell her. She doesn't say anything. Fine. I don't really care. There were a lot of great times with Stacy and I would never deny that, but she wasn't the right girl for me. I cheated on her more times than she deserved and frankly, it wasn't right for either of us. I saw my choices with drugs and alcohol taking their toll on her and she deserved better than that. "I will help you out, pay for her medical expenses for the next three months, but then that's it. There is something more going on with her and maybe someone needs to get to the bottom of it. I'm certain there is more to it than just me. You guys didn't exactly have the best upbringing, there's way more going on under the surface than you or maybe even she realizes. Get her a different doctor, move her to a different facility, I don't care, but be there with her, help her get to the bottom of this."

"I can't afford to…"

"Considering you just lost your job, I'm pretty sure you can find something closer to her. Look," I stand up from the couch, "I can't and won't help forever, three months, that's it. If at that point she isn't any better, then you need to figure out what to do from there. But if I catch you anywhere near me or find out that you're lurking around somewhere or you show up at a concert, I will call the cops. She's not my responsibility."

I lean against the wall and look at her. Her shoulders are slumped and she's completely deflated. She still doesn't say anything. I let her sit for a minute and process what I've told her. Though I am trying to be nice about all this, it's not my responsibility, not anymore.

"All right, Dex, you win."

I let out a heavy sigh. "This isn't about winning, Kate. No one is winning anything. I won't have you trying to ruin my career over something that is not my fault."

She looks me square in the eyes before speaking. "For what it's worth, I'm sorry."

I shake my head and fight the urge to roll my eyes. "It's not worth much. At least not until this mess is swept under the rug and I know I'm not going to relapse. Until then..." I don't finish the thought. I think I've made her feel bad enough already, no need to go into the fact that the familiar ache of addiction is starting to course white hot through my veins. After a beat I say, "I think we're done here."

She makes no move to get up. I look at Beck. He has concern in his eyes when they meet mine. I try to shake it off and I nod in her direction. "Get her information, make sure I have what I need to send the money to the hospital and get her out of here," I say sharply and turn toward the bedroom.

Shutting the door, I lock myself inside, heading straight for the bathroom. I need a cold fucking shower.

My hand trembles as I reach for the faucet. My heart starts to race and panic rises. *I wonder if they left any in my suite.*

It's in that moment that the guitar string snaps under the tension. I don't remember who I am anymore. Like a moth lured by the warm light, addiction has taken over my rational thoughts.

Stopping at nothing, turning anything and everything upside down.

If it isn't here...

I start to contemplate how long it will take me to score. What can I score the fastest? It's the middle of the damn day.

Shit.

Fuck.

I freeze, my body shaking, my heart racing, panic replaced by a rushing sense of relief when I find what I was looking for all along.

It's small.

It's barely enough to make a dent.

But it's more than enough to make the burn go away.

More than enough to satisfy the craving.

chapter
4
dex

"Dex!" I hear someone, Beck, shouting and pounding on the bedroom door. "Fuck Dex, open the damn door." His pounding persists. I can't move away from the bathroom sink where I stare blankly at myself in the mirror while I have a fresh line of coke stacked, a twenty in my hand, rolled and ready to go. "God damn it, Dex, don't you fucking do it," Beck shouts, but his voice is in a vacuum, having very little effect on me. I hear him, but my mind won't process his words.

My body won't move.

The monumental consequences lie before me.

The choices.

What happens right now will either be the beginning or the end.

I slowly roll the twenty between my fingers.

Staring, contemplating.

Cure the burn.
Satisfy the itch.
Destroy my career.

More pounding. Harder, more persistent. I lean forward, bringing the twenty to my nose, ready to suck the sweet powder into my system and take it all away. Wash away the pain, wash the ache down the drain and piss away years of sobriety...

"Don't."
I freeze.
"Jesus, Dex, I'm sorry. I thought we got it all."
Beck's voice is the light I need. Our eyes meet in the mirror. Compassion and pity.
"Don't fucking pity me," I bark, returning to my previous focus. The snow, laid out all nice and pretty. Ready...
"I don't pity you, Dex. Never have I ever pitied you and I won't start now. You're better, stronger than this."
"It fucking hurts."
"I know. Come on. Walk away from it. You can do it. I'll make it go away."
"It never goes away. It's always there in the back of my mind, in the pit of my stomach, the need to do it, the need to feel it coursing through my veins."
Beck comes to stand behind me. If anyone can pull me out of this, it's him. He's so close I can feel his body heat. I want to lash out at him. To fight him, to push him, to take out everything on him. His hand grips my wrist. "Don't," he whispers. "Drop it. Come on, man. We'll go find a woman, we'll go get inked, we'll do fucking anything, but not this. Not here. Not after all this time."

Every sensation is heightened, every sound is a million times louder, and everything is in slow motion. I hear my fingers snap, like a rubber band and watch as the rolled up twenty falls to the counter and unravels slowly, loudly.

I let out a long rush of air, scattering my line and I fall on my ass. "Take it away, all of it. Get it out of here."

I lean back against the wall, pulling my knees to my chest and I put my head against my knees, unable to watch Beck flush the bag.

I can hear him hustling to get rid of it as fast as he can. I jump the moment the toilet flushes.

Beck leaves the bathroom. I can tell by the sound of his shitkickers against the carpet. When he comes back again, I don't look at him but the toilet flushes again.

"It's gone," he says softly.

"All of it?" I breathe out.

"Yes."

"Good, get me the fuck out of here."

I put my hand up and Beck pulls me to my feet and he looks me square in the eyes. "We cool?"

I shoulder check him and give him a half-assed smile. "We're cool."

Fifteen minutes later, Beck, Leroy, Mouse, Peacock and myself are packed like sardines into the SUV they've acquired for the weekend. "Where we going?" I finally manage to ask. I don't feel anything like myself. In fact, I feel almost as though I'm outside looking in.

"Food," Mouse answers. I nod absently. "Then ink."

The idea cheers me slightly. I don't know what the fuck is bothering me more. The bullshit with Kate, dragging up Stacy or the fact that I've pissed on four years of sobriety and that I feel like I have to start over. What I really need is a cunt to slide my dick into, but I'll settle for the ink.

I got my first tattoo when I was 17. My left hand slides along my right side, just under my peck. Remembering the pain, remembering the torture and finally remembering how the excruciating pain was so intense that it brought me to tears. The tears I so desperately needed to shed. I'm pretty sure that my tattoo artist got an erotic rush of enjoyment out of torturing me that day. All tattoo artists have to be sadistic in some way or another. Whether it's sexual gratification or just the slight joy of inflicting pain on their subjects, either way requires a sadistic streak. Never trust a tattoo-less tattoo artist. They, in my experience, are the worst. I swear to god when they're done, they run off to the bathroom and stroke the fucking monkey.

"Here," Beck says from the driver's seat. I look out the passenger side of the SUV and we're somewhere called Fajitas. I have no idea where the hell we are, just that we're somewhere in Phoenix. The five of us pile out of the car and head toward the door. Beck stays back with me.

"Hey," I say.

"How you doin?" Beck asks.

I shrug. "I feel like shit."

"Physically or…"

"Emotionally. I feel like I've been fucking run over and I fucking hate it." He doesn't say anything in return. Beck, of all fucking people, is the one man who's always fucking there for me, bailing my ass out and sometimes getting into trouble with me too. Despite his asshole exterior, Beck's a pretty decent guy who just likes to let loose once in a while like the rest of us.

"Dude." He stops.

I stop next to him. "What?" He turns to face me and looks down. "What the fuck, dude?" I follow his gaze and see what he sees. My right hand scratching and picking at my arm. I freeze, separating my arms. "Fuck." I just stand there looking at my elbow, it's not bleeding yet, but it was damn close. "Shit," I say again.

"There is no judgement here, you fucking know that. Do I need to take you in?"

"Fuck, I don't know," I mumble. I light a cigarette. Don't go jumping down my throat. It's how I handle nerves, plus it will keep my hands busy, at least for a few minutes. I'm not my usual confident self and this is what's bringing me down. I haven't found my stride again. "No, damn it. I won't. I can do this. This isn't the first time I've fucked up, I doubt it will be my last."

"Dex, I'm serious. I'll take you in."

"What the fuck are they going to do anyway? I fucking used one time. I was drunk as a fucking skunk and I don't actually remember doing it. It's all in my head."

"I doubt that. Your body remembers more than your mind is capable of..."

"Fuck that crap. I need therapy more than I need detox, Beck." I stomp out my cigarette.

He nods his understanding. "Then let's start with food therapy."

I look at the entrance to the restaurant. The other guys are already inside. "Fine," I grumble and start walking. Beck falls into step beside me and we enter the restaurant. The guys are waiting to our right, up a couple of steps and Beck points to them, indicating to the hostess that we're with them.

"You good?" Peacock asks.

I just nod and take a seat.

Within a few minutes we have chips and salsa and alcohol on their way. The moment the chips touch my lips and the burn of the hot salsa slides down my throat, I can feel my shakes subsiding and my panic ebbing to the point that I can concentrate again.

I take more comfort in the fact that while I'm running out of painful areas for ink; I know pain therapy is in my near future.

chapter
5
dex

Pain therapy worked, but only marginally and temporarily. I long for the day when I can feel the blistering pain I once felt that cleansed me of my emotional distress. Yeah, I sound like a fucking dipshit, but whatever. If you've never tried it, maybe you should.

By the time we hit the bar that night I am slowly starting to feel at least a little bit better. Thanks to the burning sensation from my fresh ink. Though this one was small, it was a decent reminder of who I am, where I am and where I belong.

We spent the next night with Cami, Tristan and their friends, followed by an impromptu concert of sorts. Well okay, it was more for Talon and Addison than it was for me and the rest of the guys. But, whatever. My suspicions were confirmed when I watched Addison kiss Talon then turn around and kiss Kyle. I'm no dummy, I know that T & K have shared women before, but this is quite obviously different between the three of them.

In all the years that I've known Talon, I've never known him to be one for the guys, but with Kyle I always had my suspicions. Eventually I'll figure it out. But it doesn't stop me from ribbing Addison. Fuck, she's gorgeous but she'd be like every other woman who's sucked my cock. Pump and dump.

The impromptu concert was the second step in my therapy and recovering from a one night breakdown. Banging away on the drums has always been, and will always be, the best outlet for me. No matter how strung out I am, I find the pain, I find the drive to hit harder, to work harder, and to play like an animal. Though the concert wasn't for me, it was still nice to pound away. I know once we're back on the road, things will be better. I can change my focus to playing. Plus getting out of Phoenix, leaving the place where I fucked up, will make it that much sweeter.

By the time we hit Albuquerque, I am in a better mood and finally starting to feel back to my old self. I needed to get out of Phoenix and I told Beck as much. It took him a damn bit of convincing for me to stick around, telling me that the dinner with Cami and Tristan was pretty much a requirement. I wanted to fly out of Phoenix ahead of the guys, but decided I should stay. I was so fucking glad I did when Talon finally spilled the beans about 'Your Eyes' striking the top of the charts. That alone made staying worth it.

"Let me shower," I tell Mouse after the Albuquerque show.

"Yeah okay," he tells me as he returns to the greenroom.

Fuck, tonight was almost too much on me. To say that I feel strung out is an understatement. After the last few days, it's taken everything I have not to get shit faced or track down some fucking snow. I knew I was going to need something to get me through this show. But some way, some fucking how, I managed.

I step under the spray of hot water. Every muscle in my arms and chest are killing me. I haven't felt this worn out after a show in a long time. I want to crawl into my rack and pass out. But Mouse convinced me to go out tonight. It was our last show with Empty Chamber before they go on to another tour and we head into Texas.

The prospect of going out revitalizes me and for the first time in three days, my dick stirs at the thought of finding someone to suck me off. I close my eyes, soaking in the idea of finishing off my own brand of therapy by banging some chick in the bathroom.

By the time I'm done washing, my dick is hard as steel. I grip my cock hard. Holding it at the base, watching the head swell and grow darker as the blood flow is cut off. "Fuck," I groan and start to stroke it. "Fuck." I lean forward, putting my head against my forearm on the wall and stroke harder, faster, base to tip. Just let me fucking get off.

Fuck…

Ten minutes and a mind blowing orgasm later, I'm drying off. Though now that I've woken the monster, he won't subside. He knows what he needs. He needs a warm wet mouth to sink balls deep into. I snort. "Yeah, that would be fucking great," I grumble. "Because so many women have taken all of you before." I roll my eyes at myself and slide my still damp legs into a pair of ripped up jeans, and check the back pocket. Yup, they're still there. Finally I throw on a black t-shirt. Running my fingers through my still wet hair, I join the guys in the greenroom. I shake my head as Addison is surrounded by fans thrusting autograph books in her face.

I smirk. "Hey brother." I turn to Talon. "Nice job tonight."

"You weren't so bad yourself," I tell him as we take hands and bump chests. "How's she handling this?" I nod in Addison's direction.

Talon snorts a laugh. "Far better than we ever did."

"Ha! Says you. I was only looking for whose pants I could talk my way into. I didn't give a shit."

Talon laughs. "This is true. You doing all right, man?"

I look at him, serious. "I'm getting there."

"You know we're all here for you," Kyle says over my shoulder.

I release Talon and turn to Kyle. "Yeah, I know."

"We've all been there and I have no doubt that one day we'll all be back there again at some point," Kyle says and we bump forearms.

"Yeah. Let's get this over with. I need a drink," I tell them both, avoiding the conversation and the direction it's going.

When we're finally done catering to the hoard of obnoxious fans, I've found at least one so far to strike my fancy and I invite her along. Don't bother asking her name, because I'll be damned if I could tell you. I'll be damned if I give a shit. The minute they have a name is the minute I either start to care too much or don't pay attention anymore.

Pop.

Pop.

Pop.

Go the buttons on my button fly.

Shit, her hands are fucking cold as she wraps her dainty fingers around my shaft. She tries pulling me free. I grab her chin, forcing her to look up at me. Her dull green eyes stare back at me. I shake my head subtly. "You'll never free him like that, sweetheart." I release her chin and grab my jeans, pulling them down. My dick springs free and smacks her right in the face. I bite my lip to stop from laughing. The shocked look on her face is enough to make me snort a laugh, but she's too wide-eyed to pay attention to any other head than the monster.

"Jesus, you're fucking huge." She beams up at me. That's right, sweetheart, let's see how much you can handle.

Her cold hands double fist my cock and she starts to stroke. Oh come on... I wrap my hands around hers and squeeze tighter. I groan and she continues stroking me.

Within about five strokes, I'm bored.

I take my dick in my hands and position it against her lips, pressing gently and she looks up at me with fear in her eyes. "It's all right, sweetheart. You can take it."

She sticks her tongue out and strokes the purple head against her bright pink tongue. "Ahh, that's it, baby. Suck it," I tell her, hoping to encourage her.

For as fucking slutty as she was when we got to the bar, I half expected her to be cramming my dick down her throat, but we get back here and she's gun shy.

Finally I feel her warm wet mouth wrap around the head of my cock. "That's it, baby. Take it." Her hands have stilled and she's just barely working the tip in her tiny little mouth. I put my hands in her hair, hoping to help encourage her to take me deeper into her wet mouth, but

I'll be damned, she resists me. I fight the urge to roll my eyes. This is so not what I needed or wanted tonight.

Think of me as a pig if you want, but I needed a girl to worship my cock like it's the best thing on the planet and I manage to find the flirty and hesitant goody-fucking-two-shoes.

Oh... Okay, that was a little better. "That's it, baby. Yeah, suck that cock." My words of encouragement spur her on, but it doesn't improve her skills any.

I wonder idly how often girls think they're great at giving head when in reality, they suck. No pun intended.

I am about three and a half seconds away from pulling her off my dick, bending her over and fucking her stupid, but her tentative nature tells me that I'd be taking far more from her than she is giving me. There are just some girls you know are either virgins or highly inexperienced and in this case, I'm not sure which. I pray to the rock gods that someone, anyone, something, I don't give a fuck what, will interrupt this train wreck. I close my eyes, hoping against hope that not looking at her will make it feel just a little bit better.

Nope.

I grunt and groan at the appropriate places, but unless I'm going to pound it into her, I can't fake getting off.

Ring...

Ring...

Thank fuck.

"Sorry, baby, I gotta take this."

I look at the phone. Beck, thank fuck. "Yeah?"

"Dude, we're leaving."

"Be out in a minute."

I hang up.

"Sorry, sweetheart, my ride's leaving." I extract myself from her hands and mouth. She looks absolutely crestfallen, but I don't give a shit. I button up, stuff my phone back in my pocket and leave her there with a shocked expression on her face.

"Remind me to kiss you later," I tell Beck as he meets me at the door.

He laughs. "I could kind of tell." I raise my eyebrow at him. "Seriously? Dude, you're usually far more vocal than that. You sounded rehearsed."

I snort. "We actually leaving?"

"Nah, but…"

"Fuck it, let's go," I tell him and he says something into his mic, probably telling Mills we're bailing.

Twenty minutes later, I'm in my rack, my curtain is closed, my headphones are in and porn flashes before my eyes as I desperately try to rub out the hard-on she couldn't make go away.

chapter
6
dex

Sometime during the night, we pulled out of Albuquerque and headed for Galveston. We spent the better part of a day and a half on the bus. It sucked royally. Especially considering the walls on this damn thing are paper thin and Talon and Kyle make no secret of their enjoyment of Addison. Lucky bastards.

The show in Galveston went great. We wrapped up, hung out and bailed. We have a show in Dallas tomorrow night and have to get up there.

By the time the Dallas show is over, I'm covered in sweat and my arms are killing me. Drumming becomes a great outlet for sexual frustration. I even managed to gather a few sideways glances from the guys during the set. I don't give a shit; I think I play better when my dick is hard and untouched. Finally we get a night out.

We've managed to pick up a group of unruly idiots for the next leg of the tour and I don't take to them very well. What can I say; I'm not a people person. They're a bunch of douchebags. I don't pay them much attention. I just want to get out of here and find something to stick my dick into. Anything has got to be better than the last groupie.

When we arrive at the bar, there is a circle of couches in the middle and we take it over. Most of the people here tonight were at the concert, as evidenced by their t-shirts, and other attire. Not to mention the overwhelming welcome we had walking into the joint.

I barely finish half a beer before chick number one approaches me. Meh, she's cute, but there are far better in here tonight. "Sorry, sweetheart, I've got someplace else to be," I tell her. It wasn't gentle and she gets the hint. Though I can see the girl crush wheels turning in her head for whatever girl manages to capture my attention tonight. By the time I finish my second beer, I've turned down three more girls, though Mouse is charming one of them. Maybe she'll get lucky there. Though I wish he'd realize who the fuck he really is. Good looks get that man laid, but he has no skills when it comes to picking them up. I watch as Peacock surreptitiously watches Mouse from the other side of our circle. Though he isn't lacking for chicks surrounding him, there is more hiding beneath the surface for Peacock than he lets on. Who knows, maybe one day he'll finally spill the beans and come out of the closet. Then again, it's just a theory.

I watch Talon with Addison. He is ridiculously lovey-dovey with her and I wonder what is so special about her. She's managed to ensnare both him and Kyle, our band's manager. They're both chatting with Kyle. Addison eye fucks Kyle like I once eye fucked her. Oh, what I wouldn't give to conquer that piece of ass. Anyway, Kyle is turning down women left and right. I don't know why he feels the need to be so far away from Talon and Addison. I mean, shit, we all know the three of them are working something together. I cock an eyebrow as I realize Talon is looking at Kyle too. Hmmm? Could it be that they're all together, together? I snort.

Finally something I can work with approaches. Brown shoulder length hair, too much makeup, bright 'fuck me' red lipstick. My eyes travel south. I want to roll them when I notice she's wearing a modified Bottles shirt. But then my eyes land on super short shorts, the kind where the bottoms of the pockets hang out. Some very nicely shaped and tanned legs, and her feet are trapped in some black strappy five-inch heels. She smiles. I knew there was a flaw. Fuck it. She's fuckable.

"Hey, you're Dex, right?"

I put on my charming smile and sit up a little straighter. "I am, sweetheart." I pat my thigh and she takes the hint. She slides between my legs and sits down. In a seemingly innocent gesture, I feel her hand slide along my semi. Her eyes widen just a fraction. "Having a good time?" I ask.

She leans into me. "I'll have a better time when you take me into the back room."

My eyes widen marginally. "Well, what are we waiting for?" And no, I don't bother to ask her for her name. She may have said it at some point, but I'm better when I don't know. Gives me an excuse to call her names like baby and sweetheart and it seems an endearment, when in reality, I just don't know her name.

She stands up and I follow her after I set my bottle down on the table. Mouse gives me a sly smirk as we pass. When we clear the couches I turn to her, gesturing toward the back of the bar. "After you." She smiles at me again and leads the way. We weave our way through the crowd.

I can feel Beck behind me. I turn my head in his direction and smirk. Beck just rolls his eyes and shakes his head. I mouth to him, "Join us?" He shakes his head again. Pity. I look back to Red Lips and watch as she sways from hip to hip as she navigates the bar in her heels.

Finally we come to a closed door. She opens it and I hold it open, ushering her inside. Once she's inside, I close and lock it, then push her against the counter. Taking her head in my hands, I slam my lips over hers. She's taken aback briefly but quickly melts into my body. My semi grows, but only slightly. There is very little passion in her kiss. No matter. I don't stay there for long. I move my hands and start kissing along her jaw, down her neck, then along the exposed shoulder of her modified t-shirt.

My hands have nothing else to do, so they slide up her sides and she lets out a breathy moan. I twitch against the zipper of my jeans. My hands come up to roughly grab her tits. Mmm, not bad. Maybe a big B or small C. I feel her nipples harden as I realize there's no bra between us. I smile against her shoulder. "What do you want?" I breathe.

"You."

"I know that, what do you want me to do?" I roll her nipples between my thumbs and forefingers. Her back arches. I pull my hands back and lift her onto the counter. She settles in and I go back to massaging her nipples. Her back arches again and she moans. "You haven't answered my question. I won't ask again."

She still doesn't answer but instead she goes for the hem of her t-shirt. Pulling it up, I let go of her tits and she ditches the shirt. Nice. Round, perky nipples stand out at me. My mouth instantly lands on one and I suck it into my mouth, rolling the other with my fingers. I feel her tugging on my shirt. I back off with a pop and she pulls my shirt over my head. Her hands slide down my pecks to my abs and to the button on my jeans. Mmm, I love the ones that take charge.

Pop.

Pop.

Pop, go my buttons and in go her hands, trying to free me. I push my jeans down and remember slapping the last chick in the face. I fight my urge to laugh by taking her other nipple into my mouth while her hands wrap around my cock. The contact is warm and mildly firm. She tugs and pulls, eliciting a groan from me. My hands go to the button of her shorts and she pushes her hips forward, inviting me in as she continues to stroke my cock in her hands.

After a couple more strokes, I pull back from her tits and stand up, pushing my jeans further down my thighs. I step back and grab my cock from her hand and start to stroke it. "Take em off," I demand and she jumps down from the counter. She unbuttons and lowers her shorts, revealing a bright green thong and a very bald pussy. Yes.

Once she's lost her shorts, she starts to climb back on the counter. I shake my head and wave my cock at her. She smiles and lowers herself to her knees. "That a girl," I say softly as she takes my cock into her hands once again. Then her bright red lips wrap around the head of my cock. Much better, I think to myself as I close my eyes, savoring her touch and her hot mouth wrapped around my dick. "That's it, baby, suck my cock. You like that, don't you?"

She answers by humming and it tickles my balls. I groan and she continues. She keeps this up... she doesn't stop and I don't stop her. She keeps stroking and sucking. I feel my balls shrink up and my cock twitches. The head swells as I'm about to unload. One of her hands moves to massage my balls and she backs off sucking. "Don't stop," I growl. She begins sucking vigorously, intentionally trying to make me come. Fine with me. I take hold of her head and begin helping her. Fucking her mouth. It takes only a few strokes before I'm exploding with a grunt and a growl. My load comes too hard and fast for her. She chokes and I look at her just as my cum starts seeping out of her mouth.

It's a gorgeous sight. Whether they're choking on my cock or cum, it makes no difference to me. She looks up at me and she looks petrified. I guess I should have warned her before exploding down her throat. She probably thinks I'm done and it was a waste to get butt fucking naked. But once I'm finally done coming down her throat, I help her up and lift her back onto the counter before I spread her legs and bury my face into her dripping wet pussy. Ugh, I fight the gag. She tastes like she doesn't spend enough time rubbing one out. Fuck it. I'll make her come, and then I'm going to fuck her until she forgets her name. The blowjob wasn't bad, but he's hungry for something wetter and warmer.

I slide two fingers up into her pussy and she bucks. "Hold still," I tell her. She nods and settles back down. Jeez, she isn't saying anything. Oh well, all the better for me. Better to not say anything than to talk my fucking ear off.

Her hand plunges into my hair, squeezing and holding me to her. I continue fucking her with my fingers and sucking her clit into my mouth. Thank god it only takes about another thirty seconds before she's exploding, crying out my name and her pussy unleashes a flood. I milk out her orgasm for her. Bringing her down with my fingers.

When she finally settles, I reach with my free hand into my jeans pocket, withdrawing a condom. I withdraw my other hand from her dripping cunt and raise my fingers up to her mouth. "Suck," I tell her and she feverishly starts to lick her juices off my fingers. I make a show of ripping open the condom. Her eyes widen marginally as she finishes up.

"What?" I ask.

"Nothing, you already…"

"Oh, I'm not a one hit wonder, sweetheart, unless you want me to stop."

"God, no," she moans as I set about sheathing my dick in the rubber. I notice now that she still has drops of cum all over her chin and on her chest.

"Hop down and bend over," I command her and she doesn't argue. I watch her tits bounce as she hops down and leans over the counter, wiggling her ass in my direction. "Ready?" I ask.

"Mmm, yes, please," she moans, as I slide the head of my cock against her pussy. She pushes back against me; I find her hole and start sliding in. Thank god, she turned around. No wonder she's so easy. She's like the town doorknob; everyone's had a turn. Fuck it. Good thing I came already. I start pounding into her. She's managed to take a little more of me than most girls, but it doesn't matter, I can't feel shit anyway.

I'm a big fucking dude. A good nine inches and I ain't no fucking pencil. What the fuck does this girl fuck herself with? Jesus, she's looser than… Oh nope, I can… nah, can't feel that either. I close my eyes again and start fucking her harder. She bucks back into me, she's moaning loudly and if her orgasm from earlier is any indication, she's close. "Give it to me. Fucking come," I growl and she bucks against me harder. I feel her clamp down a little and the warm rush of fluid spreads over my cock and I grunt and groan. Only this time, I didn't come. At least I got a blow job. I extract myself from her and quickly pull off the condom before she can even turn around. I tie it off and grab a paper towel from the counter, wrapping up the wasted condom and throwing it away.

She's still groaning, sated and satisfied on the counter. Whatever.

I pull up my jeans, button them and throw my t-shirt back on. "Sorry, sweetheart gotta run." I quickly unlock the door and exit before she can protest. As soon as I step out of the room, Talon, Kyle and Mills go bolting past me.

"What the fuck?"

"Addison," Beck says and we slowly follow behind the hoard headed toward the ladies' room.

chapter
7
raine

My phone starts to ring with Cami's ring tone. It's after ten; I've barely crawled into bed. I debate for a second about not answering. "She never calls this late. Unless... This is Raine," I say after hitting the green button.

"Hi Raine, sorry to call so late, but I'm on my way into the office. Can you meet me there?"

"Everything all right?"

"No, but I'd rather not discuss it on the phone."

"All right, do I need..."

"Casual is fine."

"Okay, I'll be there in twenty-five."

"See you then." Cami disconnects the call.

What on earth could possibly have Cami going into the office at this hour?

I shrug it off and climb out of bed. I throw on my bra, a nicer t-shirt and a pair of jeans with tennis shoes and pull my hair into a messy bun. I grab my phone, my keys and my purse and head for the door. I stop to grab a bottle of water from the fridge and leave.

Twenty minutes later, I walk past the security desk to the executive elevator at the back of the bank of elevators that will take me straight to the top floor. I don't use this elevator often because I'm not usually in this much of a hurry. My phone chimes.

I look down.

Breaking News Alert... Trouble in Dallas with 69 Bottles PR Rep, click into App for details.

"Shit," I say as I step into the elevator. I'm going to lose service so I don't bother clicking into it as the elevator skyrockets to the top floor.

A mere fifteen seconds later, ears popping - the reason I don't use this elevator - I am stepping off into the reception area. "Cami," I shout. I don't get a response. As I round the corner I understand why. She's on the phone.

"Calm down, Kyle. Is she all right?"

Pause.

"What do you mean, you don't know?"

Another pause. She looks up at me, concern etched on her face.

"All right, keep me posted. I'm going to call the hospital and see what I can do to keep people from talking and see what information I can..." She's cut off. "Yes, I know. We'll take care of it..." pause, "okay, keep me posted."

She disconnects the call. "I got an alert, is it Addison?"

Cami leans back in her chair rubbing her eyes. She's not wearing any makeup, which for her is odd and the blue in her hair is fading out. Not a norm for her either. "Addison was attacked in Dallas tonight."

"Jesus," I say. It's all I can manage because there's a familiar burn in my chest.

"Tell me about it. The media is already swarming the hospital and my phone has been blowing up. Trinity is on her way in."

"What do you need from me?" I ask her without setting anything down.

"I need you to gather the masses. I am going to contact the hospital. See what we can do to make sure the staff doesn't speak to the reporters and try to get an update on her condition. Kyle says they're not letting them back, which usually isn't a good sign," she says softly. The look in her eyes is tortured. My first thought is that Addison was raped. God, I hope not. "We need to start answering the phone," Cami continues as she looks at her watch. "I want a press conference, from here, downstairs, so let's get the team together. There should be one already here."

"What time?" I look at my watch, it's nearly eleven now.

"I need time to gather some information. So let's say midnight. I imagine they're going to start showing up anyway." I nod my understanding. "When you're done with that, I need Zachary on the phone. We need to make some adjustments to Addison's security detail. I need to discuss this with him. Actually, strike that, for now. We'll call him tomorrow and set an appointment with him. We can't solve that problem tonight." Cami's phone rings. She looks at it, sends it to voicemail and looks back at me. "Okay, yeah, let's go with that for right now."

"No problem. Holler if you need anything else."

"Yup." She picks her phone back up and starts doing something on the computer as I leave the room. I enter the reception area and I roll my eyes as I see the phone lighting up with incoming calls. I grab the receiver and pull up an internal line. I dial the press team and wait.

It took three rings and ten minutes of explaining what I needed done before they're off on their task. I get my email and contact list open before turning on the phone and grabbing the first line.

"Bold International, Cameron Michaels' office."

Fifty something phone calls later, the lines are finally going quiet. In between calls, I called the media outlets that we want at the press conference. There are only a select few. Cami comes out of her office, it's ten to twelve and she's still unkempt. I know she will not go on the air like this. "Call down, we need another thirty minutes."

"Yes, Cami. Anything else? Any news?"

"Not really. The hospital has agreed to stay quiet, advising the staff to avoid the cameras. Fortunately for us, Addison was secluded quickly. I've been informed that she is doing all right and is being treated. Nothing more than that so far. I also spoke with Mills and got some more information on the incident." She walks over to my desk. "This is my initial press release. Can you review it for me?"

"Absolutely."

"Great, thanks. I need to go change." She gives me a sad half-smile. "Trinity is on her way up. Can you brief her for me? I'll be out in about twenty."

"Of course."

"Thanks, Raine, and thanks for coming in too, I really appreciate it."

"It's what I'm here for. If you don't mind my asking, why are you here?"

She smiles. "Tristan has some business here this week and next so we're staying in town. I hadn't planned on coming in until Monday, but apparently that's changed."

"Sorry."

She smiles again. "No worries." Then she turns and leaves.

I begin looking over Cami's press release. It's the same as the speech she'll give downstairs. When she takes the podium, it will be me sending the document out to all the outlets. A minute into it and I can tell that Cami is frazzled with the news of what's happened because it's not her usual spit and polish. Just as I'm about to redden her paper, the elevator chimes and Trinity comes strolling in. "Hi Trinity."

"Hi Raine, how's Cami?"

I smile. "A mess, but she's all right. I don't know if I've ever seen her so frazzled."

"Well, this isn't a client. This is an employee. She takes them a little more seriously," Trinity says as she leans on the upper part of my desk. "What do you have there?"

"Her release. She asked me to look it over."

Trinity winks. "Good. Where is she?"

"Getting changed. She came in pretty undone, no make-up, hair a mess." I chuckle.

"That's a first." Trinity laughs too.

"That's what I was thinking."

"All right, I'll wait in her office and I'll let you get back to it."

She leaves me alone and I go back to editing the release.

When Cami comes out, her hair is pulled up, some make-up thrown on and she's changed her clothes.

Though, given the late hour that surprises me. No one is going to give a shit. I'm typing on the computer. Cami's release was such a mess that I had to retype it for her. "How's it coming?" she asks.

"I'm retyping it now."

"Okay, great. Bring it in when you're done?" I nod. "Trinity is…"

"In your office."

"Perfect, thanks." Cami goes back into her office. I finish feverishly typing with less than ten minutes to spare before we're to be down stairs.

I finish it, print it and grab it on my way into the office.

"Yes, Kyle. All right. I talked to Mills. Though I don't know anything more from the hospital." There's a pause while she listens to Kyle on the other end of the phone. "We're going to press in ten. We will squash what we can and see what else we come up with. At least then I'll have more to go on." Pause. "No, we'll save that for tomorrow…uh huh…yup, okay, got it. Thanks." Cami disconnects the line.

I walk straight toward her and hand her the new release. "Thanks," she says half paying attention and starts looking over what I've just handed her. I don't say anything, waiting for her to decide what changes she wants. She looks at me, then back to the paper, then back to me. "Was what I wrote really that bad?"

I shake my head. "No, it was fine, but your emotions were kind of all in it. I just wanted to clean it up."

"Stale it up?" she says with a smirk.

"Yeah. I realize she's an employee, but…"

"Well done, Raine," Cami says as she hands the release over to Trinity.

An hour and half later, I'm finally leaving the office. It's after two in the morning and I'm wiped. I adore Cami and her ability to stand before those reporters the way that she did. She took no bullshit and ignored many of the inconsequential questions that were being asked. She was calm and collected and it was admirable.

I've made no secret of my desire to step out of my assistant role and into something more PR Related. No, I don't have the degree, but I've been roaming around this place long enough to understand the job, and in some cases, do it better than other reps who've had the schooling.

When Bobby was my boss, I'd confided in him my desire to return to school and get a degree in Public Relations. He was elated and vowed to help me get started that fall, when classes started. He died two months after that. With all the upheaval of the transfer of ownership from Bobby to Cami after his death, it slipped through the cracks and I just kept doing my job.

Being there to help Cami transition has been vitally important to me. I've seen six increases in pay since she took over as CEO. She keeps telling me that I deserve to be paid more. I make good money as an executive assistant, but living in California, my current salary is just barely above the minimum needed to live here. Which is why I live in a meager, two bedroom apartment not far from the office.

I've made it on my own since I was just out of high school when I decided I wanted to move to California from North Carolina. I thought the grass would be greener here and well, it took me nearly ten years to see the greener side of life. And the greener things have only been since breaking up with what's his name. Things have finally started to turn around for me. I'm single and I'm happy to be just that.

When I get home, I shed my clothes and climb into bed with just a t-shirt on. I'm too exhausted to care. Cami said that I didn't need to come in until noon, but things are going to be crazy. I set my alarm for my normal wake up time, and fall asleep quickly.

Surprisingly, I wake up seconds before my alarm goes off. Though I'm exhausted, I stumble out of bed and head straight for the shower. I know that I don't have to be in until noon, but I have a feeling Cami will need me sooner than that and I'm rather anxious for more information on Addison's condition. I'm also worried about Cami. She'd said, in a rather candid moment - shortly after sending Addison on that bus - that she was worried about her with all those guys. I didn't say anything at the time, but Addison has a reputation for being a ball buster with her clients. That at least gave me some comfort in knowing that Addison just might be all right on a bus with five men.

Thinking about Addison on that bus brings to mind my own little fantasy. A fantasy that I've harbored for a couple of years, even while with Michael. That name in my head sends an involuntary shiver down my spine. I try and push him from my mind and let the fantasy take over. Closing my eyes, my hands roam across my body, across my nipples and my back arches and every nerve ending in my body comes alive. I'm no prude when it comes to sex or my body. In my twenty-nine years, I've had enough sexual encounters to know what I like and what I don't like.

I'm a curvy five feet six inches tall, with hips that seem to go on for days and a chest that makes most men drool. I have shoulder length black - from a box - hair with a pink chunk in the front. I only get away with the hair because my boss isn't any different in that department. Her hair's usually black and blue, black and red, and occasionally black and purple. I like pink. My natural hair color is more of a dark brown, so going black isn't much of a change. The black contrasts nicely with my bright blue eyes that are usually too big and too bright, staring at the world with wonder and amazement. I'm not self-conscious about my body, it is what it is, I am who I am, take me or leave me.

With those thoughts, I let my hands continue to roam over my body, imagining my fantasy man taking the reins from me, sliding his fingers down my body, tantalizingly slow, teasing me and torturing me with the promise of what's to come. My right hand slides past my belly button, down toward my pussy. Smooth and hairless except for a tiny triangular patch just above the lips of my cunt. My fingers slide deeper until my middle finger grazes my clit. My other hand comes up to cup my breast and I roll my nipple between my fingers. The sensations are overwhelming as I imagine looking into the bright, excited grey eyes of my fantasy as he laps at my sex, flicking my clit with his tongue, teasing me, bringing me closer to an orgasm I so desperately need.

I fall into the shower wall. The coolness of the wall has my nipples hardening from the contrast of hot and cold. I moan and rub my clit with more vigor; my need to come is overwhelming me.

I moan as I roll my nipple between my fingers, tugging hard on the barbell spearing my nipple. The bite of pain is enough to send me over the edge. I scream out *his* name as my body climaxes. Dex.

chapter
8
raine

Yeah, okay so of all the members of 69 Bottles I could be infatuated with, I'm sure you're wondering, why Dex? Well, he's fucking gorgeous. What can I say? Those grey eyes are piercing to say the least. It's the bad boy image that he projects, and I have no doubt lives in. In fact, I know he does. I'm not oblivious to the ways of Dex Harris. No one in this world, who pays any attention to the media, is unaware of Dex's antics. The stuff in Phoenix is nothing new. Though with the tour it could have blown up way more than it needed to had it not been for Addison making headlines at the same time.

But I can't help it. Every girl has that fantasy man and mine is Dex. I've seen him a few times in the office. Occupational hazard. It didn't make me feel special or like I actually have a chance since he paid me no attention whatsoever while he was here. Calvin, a.k.a. Mouse, now he's another story. But when he was flirting with me, I was blissfully happy and unaware of Michael's antics with other women, so it didn't go anywhere.

I shake my head at the thought. It's been six months since I threw Michael out of my apartment and frankly, I've never been happier.

Kicking him out opened my eyes to the reality that there are more important things in life to focus on and while I'm focusing on those 'more important things', men have become a distant past. I haven't gotten laid in about seven months and the last time wasn't anything to write home about, in fact, I'm pretty sure I faked it then too. Michael was a lousy ass lay and that realization made it easier to accept the fact that we were no longer together.

I put the finishing touches on my make-up and hair before deciding to make coffee here and take it with me, rather than stopping at my favorite coffee house.

I'm usually in the office by about 7:30 every morning. Usually before most of the executive floor arrives, though after last night, I imagine I will probably be the last to arrive.

Oh boy, was I wrong. It's almost eight when I walk in and the floor is as quiet as can be. No one is here yet. Odd. I set about my usual morning routine and prepare coffee for the staff. Though this time I help myself, I'm missing my white mocha this morning and I regret not stopping. It's amazing what you get used to.

Dex invades my mind once again while I set my lunch in the fridge and clean up the coffee making mess. I really need to rid him from my conscious; I don't stand a chance in hell of ever capturing that man's attention. I mean, seriously. No, I'm not self-conscious about myself - it's simply the fact that when you compare me to the bimbos he no doubt fucks on a nightly basis, I don't even come close to their caliber. Let alone having the sexual prowess to even try.

dex

When we got to the hotel this morning, I pretty much face planted on the bed. Too exhausted to give a shit.

It was an excruciatingly long night waiting around for word about Addison and thank fucking god, she was all right. She was drugged, a little beat up, but that was about it. She wasn't raped and the moment Kyle told us all, you could literally see him deflate. It's very obvious to me that he cares a great deal about Addison so I cannot imagine what that kind of news would have done to him.

I hear the door to my room beep and click open before closing again. Beck comes barreling into the room. "Oh good, you're up. We're bugging out."

"Already?"

"Yeah, the police came and talked to Addison already. She and the rest of the guys just want to get out of here and on to New Orleans."

"That fucking works for me." I get up, still wearing my clothes from the night before. Don't judge me, I was fucking tired. "Let's roll."

Beck laughs. "You have time for a shower."

"Fuck that, I'll get one on the bus." I grab the bag I brought up with me.

"It's downstairs, you need an escort?"

"Fuck that." I side step him. "I don't need a babysitter."

"No shit." Beck, the snarky little fucker. I shoulder check him.

"Let's fly."

"I gotta hang out up here," he tells me and I shrug, holding the door open for him.

What a waste of a damn good room, oh well. Fucking New Orleans here we come.

I do my best to steer clear of the guys as they're coming on board, but when Addison climbs up those steps, flanked by Talon and Kyle, I can't help myself. "Hey Red," I say as I wrap my arms around her. "How you doin', kid?" I pull back and give her some space.

"I'm okay, really tired. Other than that, I'm good." She smiles at me.

"Make sure they take care of you," I tell her with a wink, desperately wanting to be my snarky self, but I decide now is not really the time. She eyes me suspiciously with a squint. Like she's expecting me to say something. *Yeah, I know, sweetheart, it's killing me too.*

I move out of the way and Mouse and Peacock do the same with Addison. I watch as she just lights up with all the attention. Talon stands back next to me while he watches his girl get enveloped in the guys. I jam my shoulder into his. "You good?"

I watch him out of the corner of my eye. He scrubs his face with his hand. "Not really."

"She's all right though?"

"Yeah, she's, fuck, she's better than I could have thought possible. I expected to be taking her to the airport this morning." There is relief in his voice. "I didn't think she'd stick around. Anyone else would be running for the fucking hills," he whispers to me, trying not to pull attention away from Addison. Talon is a strong man, stronger than most I know and frankly, seeing him crumbling like this makes my problems seem like fucking child's play.

"She's stronger than you give her credit for," I tell him and he softens, just a little bit. "I'm here if you need me."

He shoulder checks me back. "Thanks, bro. But I'll be all right. I think I'm still waiting for the other shoe to drop and for it to just smack her right in the face."

"Nah, stop waiting for it. Just let her deal as she's going to deal, nothing you can do about it."

Just then Addison turns around, gives Talon a knowing smile and he nods. Not sure if it's in response to what I said or Addison looking at him. No matter, he doesn't say anything else to me as he and Kyle take her back to their room.

"I'm gonna jam for a while," Mouse tells us.

"No worries. I'm passing back out," I tell him and Peacock, who is grabbing his bass to play with Mouse.

I scrub my scruff, I need to shave. Ugh, I still need to shower.

It's early evening when we arrive in New Orleans and get checked into the hotel. Mouse, Peacock and I spent the better part of the last hour or so packing up and chatting about where we are going tonight. We eventually settled on food then a bar. Mouse asked Talon if they'd be joining us but he declined. No one pressed him about it. He has hardly joined us since the tour started; I guess it's just what you do when you're entertaining a woman. But then again, Addison has several bruises on her face, has been through something pretty dramatic, I'd want to stay in with her too.

When the three of us, okay fine, five of us, if you count Leroy and Beck trailing behind us, hit the Quarter, you'd never know it's a Sunday night. Women are everywhere, there are beads on the ground, broken plastic cups spilling their contents into the gutters and the smell is very distinctly the Quarter. There are hundreds of people meandering up and down the street and we grab a bite to eat up on a balcony, watching the patrons below. It's great to people-watch from up here. Especially the chicks with the low cut tops. A perfect view.

Watching, eating and drinking... that's pretty much what we do for the next couple of days, then it's concert time.

I down two acetaminophen and four ibuprofen with a very large bottle of water about twenty minutes before the show. I crack my neck, my knuckles and stretch out my arms. Taping fingers, breaking in sticks, double checking drum heads. Ah, the story of my life. The excitement roars, the adrenaline skyrockets. There is nothing better, not even sex, than taking the stage, tapping those sticks together and kicking off a concert.

The adrenaline is usually flowing so hot and hard through my veins that by the end of the first song, I'm changing sticks because I've managed to snap them, or at least the head off. Tonight, the adrenaline is especially hot and heavy. I fucking struck out, not once, but three times in the Quarter over the last couple of days. I'm starting to wonder if I only affect women when I'm sweaty and gross after a concert. Then again, we managed to roam around the French Quarter practically unnoticed. That changes tonight.

chapter
9
raine

Checking 69 Bottles' schedule, I note that tonight they're in Kansas City after hitting New Orleans and Oklahoma City. Addison did not perform in either city but from my understanding, she is performing for the first time again tonight. I think it's a little early for her to be back on stage, but it's not my call. My day at the office is nearly done and after some much needed research on what's happening with Addison's case, I'm exhausted.

Cami comes out of her office with her bag over her shoulder. I gather she's getting ready to leave. "I have a bad feeling about tonight," she says, but it is so casually spoken, I'm not sure she's talking to me. I just look at her. She doesn't need any more prompting. "Are you busy tonight?"

I sigh. "I agreed to go out with a friend, but it's not that important, I can stay."

"No, it's not that, it's just, I might need you again tonight. At least if this feeling keeps up." Cami looks a little sad at the idea of having to call me in tonight. I am a little sad that I have to keep my plans. Erica has been pestering me for weeks to go out. I used to love going out and partying, dancing especially, but since I kicked Michael to the curb, I haven't been out much. The thought of meeting another guy in some dingy bar makes me shiver.

"No, I'll be around. Call if you need me. Were you able to get things straightened out with Zach?" Zach is the head of our security detail team. He's responsible for setting up bodyguards and additional event security for our clients. Zach is probably one of the coolest guys I know and if it wasn't for the fact that he's married, I'd probably swoon over him almost as much as I do Dex.

"Yup, everything is set. He's got a team in place. We'll probably ship them off to New York. Addison is going to need some additional help while she's there. Their schedule is getting tighter by the minute. Which reminds me, what's my schedule for tomorrow?" she asks as she leans against the counter on my desk.

I open her calendar. "You're pretty light tomorrow. In fact, after one, you're free. You said something about heading back to Phoenix this weekend, so we kept your appointments to the morning."

"Yeah, I don't think that's going to happen until next week. Tristan has some more business to wrap up here before we can head home. Schedule an appointment for me from one to two." I open a new appointment.

"With who?"

"You," she says rather nonchalantly.

"Should I be worried?"

She smiles, "Not at all."

"Well, okay then, tomorrow at one."

"Clear your schedule for the rest of the day after that appointment. You've worked really hard, take the rest of the afternoon off after we're done." I raise an eyebrow at her. She laughs. "Well, it was worth a shot." I laugh with her. "All right, I'll see you in the morning." She turns to leave

"Cami?"

"Yeah?" She looks back at me.

"Mind if I ask what this 'bad feeling' is?" I ask her, but for some reason, I grow shy and look away. Asking someone to spill a premonition or a feeling, to me, seems rather personal for some reason.

"I have a feeling that something is going to happen tonight in Kansas City. But I don't know what."

I nod my understanding. She smiles and once again takes her leave.

"Seriously? Why are you acting like this?" I ask Erica. She's a tall leggy blonde, with about three inches on me, couple that with her heels and she's about seven inches taller. I normally wear heels when I go out, but having the feeling that I'm going into the office tonight, I settled for jeans, a tank-top, one of my wide belts and my cowboy boots. We are in a country bar after all. When I mentioned dancing, I meant country dancing, line dancing. I love it. It's so much fun and it's quite the workout with the right partner. Erica and I are regulars here and tonight, most of the regular guys are around, so I've been able to take my spin on the dance floor.

"Because you need to get some dick or something. What the hell's happened to you?"

"Oh my god, seriously? Oh, I don't know, the last dickhead I picked up in a bar ended up moving in with me and sleeping with some slut in my bed. Sorry, not exactly in a hurry to relive that experience," I say with a little more snark than I intended and she gives me that 'what the hell possessed you' look. "What?"

"Nothing. I just don't like you like this."

"Girl, come on, give me some time."

"Time?" She scowls at me. "It's been six months."

I sigh. "Six months out of a six year relationship that feels totally fake. Sorry, sweetheart, it's going to take longer than six months."

"I know, I'm sorry. I guess," she takes a sip of her Cosmo, "I just miss going out, hanging out with you, dancing, you know." She's all whiney and crap.

"What's eating you?" I ask her.

"My boss," she snorts. "Well, he's being a dick. Treating me like crap, like I'm useless and I don't know what the hell I did wrong. Then again, his wife hasn't called the office in weeks…" she lets the thought trail off, staring off toward the bar.

The familiar strains of Blake Shelton's 'Boys 'Round Here' start to play and Erica gets animated, grabbing my arm and pulling me onto the dance floor.

She stops in the middle of the small mob of people. This song is one where people either know it, or they don't. It's hard to learn while surrounded by people who know how to do it. There are a lot of steps in this one but it is one of my favorites. I place my hands on my hips and start the slow wait for the singing to start. Once it does, we're off. Tapping our feet and crossing over, moving and dancing along. The more into the song, the more into the dance I get. Our conversation is long forgotten as the familiar energy flows through me. I feel my phone vibrate in my back pocket, but it stops immediately. A text.

As soon as our dance is over, I pull my phone from my back pocket and press the button…

Something's happened, please come to the office. Everyone is fine, but I'm fed up. Time to put an end to this.

"Erica, I'm sorry, I have to go."

"What? No," she whines.

"I have to go into work," I tell her as I down the last of my water.

"That's why you weren't drinking. You knew?"

I shrug. "I knew there was a chance."

She pouts but doesn't argue with me about it. "Hey, I could have cancelled completely." I wink at her and she smiles a little. We hug and I leave.

I round the corner on my way out and run smack into a guy, bouncing backwards slightly. He reaches his hand out, grabbing my elbow to steady me. "Where's the fire?"

The blood in my veins freezes.

chapter 10
raine

"Leaving so soon?"

I look up into the eyes of none other than Michael and I want to slink into the brick wall behind me and turn invisible until he leaves. "I have to go," I say, looking anywhere but at him.

"I was hoping you'd be here tonight. We need to talk."

I look at him then. His hair is a little longer than the last time I saw him, but he's wearing the same black muscle t-shirt he always wears dancing. It's a size too small, trying to accentuate his muscles. Muscles I used to enjoy licking, muscles that... I stop the thought in its tracks. "We have nothing to talk about," I state firmly.

"Yes, we do. We have some unfinished business."

"I'm sorry." I straighten my shoulders, letting bitch mode roll through my veins. "I'm pretty sure I've said everything I need to say."

"Stop that. Let me apologize."

"For what, Michael? Your apologies mean nothing to me, no matter how many times you say it, text it, email it. It's all worthless bullshit and I don't want to hear it anymore. Now if you'll excuse me..." I move to side step him and he moves in front of me. I move back where I was, hoping he'd quit this childish game he's trying to play but he moves right back in front of me.

"See, I knew you wanted to dance with me again." His hands come up, grabbing my shoulders.

"Don't touch me."

"Aw, come on, Raine, don't be like this. We just need to talk." I can see the pleading in his eyes and for a moment, I want to give in. Then I remember the sight of his ass bouncing up and down and the bimbo under him.

"I wasn't important enough to you then, what makes you think I believe that's changed? Or wait, better yet, did you run out of slutty bimbos to fuck?" I scowl at him and he scowls back.

"I used to fuck you once. Remember, remember how much you liked it?"

I fight the desperate need to cringe. "If that's what you want to call it." His hands tighten on my shoulders and it is starting to hurt. I squirm, trying to move away from him once again but he doesn't let up.

"You're a catty bitch, you know that?"

"Fuck you."

"You think you're better than everyone else, that you're not some dumb slut from the streets."

Not even realizing I'm doing it, I watch in slow motion as my hand flies up and connects with his cheek. Forcing his head to snap to his right. He's so shocked by my action that his grip on my shoulders loosens and I step out of his grasp. Moving quickly, I get out of reach. "We're not done talking, you stupid bitch," he yells after me.

"Oh yes, we are." I keep walking as fast as I can toward my car. I only look back once and he is still standing on the side of the building holding his cheek, watching me walk away from him, or rather, slowly running.

I get in my car and lock the doors quickly before starting it. The radio comes on...

"69 Bottles is at the top of their game, climbing the charts quickly compliments of an impromptu duet. Tonight, their fame climbs even higher as their Bold PR rep, Addison, and front man Talon unleash a brand new song. A duet. More details coming soon..." I drive out of the lot and turn the volume down as I drive. Adrenaline crash is making me shake. He's never been that aggressive with me before.

Not wanting to dwell on the interaction too much, I press the home button on my iPhone and Siri makes her appearance.

"Text Erica," I tell Siri.

"What would you like to say?" The disinterested voice comes back at me.

"Keep your eyes open, period. Mike is in the bar, period. Just had a nasty run in with him, period. He is going to be in a foul mood, period."

"Would you like to send?" Siri comes back.

"Yes."

I repeat the process, only this time I text Cami and tell her that I'm on my way.

73

When I arrive at the office, Cami, Zach, Trinity and some other female I don't recognize are in Cami's office. Judging by the woman's tight stance, arms behind her back, black cargo pants and t-shirt, lest we forget the thigh holster holding a gun, I'm going to guess she's one of Zach's employees. I step into the room.

"My plane will be ready to go around three. Get your team together," Cami tells the woman. "Oh, and Victoria?"

The unfamiliar woman answers, "Ma'am?" I cringe and Cami scowls.

"If anything, and I do mean anything, like this happens to her, or if she gets hurt, or otherwise attacked again, it's your ass and your job." Cami's expression is fierce and I am starting to put the pieces together. But fuck, again?

"Absolutely. I will make sure she's safe."

"Thank you." Cami nods to both of them and Victoria leaves, giving me a curt nod as she passes. Zach stays behind. "Raine?"

"Yes, Cami?"

"She's all right."

"What happened?" My voice is a little higher than I intended and I feel a new rush of adrenaline. I'm certainly going to sleep well tonight.

"Nothing, well, it was something but nothing really happened. The guy, the one who attacked her before, showed up in Kansas City and managed to get onto the bus. He set her up, but before anything could happen to her, the guys interceded and the security team took him down. He's going to jail and he will stay there. He's violated the terms of his bail and plea. Mills and his crew are doing everything they can to make sure he stays in jail."

"Jesus," I say. My whole body is shaking, especially my hands.

Cami notices. "Hey, are you all right?" she asks me and I sit down in one of the chairs. My eyes dart to Zach, Trinity and then back to her. "Can you guys give us a minute?"

"Absolutely," Zach says and he and Trinity leave the room.

"Does what happened to Addison bother you that much?" she asks as soon as Zach closes the door.

"Yes and no, but Addison is not why..." I can barely talk. The adrenaline from Michael's encounter is draining from my system and I'm crashing pretty hard. "I...uh... I was out with my girlfriend when you texted." I take a deep breath, trying to settle myself down. Cami moves about the room, stepping up to the sidebar in her office. She pours something brown into a glass and returns to me. She hands me the glass and I take it, shooting it back. "Gah," I groan as the burn sweeps through my throat and down into my chest.

Cami doesn't push me to talk and I take a minute to let the alcohol slide into my system. "When I was leaving, I ran into, literally, my ex."

"Michael?" she says casually and I'm a little surprised she remembered.

I nod. "He said he wanted to talk, that we needed to talk. I got pissed. He grabbed me by the shoulders, hard. Said some things that pissed me off, I slapped him and then was finally able to get away. I'll be all right...it's just that, plus Addison, uhm, it's all just kind of overwhelmed me."

"Take a deep breath. Do you want to call the police?" she asks me and I look at her shocked but I shake my head.

"Technically, I slapped him so..." I don't need to finish the thought.

She nods her understanding. "He deserved worse," she says with a smirk.

I can't help but smile and laugh. "Yes, he does." I take a deep breath. "Sorry about the meltdown."

"Don't worry about it. We all have them from time to time." She winks and I set my glass on her desk. "You good?"

"Better," I say as I feel the warmth of the alcohol flowing through me. Cami walks over to the door and ushers Zach back into her office. Trinity isn't there.

"She'll be right back," Zach says as he comes back into the room.

"Okay, Raine, here's what's going to happen," Cami tells me as she takes a seat at her desk. "Zach is sending four additional bodyguards to Des Moines where they will meet up with the rest of the team. This is both my requirement and at Mills' request. He called me in a panic about what happened. Apparently none of them knew the guy had been released and he was able to get onto the bus with a couple dozen roses. Obviously igniting every weakness the team has at this point." She pauses as Trinity comes into the room.

"Hi Raine," Trinity says to me and I smile my welcome at her before returning my attention to Cami.

"Zach is still here because we want to discuss a few things with you."

My eyebrows knit together in confusion and Zach moves, drawing my attention to him. "It is my understanding that you're pretty well versed in the ways of self-defense?"

I nod. "I've been teaching women for years." No need to go into the reasons why. Cami knows which is why her concern for me tonight is not unusual.

"Well, then we're going to put you to work," Zach says so nonchalant that I'm confused.

"We're sending you to Addison," Cami says without missing a beat.

chapter
11
raine

"What?" I exclaim. "That's a little redundant, don't you think? You've just sent four bodyguards after her and frankly, I'm anything but a bodyguard."

It's Zach who steps up to talk. "It's true and they'll take good care of her. Apparently my job is on the line if they don't." The smirk is a bit out of place considering Cami's threat if anything happens to Addison. "The reason we've discussed the self-defense aspect of things is because all Bold reps go through extensive courses in it. With what we want to do with you, you don't have that kind of time."

"I'm confused." I look to Cami.

"Well, I was going to discuss this with you tomorrow, but since we're here and the bus incident is under the radar and not being picked up by the media, yet. We might as well do it now while we wait and see if the shoe drops."

She gives me a reassuring smile, but I can't say I'm comforted by it. Cami leans forward, placing her hands together, her forearms are flat against the desk and she sits up a little straighter. I know this pose, she's about to get real.

Compliments of Michael's bullshit earlier, her posture has the hairs on the back of my neck rising. I sit up a little straighter. "If the event happened on the bus, I'm pretty sure the only people who know are the members of the band, maybe the crew." I raise an eyebrow asking for reassurance.

"We're pretty sure that's the case too," Trinity says with a smile.

"It's my understanding," Cami starts and I look back to her, "that my father owed you something?"

I shake my head. "I'm not sure I know what you're talking about..." I'm drawing a blank.

Cami smiles again. "If I recall from reading your file thoroughly, he promised to send you to college." My heart skips a beat.

"It... yes, he'd said he would do that, but..."

"I think a degree would be great training for you. But as someone who holds a Bachelor's, it's rather pointless." She grabs a folder from her desk. It's one of the thousands of plain manila folders we use around the office, nothing special in appearance, but its presence scares the hell out of me. "Raine, you've been hanging around this office for a very long time. You've written more press releases than probably Trinity or I have in the last year. You've sought out news articles from some of our clients, big and small, and brought their situations to the attention of their reps and when you do, you constantly offer ideas, suggestions, things to do to help with the situation."

I am sure my face looks like it's going to freeze in its confused, scared shitless state. I can barely breathe.

"You've proven yourself time and time again to be a very valuable asset to this company and it's high time we rewarded you for it," Trinity says from her chair next to Cami's desk.

"You're being promoted." Cami finally says the words.

"To what, exactly?"

"Addison's assistant."

I slouch. "How is that a promotion?"

Both Trinity and Cami chuckle before Cami continues. "You're being promoted because Addison is going to train you, show you the ropes, teach you about all the things that she does. Then, when you've learned everything you possibly can from her, we're going to give you your first client, assuming things go the way we anticipate them going." Cami grabs the folder.

"Who?" I say softly.

Cami gets a big smile on her face. "Addison."

"So she's going to train me to be her rep?"

"Something like that. The whole point of this is that we need to send someone to New York, someone to help her out, keep her on schedule and help her deal with the added things, like marketing and social media. She's going to be busy with recordings and the band's various appearances, it's going to make things difficult for her to keep up on everything. Between her own stuff and the band's, she could literally spend an entire day just on social media," Trinity says softly. Her motherly nature is comforting right now because hell if I understand how all this is happening.

"Things will probably start off a lot more of 'hey do this', 'hey can you do that' but that's all right. She's going to need someone to help her out. She's an amazing rep and the reason why we sent her to handle 69 Bottles is because we know she can handle it, but that was when she was dealing with one band at a time and not dealing with her own stuff," Cami says.

I cock my head at both of them; "She had like, twelve clients before she took on just 69 Bottles, I'm-"

"Sure you can handle twelve clients when you're sitting in an office more than being on the road." Cami smiles reassuringly. "She's responsible for more things with 69 Bottles than she is with a lot of her other clients. Like social media and all that good stuff, and that's when she's not being pulled in a thousand directions for her own career. They're in New York for two weeks. Once that time is up, you'll come back here and I will continue to work with you."

"I'm not sure I know what to say," I tell them.

"You don't have to say anything tonight. In fact, you're off the hook until Tuesday." She hands me the folder in her hands. "Inside you'll find all the details of your contract, a handbook regarding your responsibilities and Bold's expectations for our reps. There are also forms for certain things, like laptop, cell phone, expense account, etcetera that should you decide to do this, will need to be filled out. I figured that if you decided to do this, you'd want to know as much as possible before returning to the office on Tuesday."

"Why Tuesday?" I ask.

"Because I'm giving you the weekend and Monday off. No matter what happens, I don't want to see you here until Tuesday," Cami says sternly.

"Okay," I reply hesitantly.

"You and I will talk as soon as I get into the office. I've cleared my calendar. So come prepared with all your questions, write them down. If it's overly pressing or it will make or break you accepting the offer, you have my number." I nod.

"Is there salary information in there?" I ask.

"Will that make or break your decision?" Cami asks.

"No, but I am curious."

She smiles knowingly. "It's all in there. Then when we're done, your decision will decide what happens. They're in New York a week from Sunday."

I nod absently. It doesn't matter what's inside the folder. I already know my answer, but I am pretty sure that Cami will not accept that answer today, so I'm not going to argue about it. At least not right now.

"Any questions?" Trinity asks.

I shake my head. I'm in a little bit of shock over what's transpired tonight. Forgetting completely all about what happened in Kansas City.

chapter
12
raine

"Victoria, right?"

"You can call me Tori." She extends her hand and I take it.

"Nice to meet you." She gives me a small smile. She's very pretty, but carries a very deadly posture about her. She's broad in the shoulders, with strong hips and thighs that could probably squish a grown man. I casually note that one of the other guards is eyeing her. The look gives me the impression that he's impressed by her. "Is she here?"

"She is. I'm assuming you've been told?"

I give her a quizzical look. The only thing that Cami told me over the last week is that Talon, Kyle and Addison are all together. I think she wanted to warn me or give me a chance to put aside any preconceived ideas I may have had. Honestly, I think it's great. If they can make it work. "About Talon and Kyle?" I say hesitantly.

She cocks her head, appraising my intrigue. "I'm going to say that you haven't been told. I'm sure Addison will."

I raise an eyebrow at her, just as two doors open behind me. "You ready?" a deep voice calls.

"Yup, let's roll." That has got to be Mouse.

"Start downstairs?" another voice says and I finally turn around, only to have my heart skip six beats in my chest at the sight of Dex. I quickly turn back to Tori who has a knowing smirk on her face. There is some commotion and then finally I hear the elevator chime, the one I just came off of, and then the doors open. Some more footsteps and then finally the closing of the doors.

"Don't let them intimidate you," the guy who was looking at Tori with reverence a few moments ago says. I blush. "Sorry, I'm Rusty." He extends his hand. I take it, distracting myself and washing away all thoughts of Dex Harris.

"Pleasure to meet you." I smile sweetly at him.

"I'm one of the guards. You'll probably see me and Tori more than the other guys. Addison is Tori's responsibility and I'm on Addison's detail. If you'd like, we can arrange a meeting later today or tomorrow so that you can meet the entire staff. Well, with the exception of the road crew." He gives me a reassuring smile.

"That would be great, thank you. I just came by to say hello to Addison, let her know that I'm here and then leave them to their evening."

"They're expecting you," Tori says as she knocks twice and slides her key card into the door.

Stepping inside the suite, I'm met with a hallway and Tori follows me in. "Addison?" Tori says.

"Come in, Tori," calls the familiar voice of Addison. It's only familiar because I've been speaking on the phone with her these last few days.

"Raine is here."

"Perfect, bring her in," Addison says then I hear her giggle. "Stop it," she says and I want to roll my eyes because I can about imagine what's happening just on the other side of the wall separating us.

Tori leads me into a wide-open sitting room that has a very pleasant view of Manhattan. Trying not to get distracted by it, I look for Addison who is sitting on a couch between Talon and Kyle. Her face is bright red, almost as if the boys have done something scandalous, confirming my suspicions from a moment ago. She stands up and comes toward me. "Hi Raine."

"Hi Addison. Good to see you again. You look well."

"Thank you," she says then she nods to Tori. "How was your flight?"

I chuckle. "Long."

"I've taken that flight more than a few times. Have you met Talon and Kyle?"

"Not formally, no."

She laughs. "Nothing formal about these two," she says turning toward them. Talon and Kyle stand up like dutiful men and come towards us. Each of them wraps an arm around Addison's back and holds her to them. "Talon, Raine." She gestures between Talon and me. I take his hand.

"Nice to finally meet you, Talon." No need to mention that his overwhelming good looks and celebrity persona is making my breathing ragged.

"Likewise. This meathead," he pokes Kyle in the ribs, and he jumps, "is Kyle." He has to remove his arm from Addison's back in order to shake my hand.

"Don't listen to him. It's nice to meet you."

"Thank you, you too."

I'm surprised that my voice doesn't sound like the crazed lunatic I feel like on the inside. I don't know how she does it. I can't even think straight with these two looking at me, let alone function.

"We'll leave you two to talk," Kyle says and both he and Talon kiss Addison on the cheek simultaneously and she flushes. They both leave the room, heading for the bedroom, maybe.

"Come, sit down," Addison says to me.

I follow her toward the couch and we both sit down on opposite sides. "I'm not sure how you do it," I say while fanning myself and surreptitiously looking at the door they just went through. The words tumbled out so fast, I blush like an idiot.

"Sometimes I have a hard time with it." Her smile is warm, comforting. "But the bottom line, they're both amazing and I love them dearly." My heart melts at her declaration. "Let's talk shop for a minute," she says and we launch effortlessly into a conversation about business, but the attitude between the two of us is like we're best friends.

We discuss the schedule for the next few days, she lets me know what she wants me to take care of and take over completely and I have no problem with any of it.

"Next week is going to be the real madhouse," she says with a smile. "We have several appearances and the schedule is really tight. I'm going to need your help with making sure the guys get where they need to be. In some cases, Talon and Kyle will need to stay back, but the rest of the band will need to go on ahead. I will handle Talon, if you can manage the other three?"

"That won't be a problem. So long as they don't give me a hard time."

"Don't worry about them. They all try to act like a bunch of ball busters, but in reality, what they do is really important to them and that drives their willingness to listen and do what they're told." She smiles.

"Good." I laugh.

"Now, for the last bit of news I'll leave you with for tonight." I cock my head at her. "It's still new, and still setting in and only a handful of people know. I am going to tell you because it may or may not affect certain things." She starts wringing her fingers.

"Whatever it is, Addison, you can tell me."

"Well, honestly, you're the first person I've told straight out." She gives me a smirk. "I'm pregnant."

Whoa, jeez. "Congratulations." I beam at her. "That's awesome, Addison."

She lights up and smiles wide. "Thank you. I haven't told Cami yet. In fact, it scares me."

I chuckle. "I wouldn't worry about her. Tell her in your own time. You'd be amazed at what she'll have to say about it." Addison looks nervous all of a sudden and as if sensing her distress over something, the guys come out of the bedroom. I reach out and pat her worrying hands, gripping them slightly so that she stops and looks at me. "Honestly, do not fret about it."

She grins and mouths a thank you as the guys come up. I pull my hand back. "Everything okay?" Kyle says looking between the two of us.

"It's perfect. Thanks for letting me borrow her." I smile at her and the guys as I stand up. "I'm going to go grab a bite to eat and get settled in, I'll see you guys in the morning?"

"Absolutely," Addison says, the worry about telling Cami is gone from her eyes.

"Wonderful. Enjoy your evening." I tell them and take my leave.

When I exit the suite another guy is standing guard. This one is taller with a severe expression on his face. Jesus, he's gorgeous with broad shoulders, thick-corded muscles rippling under his tight black t-shirt. I can see his nipples because the shirt is so tight. He straightens a little more as I rake my eyes over him and I can see a smile tugging at his lips. Finally the awkwardness, though only two seconds, breaks when the door shuts behind me. I yelp and he laughs. "You must be Raine?"

I can't help but laugh. "That would be me. And you are?" I take a step toward him and watch as he looks me up and down. I feel my nerves flash and that little ball of nerves that is my clit throbs. My nipples tighten.

"Beck." He extends his hand to me and there is a fire that ignites with the contact. It's not lightning, but the slow burn of lust. Beck's body screams sex and my body is betraying me.

"Nice to meet you." My voice comes out a little softer than I intended which of course causes him to smirk at me.

Just then a door opens and slams shut. I peer around the man standing in front of me and into the steel grey eyes of none other than Dex Harris.

dex

Who the hell is that?

Ice blue eyes stare back at me from around Beck's body. Looking into her eyes has my dick twitching to life in my jeans and all I can see is her forehead, her black and pink hair and her eyes, those eyes. Those fuck me eyes. I see Beck turn toward me then back to the woman, who straightens. I can't see her anymore. Thank god. "Let's go," I say sharply.

"See you later," I hear Beck tell her, quietly. I turn toward the elevator and I feel Beck fall in behind me. I don't turn back, despite the need to see what else comes with those eyes. While standing there waiting for the elevator, I hear the familiar beep and click of a door.

So she's staying on this floor.

The elevator arrives and I step in, turning to push the button and the door just beyond Talon and Kyle's suite swings closed. *Great, now I know what room she's in.*

"Who the hell was that?" I say to Beck who is standing stiff as a board next to me. He doesn't answer. "Oh, come off it. She's obviously now one of us. Kate's replacement?"

"Addison's assistant." His voice is steel.

I shoulder check it. "Come off it. She's just a chick."

"That's precisely my problem. To you she's just a chick, just a receptacle."

"What the fuck has gotten into you?"

He shakes his head and loosens up. "Nothing."

"Yeah, right."

chapter
13
raine

What the fuckity fuck just happened? I fall back against the closed door.

Beck? Dex? Beck... I look at my hand, almost as if I'm going to see it on fire from his touch, but it's the same bland hand that I always have. I rub it on my thigh, trying to squash the burn. Beck is definitely more my speed. I mean, come on, Dex is a fucking playboy. He treats women like shit and he's a fucking celebrity and I'm, what? A broke assistant?

Though taking this position has increased my salary by more than double what I was making as an assistant, I've yet to see that reward. My first paycheck doesn't come until Friday.

I push myself away from the door and the motion reminds me of the tightly bound nerves in my clit. I groan as I grab my suitcase. Hoisting it onto the bed, I go digging for a change of clothes, my bathroom supplies and… my vibrator.

I don't think I've ever stripped out of my clothes faster than I just did. The chill in the room making my nipples hard and my clit throb, as I lie sprawled out on the bed, naked, vibrator plugged into the wall. Drifting into fantasy land is easy. What surprises me most is that Dex isn't the only star of my fantasy. Beck and Dex…together are the stars in my private show.

dex

"Have you seen Addison's assistant yet?" Mouse asks all of us.

"She's fucking hot," Peacock replies back. For some reason, irritation ripples through me. What the fuck?

"Yeah, she is. But she's off limits." Mouse takes a drink of his beer.

"Says who?" I counter.

"Says anyone. She's Addison's assistant for one, for two, she's only with us while we're in New York," Peacock tells all of us.

"All the better for her to be in limits," Mouse retorts. "She'll be gone and back to wherever it is she came from before we're back on the road. Another notch, right Dex?"

"Mmm." I nod and drink my beer.

"What about her?" Mouse nods his head toward the bar. Our eyes travel to a group of women sitting across the bar from us. They're giggling like idiots but they keep looking this way. There are three of them. A blonde, an unnatural redhead, and a brunette.

"Not bad. Three for three," I grumble and go back to my beer. Beck's attitude in the elevator has me on edge. He's actually staking a claim and bent over the fact that I just might be interested, but the fucked up part about that is her eyes are the only part of her body I've seen.

"Yo. Dex?"

"Hmm." I look up to Mouse.

"Where the hell are you? This bar is crawling with chicks and you're all..." he waves his hand at me, "whatever you are."

"Just thinking. When did you guys see Addison's assistant?" I ask, curious as to when they may have seen her.

"She was in the hallway when we first came down here, talking to Tori," Peacock says behind his beer. "She's also Cami's assistant." I raise an eyebrow in question. "Bold? Our representation. Jesus, you mean to tell me you didn't notice her all those times we were there?"

Peacock is not known for being subtle. "Um, should I have?"

"How could you not?"

"That's easy, I wasn't trolling."

Mouse shrugs. "Neither was I, but I fucking noticed," Mouse says, and now all of sudden I feel like I have three times the amount of competition. Beck, Mouse, okay two times. Peacock just needs to come out and get over it. I drop the subject and go back to brooding.

A couple minutes later, the waitress returns with a tray full of beers. I grab one and offer it to Beck who turns it down. "You guys going out tonight?" he asks me with a raised eyebrow.

"Probably," Mouse answers him.

"Then no." He pushes the beer back at me. He's standing behind me, Troy is behind Mouse and Casey is behind Peacock, which is rather odd because Peacock is bigger than Casey is. Troy and Casey joined us when Addison's personal bodyguard, Tori, showed up in Des Moines after Addison was nearly attacked for the second time by the same man. There's another guy, Bruce, but I haven't seen him since Philly. They overloaded us with bodyguards, if you ask me. Now we all pretty much have our own. Peacock and Casey hit it off pretty quickly, making me wonder if there could potentially be more between them than just something professional, but meh, not my deal. Leroy and Troy take turns around Mouse. My guess is because they have nothing better to do. I have a feeling sometime in the coming days, with Victoria around for Addison, that one or two of these guys may be shipped back home.

I hear someone whistle and I look up. Peacock and Mouse are both looking off in the same direction. Then I feel Beck nudge my shoulder. I look toward him and his eyes too are in the same direction as the other fuckknuckles. I follow their gaze and my eyes land on a pair of delectably shaped hips, thighs and quite possibly the best bubble butt I have ever seen in my life. Her waist is narrow, leading toward the top of the most perfect hourglass shape I've ever seen.

Her hips are clad in a pair of jeans that I'm immediately envious of. How I'd love to be wrapped that tightly around that body. She's wearing a couple of tank tops and her jet black hair is pulled up into a messy pony tail. There is something peeking out from under her tanks, thick black lines extending up and wrapping her shoulders. There isn't enough to be able to tell just what she might have there.

The tanks are more like colored A-shirts men wear than spaghetti straps. I watch her as she leans against the bar; she's talking to the bartender who is flirtatiously smiling at her while he makes her a drink. Then she shifts her weight to one foot and kicks up the other. That's when I see a pair of cowboy boots and I nearly want to look away. I'm more of a slutty heels kind of guy. But then she turns her head.

Cowboy boots be damned…

All it takes is a tiny glimpse of the bright pink in the front and I know immediately that I am admiring the backside of Addison's assistant. "Fuck," I exclaim in a rush and look away. Jesus, she's fucking gorgeous and like a moth to a fucking flame, I look again, but before I can turn my head I feel three sets of eyes on me. "What?" Nobody says anything to me. "Oh, come off it. She's fucking gorgeous."

"That's her assistant?" Mouse says, and it's a question not a statement of fact.

"Yes," Beck says behind me. "Her name is Raine."

My dick twitches in my jeans.

I make my best attempt to keep looking at her, but it's hard. I'm watching from the corner of my eye because my line of sight to her is ridiculously bad and would give it away that I was still looking.

Finally I can't take it so I look up. Apparently at just the right time, or maybe it is the wrong time, either works for me because when I do, she turns around and my jaw, I swear to god, falls on the floor.

"Jesus," I hear Beck and Mouse say at the same time as I think it.

Her tank top is low cut in the front accentuating the upper swell of her breasts; she's at least a C cup. She has to be. Her nipples are hard and I shiver, causing my dick to stir even more. When my eyes finally meet hers, she stops mid-stride and then smiles. But she isn't smiling at me. No, her eyes are over my head, she's smiling at Beck; of course she'd smile at him. I growl under my breath. *Jesus, what the fuck is wrong with me?*

I watch as she starts walking again, coming closer to us with her girlie drink in hand. I can hear Mouse and Peacock saying something but they're not talking loud enough for me to make it out over the dull roar of the bar.

I think she's going to talk to Beck but instead she comes up, stands next to me and I'm assaulted with the glorious scent of something that is distinctly her. A cherry chocolate scent that makes my mouth water. "We didn't get a chance to meet earlier. I'm Raine." She extends her hand to me and I stand, all gentlemen like. I tower over her and her eyes flare slightly at my height. I take her tiny hand in mine.

"Dex." There is a lightning spark that tingles in my hand the moment they meet and my heart is pounding in my chest. *What the fuck?* It's like I've gone from one night stand to love struck puppy. Nope, so not going to happen. "Have you met the rest of the guys?" I manage to ask.

She shakes her head. "Not yet."

"Let me introduce you." Hoping against hope that I can set her sights on someone else. It's almost as if somewhere in the back of my mind, I know that I cannot simply fuck this girl. *Oh, who the hell am I kidding?*

I introduce her to Mouse and Peacock. Mouse does a great job of capturing her attention and before I know it, Raine is sitting between Mouse and myself, only closer to Mouse.

I suddenly feel like I need a cigarette. Without a word, I get up and leave the three of them to their conversation.

chapter
14
dex

"You all right?" Beck asks me as I step out into the chilly New York evening.

"No," I say sharply and light a cigarette.

"She's fucking gorgeous," Beck says.

"Too fucking gorgeous. I'd fuck that girl up." I lean against the building, propping my foot against the wall and pull a long drag off my smoke.

"Can I have one?" I raise my eyebrow at him.

"She got you that bad too?" I suddenly start to understand what Talon and Kyle went through when they both met Addison. I look at Beck... yeah, no, there ain't nothing there. But Raine certainly wouldn't be the first woman we've shared.

"Something like that. Did you see that ink?" He smirks like he has a secret. The fucker.

"What little I could, yeah, I saw it. I'd love to find out what's really under that tank top."

raine

"See you later, Raine," Mouse says as he and Peacock take off, their guards in tow. Dex took off like a bat out of hell. I knew it was foolish of me to think that I could honest to god turn his head. I down the rest of my drink just as the waitress comes over to clear off the guys' beer bottles.

"Can I get you something?" she asks with a smile and I smile back.

"Yes, please, another Cosmo? Actually, keep 'em coming," I tell her.

"Room number?"

I give her my room number and her eyes flare slightly. No doubt she knows full well who her previous patrons were and who is actually on the seventeenth floor of the hotel.

"What's the name on the room?"

I roll my eyes, give her my name and hand over my license.

"Sorry, we just have to be sure." She hands me back my license.

"I understand." With that, she takes her full tray and returns to the bar. I watch her, just because I have nothing else to do, as she puts in my information. No doubt seeing the previous Cosmo on the bill and realizing that I wasn't kidding her. The seventeenth floor is completely off limits to the public. Requiring a keycard in the elevator and no other guests are allowed to rent the rooms on the floor. Though I think between the band members, the guards, and me, it's full anyway.

My phone chimes. I pull it out and look at the information that's coming from Cami, followed by a text.

Cami: Hope you made it safe, hope all is well.

I reply back.

Raine: Here, safe and sound, in the bar.

Her reply is almost instant, indicated by the three little dots in the bubble.

Cami: That bad?

I snort a laugh.

"Something funny, sweetheart?" I jolt at the sound of Dex's voice and look up to meet a pair of steel grey eyes penetrating me. Next to him are another set of gorgeous chocolate brown eyes.

"Depends. I think it's funny." I smirk and turn back to my phone.

Raine: LOL, not yet, but we'll see.

I press send just as the waitress arrives with my drink. I take it from her and before she has a moment to straighten and turn to Dex, I down my drink. It freezes my esophagus on the way down, compliments of the ice bath it got before being poured. "Oomph," I grumble and hand her back the glass.

"Another?"

"Please."

The waitress nods and leaves with Dex and Beck's orders.

"Aren't you guys going with Mouse and Peacock?" I ask. There is an edge to my voice that I didn't intend to come out, but Dex running off moments after meeting me told me all I needed to know. This is, and always will be, a one way attraction.

"Nah, the scenery is better here," he says pointedly looking at me, then I watch his eyes dart around the room.

And let's just drive the nail home. "Very nice. Well..." I stand up and continue, "I was saving your seats just in case. Enjoy your evening." I skirt Dex, heading toward the bar. A hand grabs my elbow and ice freezes my veins and locks me down completely. I don't move. I know his intention isn't malicious, but I cannot help my body's reaction. He lets go and fire replaces ice.

"Stay?" I hear him ask.

"Good night, gentlemen." I walk away from them and go straight for the bar, capturing the waitress's attention as I take a seat on the opposite side. I can see him and Beck, but barely, which is fine by me.

I watch as they both take a seat, the waitress brings me my drink and then immediately takes them theirs. From where I'm sitting I can see just enough to not make it obvious that I'm looking in their direction. I watch as the waitress shows me her ass and Dex her best assets. I watch as he takes his beer from her and smiles flirtatiously at her. "That fucker," I breathe.

"I'm sorry, what?" the guy next to me says and I turn to look at him. Well, Dex was right about something, the scenery sure is nice in here. I strike up a conversation with *Mr. Stranger In a Suit* and do my best to ignore the two men I just left. I idly entertain the idea that with enough alcohol, I can throw all my inhibitions to the wind and sleep with some random stranger.

Then I feel eyes burning into the side of my head from across the room and I am reminded of what a one-night stand with *Mr. Stranger In a Suit* will do to me tomorrow.

I can't help but wonder what Dex's problem truly is. I mean, he's looked me up and down, made a point about better scenery and looked as though it pained him to look away from me. He wasn't exactly flirtatious with me, but I can't help wondering if there isn't something more to him. I frown and go back to *Mr. Stranger in a Suit.*

dex

What the fuck is she doing?

Why the fuck do you care?

I shake my head and pull my attention back to the blonde bimbo in front of me. Jesus, talk about hypocritical. Now to ditch the bitch.

"Thanks for the drinks, love. I'm sure you have other tables to service."

She takes my hint. "I'll be back with more beer."

"Thanks," Beck tells her and she leaves.

"What a fucked up night this is going to be."

"Wanna go someplace else?" Beck asks.

I rub my eyes. "Nah, but go if you want," I tell him.

"You know I can't leave you down here."

"Then fucking call someone to replace you. You don't have to babysit me. Take the night off, go find your own piece of ass."

He snorts.

"When was the last time you got some?" I ask.

"Too fucking long ago."

"No wonder you're such a prick."

He laughs again and finishes his beer. It doesn't take us both very long before we're staring back at Raine like idiots. Watching her flirt with the guy next to her. She's smiling and laughing. *What the fuck is wrong with me?* If I want her, all I have to do is put on a smile and she'll be spread eagled under me, taking my cock hard and fast. My cock hardens again. If I keep this up, I'm going to end up with a serious case of blue balls.

When the waitress returns with more beers, I order more and something special on the side.

Ten minutes later, Beck and I are both drooling as we watch Raine savor the taste of my something special on the side. When she received the drink, she raised it to us. Watching that woman taste alcohol is something else entirely. Watching her eyes roll up into her head as she takes in the succulent flavor of a Caramel Apple Martini. I start to count how many drinks I've seen her have. She's up to number five or six and she looks like she hasn't touched a drop. Lucky bitch. I'm starting to feel the twelve or so beers I've had so far.

When she's done with her drink she smiles at us and goes right back to talking to the *dumbass* next to her. So much for that plan.

Within another ten minutes, three girls have joined us on the couch. Beck and I have no trouble whatsoever engaging in conversation with them. Ironically enough, none of them seem to know who I am, and I take complete comfort in that. The one chick - yup, don't ask her name - is very flirty with me and I take to her quickly. The other two girls are flirting very nicely with Beck who is enjoying their company.

Out of the corner of my eye, I see Raine stand up from the bar. She sways a little and the guy in the suit steadies her by grabbing her elbow and once again, she locks up. I wonder what that's all about but I don't get to dwell on it before my attention is brought back to the redhead half sitting on my lap. She's subtly grinding her ass against my thigh, my already hard cock throbs that much harder and I try to capture Beck's attention. Our waitress does that for me by coming back to the table, only this time she has a glass of amber liquid with ice rattling around.

"This is from the lady, the one you were buying drinks for earlier," she says with a little bit of a sneer. Shit.

Without any warning, the waitress dumps the drink over my head at the same moment Raine saunters past me, laughing. The woman on my lap jumps up and ice cold Crown slides over my head, down my shoulders and chest. "Fuck," I growl.

I scowl at the waitress who is working overly hard on not laughing. I catch Beck's shocked expression but he too is fighting a laugh.

"Excuse me, ladies," I say and stand. Beck is hot on my heels. Rather than going to the men's room, I follow Raine out of the bar and to the elevator of the hotel. I keep my distance and I can still hear her laughing softly at her little stunt. I hold Beck back. I want to time this just right. Not giving her an escape. Beck will be with me the whole time and I take a little comfort in that.

Surprisingly, I'm not pissed at her for her stunt. No, I'm so fucking turned on that it is going to take everything I have not to fuck her in the elevator on the way up. She wants to fucking play ball. Let's fucking play ball.

Finally the elevator arrives. I catch a glimpse of her stepping inside and Beck and I bolt for the doors, catching them just as they start to close.

I am met with terrified ice blue eyes. The smile, the laughter, is gone and I don't like that. Beck and I step into the elevator, trapping her from escaping before the doors close.

My eyes are locked on hers. Fear, excitement, panic, desire... every single emotion plays across her features before the doors finally close.

"I have to give you more credit. I didn't think you had it in you," I tell her, breathing heavy. The cool elevator air is making me shiver. "Now I'm cold, and need to be warmed up."

I reach for her wrists and she doesn't fight me, her eyes are locked on me. She shivers when I touch her. I feel it too, but I don't linger on it. I lift her arms above her head and push her against the back wall, pressing my body against hers and she moans. A perfect fit. My lips slam down on hers. She freezes for a minute but then relents, giving in to my kiss. Her body writhes beneath me. I slide my knee between her legs and immediately she starts to grind against my thigh.

My blood boils. My cock is rock hard and she melts against me. Her breathing becomes ragged and uneven, right along with mine. She wants me. I want her. No, fuck that. I need her.

I pull my head back, reluctantly releasing her lips. My breathing sounds like I've run a marathon. My heart is going to burst through my ribs. She whimpers at the loss of my lips and my dick twitches once again. I look at her a little more closely, and Jesus, she's fucking gorgeous.

chapter
15
raine

It was an unguarded moment of complete jealousy that caused me to pay the waitress two hundred dollars to dump the drink on Dex. I could have, should have, just done it myself, but fuck that, it was more fun to watch from a distance.

Staring into his eyes, I can feel the fury radiating off of him, which ignites all of my girl parts. The burning desire coursing through my veins was the last fucking thing I expected to feel after my little stunt.

When his lips landed on mine, I was too stunned to close my eyes and I watched Beck as he watched us. His breathing altered at the same time mine and Dex's did. That told me that him watching us kiss was just as hot to him as it was to me.

"Feel better?" I finally manage to breathe.

"I'll fucking feel better when you're underneath me." The growl in his voice implies all I needed to know. The jealousy I felt was a game, a ploy, he was purposely baiting me. A part of my mind registers that I should be furious at that, but I can't find it in me to feel that way.

"What are you waiting for?" The words are out of my mouth before I can stop them. Can I do this? Live in the fantasy for one night? What the fuck do I have to lose? My job. Yeah, I took that chance the moment I had the waitress dump that drink on him.

The elevator beeps. He releases my wrists from against the wall, but he doesn't let both of them go. He takes my hand in his and pulls me from the elevator.

I can do this, and I know exactly how I can do this. I can do this and get both of these men out of my system and move on. I grab Beck's hand as I walk past him, pulling him along behind me. He hesitates only for a second and then quickly falls in step behind us.

I watch as Dex fumbles with the key and the door. Beck interlocks his fingers with mine and that burning lust is back, brighter and more desperate than it was before. Jesus, this is going to kill me. But I can't do this with just Dex; just Dex will destroy me in ways I will never get over. The man you've fantasized about for the last few years, equally as desperate to sleep with you as you are with him, at least that's the perception, is nearly too much to handle.

Finally Dex gets the door open and he ushers me inside. "Oh no," Dex says.

"Oh yes, you want me, he comes too." I watch him war with himself, looking between me and Beck and back to me again.

"Yeah, all right," he says and Beck and I step inside the room. As soon as we're clear of the door, Beck scoops me up. I wrap my legs around his back and he pushes me against the wall. His lips and erection slam into me at the same time. My breath leaves me in a rush. His lips are soft, softer than Dex's, but the kiss is different. It's filled with passion but there are no sparks with Beck. Nothing close to what I felt with Dex and I know this was the right choice. Beck will keep me grounded; keep me from running away with the emotions of a lovesick teenager when it comes to Dex. The kiss does nothing but suck my breath from my body. I'm panting as Beck slides his tongue past my lips, finding mine. He tastes like beer, and I no doubt taste like hard liquor.

Beck turns, pulling me away from the wall and pushing me into Dex who helps to hold me up. His hands are rubbing along my ass, up my back and back down my sides. I let my legs go, indicating that I want to be put down and they honor my silent request.

I can barely stand up steady enough, but I don't have to, both men drop to their knees, making it easier for me to see and kiss Beck. And I do. Dex's hands slide up under my tanks. Gently massaging along my back. Climbing higher. Beck's hands roam north, finding the underwire of my bra and following it around my back. I feel his fingers fumbling, looking for the hooks and I smile against his lips. Pulling back, I pull on my tanks, lifting them over my head and I hear Dex growl behind me. "Fucking hell."

He pulls back from me, sitting on his haunches. Beck smiles against my stomach as he licks and kisses me. His hands roam north again to find the front clasp of my bra.

"Get that off her," Dex says hurriedly. He's eager to share what he's found.

I feel the clasp of my bra come undone and immediately my tits fall free. My left nipple is quickly captured in Beck's mouth and I moan, my knees shaking.

"Fuck," Dex groans. Then I feel him pushing on my hips, desperate to turn me and Beck releases me with a pop.

"What's so fucking-," Beck falls silent, the only sound in the room is our ragged breathing, but with the way my heart is pounding, I'm sure it can be heard in China.

I cover my chest and lean into the wall. Alcohol runs wild in my veins. I press my cheek to the wall and let them admire the show. I reach for my belt buckle, undoing it quickly, followed by the button and zipper on my jeans. I lower them, leaving the black thong in place so that the entire piece is in view.

dex

Sweet Mary mother of..."Jesus," I breathe, watching Raine lower her jeans just a little. Showing off the black thong she's hiding under there. My hands roam up her back, taking in the gorgeous tattoo that covers her back.

On the back of her neck is a star. That's only where the tattoo starts. Covering her shoulder to shoulder, from her neck down to two very sexy dimples on her hips are thick black lines, drawn into tribal wings. The wings wrap around her shoulders, and the trails of the wings wrap around her sides onto her stomach, though I haven't seen that side of her yet. A line of flowers breaks up the lines, simple yet elegant just the same. The flowers grow in beauty and intensity as they travel down her back. There is more to the tattoo than what we can see at the moment.

The flowers continue downward, toward her butt before disappearing.

"I've seen some amazing tattoos in my day, but this takes the cake," Beck says as his hands join mine. She moans at our touch. Her back arches and she writhes beneath our hands.

I slide my hands down, tugging on her jeans, pulling them down further. As if the back wasn't a total, knock me on my ass surprise; the flowers that continue down her thigh are just as gorgeous. On her left thigh, running from hip to, ahh there it is, knee are several lilies in a line going from large to small as it descends down. The lilies are mostly black and shades of grey, but there are hints of pink in the middle of the flowers. I run my hand along her thigh gently and I watch as she shivers at my feather light touch. "Any more beautiful surprises, sweetheart?"

I'm momentarily taken aback by the endearment; it's the same name I call every girl I sleep with. But for the first time in my life, it actually feels wrong. Trying to brush it off and focus, I tap her foot, she lifts it and I remove her boot, then her sock before finally sliding her jeans off and repeating the process with her other leg.

She is huddled into the wall, hiding her front from us. "Turn around," I tell her, though looking up and seeing all her glorious ink has my boxers soaked with pre-cum and my cock is as hard as granite. My balls are starting to ache.

She slowly turns around, but keeps her arm over her chest. Beck reaches for her wrist to pull it away and she lets it go. "Fuck," I growl and stand on my knees. Her nipples are pierced and I cannot control myself anymore. I start to lick and her back arches, then I suck her dark pink nipple into my mouth. Beck joins me, taking the other just as I have and her whole body quivers. I reach for her hip to help steady her, but decide that she should probably lie down.

Releasing her nipple with an audible pop, I look into her ice blue eyes. For a moment, everything in the world fades away. "Lie down," I breathe.

Beck releases her other nipple and she sidesteps us and climbs up onto the bed to lie in the middle of it. She is uninhibited or maybe just inebriated, but it doesn't matter. The beer is making my head spin just a little.

Beck and I look at each other. No doubt the lust I see in his eyes is reflected back in mine. We stand. I pull off my shirt and Beck quickly follows.

"Ahhh," she moans from the bed and we watch as her hand slides down her stomach and disappears behind the thin scrap of her thong.

"Enjoying the view?" Beck says in a growl and she moans, arching her back, her other hand going to her nipple, tugging and pulling on it. I shed my boots and jeans. Leaving my boxers, though it's a moot point and climb onto the bed between her legs.

'That is mine," I mumble to myself and her hand stills. Our eyes meet again. Confusion and desire. So, I'm not the only one who's getting mindfucked over this mess. I grab her wrist and pull her hand free of her pussy and immediately slide my tongue along her fingers. Holy fuck, it's not like anything I've ever tasted before. She tastes amazing. Sweet and delectable. I make quick work of cleaning off her fingers while she watches me.

Beck climbs onto the bed at her side. His hand roams over her stomach, along her hip and finally up to replace her hand at her breast. I watch as he leans down and pulls the nipple I had in my mouth only moments ago into his.

"Ahh." She mewls and moans as her legs scissor together as I clean off the last of her juices from her fingers.

I can feel her trying to pull her hand away, to go back to what she was doing, but I won't have that.

I release her hand and immediately go for her thong. In my rush to shed her of her panties, I snap one of the strings. "Shit." I hear Beck snort a laugh against her chest, but he continues assaulting her nipples.

She chuckles. The widest, brightest smile spreads across her face spurring me on so I snap the other side to keep her smiling at me like that.

The moment the material falls away, I am treated to a perfectly smooth pussy, except for a small triangle above a delectably swollen clit. I lick my lips and waste no time sliding my tongue from her opening to her clit and I feel her tremble. "Oh fuck," she moans out and I continue my slow assault on her pussy. Desperate to make her come for me. Desperate to have her juices on my tongue.

chapter
16
raine

Dex's tongue spears me, setting fire to my nerves. My whole body trembles with an overwhelming need to come.

Beck's mouth gently travels from one nipple to the other and back again. With the hand that Dex was sucking on, I find the waistband of Beck's boxer briefs and slide my hand inside, taking hold of his rock hard erection and stroking him.

I've never wanted two men at the same time but Jesus, I don't know if I can go without it after this.

Beck moans against my breast and I continue to stroke his cock. He's not overly huge, maybe a little bigger than average.

Dex's tongue hasn't stopped assaulting me. I writhe and moan, rocking my hips into his mouth until he uses a hand to hold me down. When Beck moves to my right breast, I am greeted with a pair of beautiful steel grey eyes looking up at me, watching me. I'm surprised by the fact that he's watching me, but when our eyes meet, the rest of the world falls away.

The fire ignites in my veins, and Dex knows I'm close because he is concentrating on sucking my clit. Flicking his tongue on that special sweet spot that makes my legs twitch involuntarily. That's when I feel a finger pressing against my entrance, his eyes silently begging for permission and I flick my hips just enough to tell him to continue and he does.

His finger sliding in is enough to bring me over the edge. Setting fire to my veins and igniting fireworks behind my eyelids. I can no longer keep them open and I writhe against his mouth and fingers as he slides deeper inside of me. He doesn't let up and Beck pulls his mouth away from my nipples. I start tugging on his boxer briefs. I want to suck on his cock. Beck takes the hint as Dex's continued ministrations keep me on the edge of another orgasm.

While Beck sheds his shorts, Dex slides a second finger inside, deep, rubbing along my g-spot as his tongue flicks at my clit. "Oh god," I moan out, "don't. Stop." I squirm against him. Quite possibly the biggest orgasm of my life is building inside me just as Beck returns to the bed. I grab his shaft and tug him toward my mouth, telling him what I want and he complies. Saddling up to me, I see his cock for the first time. His head is slightly purple and there is a bead of cum dancing on the tip. I lick it off and he falls forward, placing his hands on the wall above my head. I watch his eyes roll up as I wrap my lips around his shaft. At the same moment, Dex's tongue halts against my sex and I feel a rush of hot air. It sends a shiver across my skin for an unknown reason. I don't understand his reaction.

Beck groans above me, it's enough to distract me from analyzing Dex's hesitation. I close my eyes, and in that moment, I'm on fire again. The orgasm that I know is going to shatter me, simmers deep down, ready to consume me in a wild explosion and I'm now desperate for it.

I moan around Beck's cock and he groans above me. "Your fucking mouth is amazing," he groans and I feel him thrust his hips slightly, indicating his desire to take control. I relax my throat and pause, giving him permission with my eyes and he slowly starts to thrust in and out of my mouth with small motions.

Then, out of nowhere, I feel the soft scrape of teeth against my clit, the pressure is intense and I can no longer hold back. I explode into orgasm. My eyes slam closed, Beck's cock slips in and out of my mouth, I can barely breathe as I feel the hottest rush of juices spill from my pussy and Dex moans against my sex. I pull my head back, releasing Beck and I scream. My entire body rocking with aftershocks of an orgasm unlike anything I've ever felt before.

I'm not entirely sure what happened after my explosive orgasm, but I'm brought to when I feel someone rolling me over onto my stomach. "Lift up," Beck says. There is no real command in his voice, which is fine. It's almost this detached person who's now settling between my legs. For some reason I don't truly understand, probably compliments of the alcohol, I don't really care. I'd already managed to talk myself into this shindig and talked myself into understanding and realizing this is a one night stand.

Though my desire for Dex has only grown that much hotter, causing me to start to regret this decision.

The ripping of a foil packet brings me out of my inner musings. Every nerve, every sense comes alive and I listen in the eerie quiet of the room as Beck sheaths himself in rubber. When he's done, he leans over me. The bed dips as he holds himself above me, bracing his weight on his arms. I feel the head of his cock pushing and probing, seeking entrance without assistance.

Then he lines himself up and slides home, hard and fast. I cry out and freeze. Tension knots in my shoulders and I fight the rising panic.

dex

"Are you all right?" I hear Beck whisper to her.

"Just go slower," she whispers back. There's a tension in her voice that I don't quite recognize. I watch him, buried inside her and the thick green sludge of jealousy washes over me as Beck slides in and out of the one and only place I want to be.

The minute I'd gotten up to shed my shorts, he flipped her over, barely giving her a chance to come off of the shattering orgasm I gave her. Shattering is barely the right word for it. I can still feel that rush, that spray. I lick my lips, tasting her essence and my cock throbs.

Beck looks over at me, but I ignore him. He's got that wicked look in his eyes, probably the same one I always have and for the first time in my life, I'm bothered by it.

What is so fucking special about this girl?

That's easy, I saw it in her eyes. They say that our eyes are windows into our souls and hers were wide open, ready, wanting and willing to surrender to me. Normally

I'd shrug it off, I've seen the look before, but it was almost as if our two souls were sliding into one. Two halves becoming whole for the first time in my life. Which is forcing me to fight the urge to shove Beck off of her and claim her for myself.

"You're so fucking tight," Beck groans as he starts to really slam into her.

I watch as she pushes back against him with each of his thrusts in, taking him, absorbing him, moaning out her pleasure. Pleasure available for him to take.

"Dex," she moans out. Her hands go wide so that her chest is pressed hard into the mattress. I'm frozen. She's got Beck pounding into her and she's calling my name.

"I'm right here," I manage to get out.

"Come here," she commands. Though her voice is soft, I feel the twinge of resolve weakening. I wanted to watch. I wanted to watch because the closer I get to Beck, the higher my drive to deck him becomes. "Please," she begs and I can't deny her.

My body, my dick, take over and I walk the few feet to the bed. "What do you want?" I ask softly.

"I want to...ahhh, suck your cock." Her head turns in my direction and our eyes meet. I stand before her stroking my cock and she surprisingly maintains our eye contact. "Please," she begs again and I'm lost in her blue eyes as I climb onto the bed. She gets her arms under herself and lifts up. Beck grabs hold of her ass and holds her in place as he continues to pump into her.

I'm unintentionally taking my sweet time. I need Beck to finish. I need to be inside her so bad. I don't normally take seconds, but tonight, I could be the hundredth guy and still be satisfied. If Beck thinks she's tight, she's not felt anything yet.

Suddenly, without warning, embarrassment floods through me. *Fuck me. What the fuck is wrong with me? Since when have I ever been embarrassed about the size of my fucking junk?* I have absolutely nothing to be ashamed of, but suddenly it feels almost as though I'm going to be too big for her. Then it's almost as if I am awash with the idea that I am no good for her.

Turn it off, you moron. Get your fucking rocks off and move the fuck on.

Raine's eyes remain locked on mine as I touch the head of my cock to her lips. She opens, sticking her tongue out to swipe across the head of my erection. Fuck! Her mouth is warm, wet. Hot breath caresses my cock as she pants in time to Beck's thrusts.

Lust and need to come overtake me as I break our connection and look down just when her mouth wraps around my cock. Her eyes go wide and they dart down. I pop free of her mouth and she gasps. Not in lust or orgasm, but shock.

It doesn't last but a second before her delicate hand wraps around the base and her mouth is hotly licking, sucking and worshiping the beast.

I close my eyes and savor the sensations as she sinfully works to get me off. It isn't going to take much before she has me unglued.

Her moans are muffled by the fullness in her mouth. I can't help but take her head in my hands to help her out a little more. She moans and I feel her jaw relax. "That's my girl." The words tumble from my lips like a bucket of marbles, but I don't give a shit as I start to slide in and out of her hot mouth. "Your fucking mouth feels so... ahh...good," I groan and Beck's pace falters and picks up in double time. He's close and I can feel a now familiar tremble in Raine's body and her moans are stronger and more intense. She's going to come. Beck is going to come and..."Ahh fuck...I'm..." She sucks with more intensity, if that's even possible. Beck's pounding slides her mouth further down my cock. Her body locks down, I take over, Beck growls out his orgasm, faltering his thrusts and I silently explode down her throat.

Beck pulls free and falls to her side, spent and breathing heavy. Raine continues milking the last few drops of cum from my cock, causing me to twitch so I pull myself free of her grip. Her eyes meet mine and she shivers, disappointment rolls off her in waves. When she'd finished milking my cock, he went soft. Probably because somewhere in the back of my mind, I know I'm not good enough for her and I'm sure it's reflected in my expression.

"I should go." She sobers quickly.

"No, stay." Beck groans from beside her in a half-ass attempt to reach for her. He misses as she slides out of his reach and goes to the pile of clothes we've left closer to the door. I should stop her. I need to stop her, but I can't. I can't move. I have never in my life felt the stabs of rejection.

Dozens of woman... *yeah, keep telling yourself that, asshat*...and never once have I been rejected, turned down, or been walked out on. Yet here she is, slipping back into her cowboy boots and her shirt. Jeans are already pulled up. The fact that she's leaving pisses me off.

She looks at me one more time, her eyes pleading with me to stop her. I give her a dismissive wave and slide down onto the side of the bed, putting my head in my hands as she opens the door to the room.

As soon as it clicks closed I tell Beck, "Get out."

"What crawled up your ass?" he grumbles as he sits up.

"Forget it. I'm tired."

"Man, you fucking missed..." I know the look I give him is cold when he steps back. "Yeah, you're either too fucking drunk or something is seriously fucking wrong with you." He rips off the used condom, ties it off and throws it in the trashcan by the dresser. I bend down and grab my shorts, but I don't manage to get them thrown on before he actually leaves the room without another word.

I drop my shorts, turn out the light and stand, pulling the covers back on my bed and I crawl in.

The last thing I see is visions of Raine's beautiful eyes staring straight into me. Crawling her way in and shattering everything I ever thought I knew or understood about women.

When you're sticking your dick into something unknown and nameless, the looks are all the same, disconnected and haunted, but no, not Raine. No, hers are filled with something else, something unknown, something I have to figure out. Something I don't know if I will be able to figure out.

chapter
17
raine

I have never been so thankful in all my life when I stepped out of that room and the hallway was clear. My guess is the guys haven't returned from their evening out. No matter, the sooner I get away from this room, the better.

When I get inside my suite, I fall against the door. Cold shivers wrack my entire body. Fear, panic and something close to hysteria overtake my body. Compliments of my alcohol induced state; I couldn't stay there for long. Alcohol has never had me puking before, but combined with the shame running through my veins; I'm done for.

Once I finally stop dry heaving, I'm rung out, but I have no choice. I have got to take a shower. I have to wash the disgusting feeling off of me. I know it's all mental but short of running steel wool all over my body, I don't know what else to do.

I'd invited Beck in, expecting him to be the one that would ground me. Instead, he made me feel the most insecure about my body and myself. He wasted no time in staking the claim that he wanted on me and from the moment he slammed into me, nearly tearing me apart, I knew I'd made the wrong decision. I could feel the penetrating eyes of the man I really wanted to be with. The man who stood in the corner and watched. Then when he finally came to me, he wasn't with me, at least that's how it felt. It was cold and yet something was lying just under the surface, just out of reach.

When he came down my throat, shame, revulsion and the word whore came sliding into my mind and consuming my body like I'd been bathed in ice water. I had no choice, I had to leave.

When I finish my shower, I pull on a pair of shorts and tank top and slide under the covers. Desperate to put tonight behind me and praying to the god of hangovers that I will have the worst possible hangover with absolutely no memory of what happened tonight, I fall asleep.

"No, don't!"

"Stop!"

"What are you doing to me?"

"Taking what you've been flaunting in front of me all fucking night!"

"Get off of me!"

"That's exactly what I plan to do, get off on you."

He's drunk and his words are slurring together, maybe I can...he pins my arms down, holding me hard to the ground. His knees press down on my thighs, holding me immobile.

Bile rises in my throat when he licks along my cheek, then down along my neck. I need to get out of here; I need to get away from him.

I struggle.

I fight.

The weight of a thousand tons is on my body and I can't move.

Finally I feel his hand on my wrists loosen. Taking advantage of his momentary distraction, I free my hands and manage to knock him off balance and he falls on top of me. Shit!

Then in a moment of sheer adrenaline I'm able to free a leg and...that's it, right. Bam!

"Argh!" he rolls off of me. "You stupid fucking bitch, you're going to pay for that," he groans, grabbing his cock in his hands. Praying that he's incapacitated enough, I take off running, naked, through the park.

Screaming for someone to help me.

No one is around.

That's when it happens... a hand grips my elbow so hard, my hand goes numb almost instantly and I am spun around hard and fast.

Whack.

Black...pitch black.

I jolt awake. Breathing heavy, breathing hard, deep, like the oxygen has been sucked out of the room, I can't find it. Where am I? I look around, looking for something familiar, something to ground me to where I am at this moment.

My suitcase.

My suitcase...A hotel room...vague decorations...yes, hotel.

New York…

Working…

Addison, assistant…

I scrub my face. It's been a long time since I had that dream. A long time since I've felt the dirtiness of… I cannot even begin to say the word. Five years of therapy. Five years of discussing it, five years of reliving it over and over again had put it out of my mind. Five years of discussing the events of that night, the events following that night and ultimately what led to my moving to California. To running away. Though the therapy came after I moved when I was finally convinced by a friend to seek help. I guess if it hadn't been for her own personal experiences, she wouldn't have been able to convince me to go.

In the end, I was glad I went and it wasn't until Beck slammed hard into me last night and I saw stars that I realized I have additional triggers besides my elbow being grabbed. But it's only one, just that one. Sometimes I wonder if I have permanent bruises on my arms to constantly remind me of what happened that night.

When my breathing finally returns to normal and I'm ready to get up and take yet another shower to wash away the sweat and the dream, there is a knock at the door. "Who is it?"

"It's Beck."

Oh, for fuck's sake. I look at the clock, Jesus, it's barely eight o'clock. What the hell does he want? I walk over to the door. "Whatever you have to say, I don't want to hear it."

"This isn't about…shit, Raine, let me in, please."

I scowl at the door. I let out a sigh of frustration and open the door, placing my foot behind it, hoping to make it harder for him to push his way inside. "What?" I say in a pretty snotty tone.

He scowls at me. "I'm not the one for you to be pissed off at, ya know?"

He's right of course. "Yeah, I know. What do you need?"

"Can I come…" The shake of my head and the look in my eyes has him stopping mid-sentence. "Look, I don't want to talk about last night, something's happened."

"Is Dex…"

"He's fine." The scowl deepens just a little bit. "Kyle's gone."

"Whoa. What are you talking about, he's gone?" I move my foot from behind the door and open it a little further. I pick the wrong moment to peak my head out into the hallway.

"I don't give a shit what you do or how you do it, find that son of a bitch and drag him back here kicking and screaming if you have to." It's Talon, yelling at some of the security guys. Then all of a sudden, Dex's door swings open.

"Some people are trying to…" I hear him say but I can feel Talon's wrath all the way down the hallway and Dex stops, no doubt he's feeling it too. "T? What the fuck, man? What's going on?"

"Have you seen Kyle?" Talon asks him and I move to stand in the hallway a little more. Making it more obvious that I'm actually there and listening to what's happening.

Make this the second bad idea I've had so far today and I've been awake for ten fucking minutes. Dex steps into the hallway at the same time. I try to slink back into my room but he pins me down with that penetrating stare of his and I have a nearly uncontrollable urge to fall to my knees and grovel like an errant school girl and yet, I don't feel like I've done anything wrong.

"Talon, we're doing everything we can," the tall one in the middle says. Mills, if I recall correctly. He's Talon's right hand man and also the head of the security team that surrounds the band. "We don't know where he went after leaving the hotel. We're working on tracking his cell."

"Fuck it. Let him be. He has twenty-four hours to return or call. If we don't hear from him, we'll send out the dogs." I watch as Talon's shoulders slump and pain takes over.

"How's Addison?" Dex asks in probably the sweetest voice I've ever heard and my heart breaks for what I did to him last night. He is a manwhore, there is no getting around that fact, but something about his concern and tenderness is pulling and tugging at what little resolve I had when I went to bed last night.

"She's a fucking mess. We have to be at the studio in a few hours."

"Cancel that shit," Dex tells him, but Talon shakes his head.

"I need it, even if she doesn't go, I...fuck, I have to outlet this somehow." The wrath I felt earlier turns to sadness and I want to go to him, hug him, tell him everything will be fine, but the weight in my legs is too much when I see Dex hug Talon.

Who was I kidding?

God, I barge into this group of people, this fucking family, as evident by the hard-nosed assholian that is Dex Harris hugging his best friend.

I try once again to slink back into my room unnoticed, but I manage to capture Talon's attention. I brace myself for the fury from my eavesdropping on what's going on but instead he gives me a sad smile and pulls back from Dex. "She's going to need you today," he tells me softly and I nod. Dex smiles.

chapter
18
raine

Knock, knock, knock...

"What?" I hear from the other side of the door.

"It's me."

"What do you want?" This time the voice is closer to me than it was the first time, so I know he's moved to the door.

"Can you open the door, please?"

I hear the click of the security lock, the turn of the deadbolt and then finally the turning of the handle. When the door opens, the most sensual, sexy, tanned, tattooed and toned chest I've ever laid eyes on greets me. Though I've seen it before, my mouth still waters. I can't stop staring, probably looking like a fool. There is a light sheen of sweat or water marking his skin. He's either just gotten out of the shower or finished a workout, one of the two. No matter, I have the urge to lick the water from his chest.

"My eyes are up here, sweetheart," he says in that slightly amused, slightly detached voice.

"Yeah, I know, I'll get there," I grumble and my eyes dart to his. He's got a Cheshire grin on his face, but it doesn't reach his eyes. "Hi," I breathe.

"Hello." His voice is harder, cooler than I thought it might be. After returning from the studio with Addison, she asked me to leave her be and gave me a list of things she would like me to do today. A list of things that will take me probably fifteen minutes to complete.

"Can we talk?"

He leans against the wall, crossing his arms. His leg is holding the door open. "Not sure we've got anything to talk about."

"I think we do."

He gives me a disinterested look and shakes his head, a slight frown marring his beautiful face. It's a look I'm deciding right here and now, I don't really want to see again.

"It's done, it's over with, and nothing we can do to change it, nothing to talk about." Then he leans in and whispers, "You gave me head. Big fucking deal."

"I think I should explain why I ran off so quickly last night."

"Not sure I know what you're talking about, sweetheart. We were done. I got off, Beck got off, and I think even you got off a few times. We all had orgasms and life moves on."

His words twist like a knife in my back, but I guess I shouldn't be surprised. I came here hoping that what I feel when it comes to him is really real and not some infatuated fan girl moment that managed to suck off the sexiest drummer on the planet. In the distance, in his room, a phone rings. "If you'll excuse me." Unable to say anything further, I let the door close in my face and I lean my forehead against it. So much for the smile he gave me earlier. Something strikes me. Maybe I'd misread his smile. What if he was smiling, not at me, but at Beck? I'm such an idiot.

I go back to my room, dejected from my lack of conversation with Dex, though I'm not sure I really knew what it was that I was going to say to him.

Regardless, it was stupid of me to think that what I was seeing in his eyes last night was real. I go back to my room to lick my wounds and get back to work.

I work throughout the afternoon on the project Addison gave me. Updating some social media and making a few adjustments to her schedule. She looked awful. I hate to say that, especially about a woman as gorgeous as Addison, but she barely spoke to me or anyone else today. I can't imagine what she's going through; at least I'm not sure I want to try. Hopefully things will rectify themselves and get back to normal for her or she'll be able to find a way to cope with a new arrangement. Though the way she looked today, I wonder if she'd ever be able to handle the loss of Kyle from their relationship.

About the time I'm wrapping up, Tori comes to my door and asks me to join her and the rest of the team in the hallway. I'm introduced to the entire security team. I recognize Casey and Troy from the bar last night. They were with Peacock and Mouse and they left with them too. Mills, I've met before, Bruce and Leroy are two of the biggest men I think I've ever seen in my life. Troy, Casey, Rusty and of course Beck were also there. Beck didn't even make eye contact with me. Whatever, it just reiterates that Dex's smile wasn't meant for me and Beck's avoidance tactic was either professional versus personal or an "I've already fucked you, nothing more needs to be said".

After finishing my projects, I get really bored. I mean fuck; I'm in New York City of all places. I can go where I want and do what I want.

I decide to put on my walking shoes and meander around Times Square, maybe go do a little shopping in SoHo. Who knows, but it's up to me to do what I want.

When I leave the room, Tori and Rusty are standing in the hallway talking. Though I don't really know what about and I don't care all that much, they stop and look at me when I come walking down the hall. I have my messenger bag slung over my shoulder and my coat hanging over my arm. "Going somewhere?" Tori asks with a half-smile.

I shrug, "It's been a while since I've been to New York, thought I'd go wandering around for a while."

"Alone?" Rusty asks.

"Yeah, why not?"

Both of them scowl at me. "Let us send someone with you."

I smirk. "Nah, I'm good."

"Mills insists on it," Rusty says very straight faced. I scowl at him. "No one out alone."

"Kyle's out there alone." Both of them look crestfallen at my statement. "Look, I'm a grown woman…"

"So is Addison." That's all Tori had to say. I remember Dallas and then again in Kansas City. "One of us will lose our jobs if we let you go alone."

"What would you have done if you weren't in the hallway when I tried to leave?"

Rusty shakes his head. "That doesn't happen very often."

I raise an eyebrow at him. "Really? Because I managed to walk from Dex's room to mine early this morning and no one was around."

Rusty gives me a knowing smile. "Yeah, um," he turns toward the elevator, "see the..." I cover my mouth in shock. "I was sitting down there, you just didn't see me and me being the gentleman that I am..." He doesn't finish, he just blushes slightly and I go red as a fucking cherry.

"Well, okay then, um, who did you have in mind?" I ask.

"Beck's free." I cringe and they both catch it. "We could send Casey or I guess I could go," Rusty says. "I'm just coming on to take the night shift, but..." He looks to Tori for confirmation, she nods. "Or we have Casey. I can swap with him to take Eric and Calvin."

"Anyone but Beck. I'll let you guys hash it out while I go check on Addison. Is Talon back yet?"

"Not yet, but he should be shortly," Tori replies.

"Okay, good. Can you let me in?" Tori turns and puts the key card in the slot, knocks, then opens the door.

I step inside and the door closes. "Addison?" I call out and get no response, at least not one that I can hear. I step deeper into the suite and most of it is dark, curtains pulled tight and only a light on in the second bedroom. I head for that light and see her sound asleep on the bed. I don't really want to wake her, but I need to make sure she's all right. I don't make it as far as I need to in order to reach out and wake her.

"I'm all right," she says softly. She's been crying. Her voice is shaky with emotion and her eyes are red.

"Can I get you anything?" She just shakes her head. "I'm going to go out for a little while. I gave the detail my number, and you have it too. If you need it, call me and I'll come right back."

She nods. "Be careful."

I smile. Even in her state of distress, she's still thinking about other people, so I guess that's good. "Want me to check on you when I come back?"

She shakes her head. I'll decide later about that. "I do need you to do something for me though."

I smile. "Anything."

"Go to the studio tomorrow with Talon, he's going to need some help." She looks at me then, pleading with me and I can tell that her asking me to do that is a real struggle for her.

"How about we see how you're feeling tomorrow and go from there?"

She nods and rolls back on her side. "I'm here, you know, if you need someone to talk to."

"Thanks." She gives me a very weak smile but says nothing further.

I leave her alone in her bed and step out into the hallway. Once again colliding with Dex and Beck. Shivers slide up my spine and I feel my nipples harden. I move my jacket to the front and interlock my arms, hoping to hide the evidence that seeing them both, together, turns me on. But unfortunately, it's the asshat drummer I can't take my eyes off of.

chapter
19
dex

There is one thing that can be said for sleeping with nameless strays and groupies. You never have to see them again. But this one...she keeps popping up everywhere, and every time I see her, my dick gets rock fucking hard and it takes every ounce of willpower I have not to slam her against the wall and fuck her.

When she came knocking earlier, I'd only, not three minutes before, decided to let it go. Move on, go out tonight and find another nameless chick to get lost in, to extinguish this one from my mind, my body, and even my fucking sense of smell. I only pray that the maids actually changed the sheets so that her scent isn't still clinging to them.

"Am I ready to go?" she asks. *Wait, where is she going?*

"Just about," Rusty says then he turns to Beck. "She's going out, I'm following her."

"We'll go too," I blurt and just like that there are five pairs of eyes looking at me. Beck, Rusty, Tori, Mills, and lastly, the ones I'm trying to ignore, Raine's. *Why the fuck did I just say that?*

"No thanks," she says to me, rather coolly and maybe even a little too sharply and all eyes shift over to her. "I'm going out to have a good time, by myself." With that she turns to leave, headed toward the elevator and I grab her elbow. She freezes up again and I release her elbow. "On second thought, I'm just going to go back to my room," she says through clenched teeth.

Just like that there is a flurry of concern amongst everyone over her reaction. I freeze, realizing that I'm still holding her elbow. I let it go and she relaxes, but she turns back around and heads toward her room. "Raine, wait," I say.

"No," she states firmly and keeps walking. I start to follow after her and someone grabs my shoulder. I turn to see the hand is attached to Mills who shakes his head.

"You know the rules," he says in a whisper and I nod. Mills is now going to go talk to her.

But he doesn't move, he turns to Tori and nods. She dutifully follows after Raine who is shaken and fumbling with her keycard. My heart hurts. Concern rises in my chest and I can't help the urge to go to her, but Mills, being the dutiful bodyguard that he is, won't let me. The rules are simple, security handles it first. I watch as Tori gently takes Raine's keycard from her and her eyes shoot up. There is panic in her eyes, but she relaxes quickly, looking back at what Tori is doing and when Tori opens the door, Raine rushes in.

"What was that all about?" Mills' tone is accusatory.

"Your guess is as good as mine," I say, still looking at Raine's door.

"So what just happened has nothing to do with you?"

"Probably does because you know what an asshole I am. But she froze up the first time I touched her elbow, well before anything happened. It also happened later in the evening, way across the bar from us by an unknown man. It's obviously a trigger for her, but I…" My blood runs cold and I look back at her door. "What I wouldn't give to be a fly on the wall," I mutter.

raine

Tori follows me in. "It's our policy to know everything we can about our clients."

"I'm not a client," I snap.

"Yes, you are. The moment you showed up, you became our responsibility while you're here and with us. Care to explain what just happened?"

"Not particularly." I sit down in the chair opposite the room from Tori and curl my legs up underneath me. Compliments of that fucking dream last night, I am strung tighter than a violin. I had no business reacting that way.

"Was it Dex?"

"No."

"Does it have to do with last night?" she asks.

I look out the window, overlooking Times Square below me, wanting to be down there walking around, but instead I'm having a mini panic attack. "Not directly, no."

"I need you to explain."

I give her a cold look. "I got drunk, decided to indulge in a fantasy that escalated to a semi-threesome with Beck. That ended up with me being fucked by Beck and Dex shutting down completely after he got his rocks off and I got my jab in before he could by leaving. I made the decision. I suffer the consequences of that choice. But the emotions it brought out in me were emotions I hadn't felt in a long time." I let out a slow breath. "I felt like a whore," I breathe.

"You're anything but that, Raine. Dex has a way of making women feel that way. Though I'm sorry you were trapped up in that, it's how he operates."

"Yeah, I know and I knew that going into the little adventure. I was drunk, uninhibited by my usual shyness and by the way he was acting, well, I figured it would be easy to deal with it and in all honesty it was. I just woke up screaming this morning." By the time I finish my little speech, I'm whispering.

"Are there other triggers we need to know about?" she asks softly.

I look her square in the eye. "How?"

She gives me a half smile. "There are usually only two reasons a woman reacts to triggers… one is abuse and the other is an attack or…"

"Rape." The word falls from my lips.

"That."

She takes a seat on the end of my bed. She is the first person, aside from my therapist who hasn't looked at me with pity in her eyes, only understanding.

"Other triggers?" she asks me.

"None that you need to worry about."

"I think I do. I think we do."

"No, it's more physical, while being intimate. Which ultimately is what led to the start of my panic last night." I go back to looking out the window.

"Which was? Did either one of those two hurt you?" Her voice is stern but not demanding.

"No. At least not intentionally." Rather than beat around the bush, "Beck slammed into me really hard. Like I said, it wasn't intentional."

"All the same, we need to know."

I look at her again. "I think it's moot because I don't intend to sleep with either one of them again while I'm here." She nods her understanding. "This conversation…it's…"

"It's between us. I just need to let Mills know and pass along the elbow trigger to the guys, so that they can be aware of signs of distress while with you."

I nod, fighting tears. "It's just my left elbow. It's like it's permanently bruised, so any grabbing sends me into a panic."

"What about the right?" she asks, true curiosity in her voice. I smile a little.

"No."

"Will you be all right?"

I nod and go back to looking out the window. "I just need some time to myself. I'll decide in a little bit if I'm going to go out or order room service."

She nods and stands. "We really are here to protect you. If Dex or Beck is bothering you, will you let me know?"

I nod again. She leaves the room quietly and the tears start to flow.

Who knew that ten years later that asshole would still affect my everyday life from something as simple as having my elbow grabbed?

chapter
20
dex

Shortly after Tori went into Raine's room Mills moved down the hallway to be near the door. Rusty and Beck start chatting and we're quickly joined by Casey, Troy, Leroy and Bruce. "What's going on?" someone asks. The deep voice says it's probably Bruce or Leroy, but I don't turn around to find out.

"Tori is talking to Raine," Rusty says. "We're waiting for the results of that conversation."

I want to just go back to my room, or the bar, but I need to know if her reaction has anything to do with me and I need to make sure she's all right.

Finally after what seems like a lifetime, a door opens. But it isn't Raine's. I turn to see Talon, beaten up emotionally, standing in his doorway. "What's going on?"

"Nothin man, no worries," I say. "Go back to your girl. How's she doing?"

"Quite possibly better than I am."

"You need anything?" Rusty asks him and Talon just shakes his head. "Holler if you do, we'll take care of it." Talon nods and quietly closes the door.

"Jesus, he's a fucking mess," someone says.

I turn around and address whoever it was. "You would be too if you were dealing with what he's got going on," I tell them. "Just leave him be."

My defense of Talon doesn't come as a shock to anyone. Though I fucking wish Kyle were here. Maybe none of this would have happened because we'd have all been out to dinner having a good time instead of dealing with all this drama.

We all wait with bated breath when we hear a door click, this time quieter and further down the hall. Thank god, we have the fucking floor to ourselves.

Tori steps out of the room and quietly closes the door behind her. "She all right?" I say a little too loudly and I get shushed.

Tori looks at me, gives me a sad smile and nods her head. Fuck me, what the hell is this all about?

Tori steps closer to Mills and they turn around, talking quietly. I don't get my panties in a bunch, Beck will tell me eventually. Provided he finds out. The circumstances of the situation will determine if Mills tells the crew or not.

I'm nearly crawling out of my skin, ready to totally rip it to shreds and fuck if I know why.

Because this one means something to you...

I want to scream at the fucking voice in my head, tell it to shut its pie hole and stop fucking around with me, but I know damn well, it's right. My standing here, waiting on bated breath is proof of that fact.

They turn around and start walking toward us. Mills has his normal game face on and he's looking at all of us, then his eyes land on me. "Dex?" He stops halfway between Raine's room and where I'm standing. I feel like I've been called before a firing squad and my legs feel heavy as fuck. *What the hell did she tell her?*

Beck was there, I guess this is where I figure out what kind of friend he really is.

I get closer to them and finally come a stop. "Yeah?"

Mills straightens a little bit. Why do I all of a sudden feel like a child who stole the last Twinkie in the box? Oh wait, because I've been that child. "You're fine," Mills says quietly. "So is Beck."

The air in my lungs leaves in a relieved huff. "So then what's the deal?"

"I can't tell you that."

"Fuck you, you can't tell me. I'm the one that touched her, I'm the one that made her freak out and ruin her evening."

"No, I really can't tell you." Tori steps up. "There are certain things that should be heard straight from the horse's mouth. You need to let her tell you, if that's what she wants to do."

I try to sidestep both of them and go to her room, to fucking apologize, to talk to her, anything. "No." Mills' voice has that stern command in it and like a stupid love struck teenager meeting the parents for the first time, I freeze.

"She's asked for some privacy, some time. Let her have it," Mills says and I deflate. "Believe me, the more time and space you give her, the better off you'll be."

I nod.

"Just do your best to keep your hands off of her," Tori says, though there is no malicious intention in her voice, the threat is implied.

"That might be easier if I understood," I bite back.

"Well, you'll have to take it up with her, another time," Mills says and finally getting the hint, I turn and head for the elevator just as Mouse and Peacock exit their rooms. I hit up instead of down. I'm going to the roof. I need the fresh air and the view.

Somewhere in the midst of all this, I started to care. Somewhere in the midst of what the fuckity fuck is happening inside my head, I'm losing my edge and it's pissing me the fuck off.

Surprisingly, I manage to make it onto the elevator alone. I slump against the wall after pressing the 32 button. No doubt they'll know where I'm headed. I mean, where the hell else am I going to go? When the doors open, surprisingly the rooftop bar has more people in it than I expected, but whatever. I head up to the bar and order two Scotches and a book of matches. I need a smoke.

The bartender slides me the drinks and the matches, I slide him back two twenties. "Keep it." He nods and I turn around for the door to the open air patio, though it's caged, there's some comfy as hell seats out there and I can smoke. If I can't shoot it or snort it, might as well smoke. And no, I'm not talking about smoking drugs, I just want to smoke a pack of cigarettes and get drunk off my ass. So drunk in fact that someone will either leave me on the rooftop passed out, or have to carry my drunken ass to bed.

It's chilly out here. I mean, shit, it's fucking what? April, in New York City? It's not Los Angeles. But the cold drives patrons back inside faster which fucking works for me.

It's obvious that Raine has some deep secrets to keep. I snort to myself. Don't we all? But what do these secrets really do to her.

Somewhere around my fifth or sixth shot, Beck finally shows up. He doesn't say anything, he just fucking slumps onto the couch, a beer in his hand.

"It's my fault," he finally says after I light another cigarette.

"What? The elbow thing?"

He shakes his head and sips his beer. Leaning forward on his elbows, he grabs a cigarette from my pack and lights it then leans back again. "What, dude? Seriously?"

"That she bailed out on you last night."

"Huh?" I look at him, raising an eyebrow.

"I don't know the details, but I spooked her somehow." He takes a drag.

"So they tell you that, but can't tell you why or what?"

He shakes his head. "No, but I will ask her. The next time I see her. They also told me that she specifically requested that I not escort her tonight."

I squint at him. "What the fuck did you do?" I look at him, the alcohol finally kicking in and taking hold. Though the warming took effect almost immediately, my brain is starting to get a little fuzzy.

"At first I wanted to think that she figured if I escorted her that you'd come along. Then I thought maybe she was really just giving me, or us," he corrects himself, "a one night stand. Stuffing it back in our faces the way we do it to so many women, but I honestly think there's more to it than that."

I finish off my latest glass just as the waitress arrives with another. I tip my head toward her and raise my glass, then point between Beck and I. She nods and takes off for the bar once again. I down half the new glass in one big gulp. "Well, I was told that if I wanted to know the answers, I had to ask her myself. So whatever it is, they're doing a damn good job of hiding it."

"As they should. Listen, there are certain things that we know about each and every one of you guys, even maybe stuff you might not even know or be aware of, but the whole point of the matter behind that is so that we have a better idea of the people we're trying to protect. You may think I tell you everything, but I don't. In fact, nowhere near everything."

"Are you telling me everything now?"

He takes a big long drink of his beer, finishing it off before answering me, "yes."

As much as I want to accuse him of bullshitting me, I have no doubt he's telling me the truth. If Raine's private matters won't be told to the person who actually caused the reaction, I doubt that they told the guys either. Or because Beck is central to the story, they didn't include him.

It isn't until two drinks later that Beck finally moves onto the hard shit, trying like hell to catch up with my state of inebriation, but I'm too fucking drunk to give a shit. I also only just now notice his ear piece is out. "You're off duty?" I question him.

He nods. "Why do you think I'm getting sloshed?"

I laugh at his choice of words. "Who's..." Then I look through the glass of the bar and see Bruce and Casey standing there, trying to look all nonchalant and shit. "Fuck this. I'm going to bed."

Drinking and standing... standing and drinking, drinking and walking, yeah, none of those are advised to be done simultaneously as I stumble my way into the bar, toward the elevator. Bruce is hot on my heels. No doubt Casey will stay behind to keep an eye on Beck.

Once we're in the elevator, I half sit on the bar that divides the wall. "She still in her room?"

"No," Bruce says short and sweet.

"Good, she went out then."

He doesn't answer or say anything else. Our elevator arrives on the seventeenth floor and I stumble out. Just in time to see Raine standing in front of her door. I need to apologize to her, I need to make this right, but I can barely walk, let alone talk, and she can see that. She slips inside her room, closes her door and throws the chains. Shutting me out.

"Fuckin' A," I groan as Bruce lets me into my room. I manage to strip off my shirt, boots and make a half-ass attempt at my jeans before I fall hard and heavy onto my bed, face down. Turning slightly, I fall asleep with visions of those bright ice blue eyes and luscious lips.

chapter
21
raine

Waking up Tuesday morning, after a nightmare-free sleep, I feel revived and refreshed. All the craziness of the last twenty-four hours finally seems to be lifting. Though I am certain Kyle hasn't returned. I don't need someone to tell me he hasn't to know, only because someone would have told me if he had.

After my shower, I stand before the closet that I finally managed to unpack myself into and I try to decide what to wear today. A birdie, namely Rusty, told me last night that Dex would be going with me and Talon to the studio today and that Addison wasn't needed. If it weren't for the fact that Addison had asked me to go to the studio to help, I'd stay back and help her.

So when I crawled into bed last night, I gave myself two choices. Option A - make it impossible for him to resist me. Suck him in. Make him crumble. Or option B - ignore him.

On the exterior, Dex is a hard ass, an assholian, a complete and total dick, but there is something simmering just under the surface with him. He looked desperate to come to me last night, but he was too drunk to really be able to do anything about it. So I am going with option A. Make it impossible for him to resist me. Make him come to me, begging for it. Then, string him along. Okay, I'm not a total bitch, but the reality of the situation is if he really wants this (meaning me) then he's going to have to work for it and work pretty fucking hard.

I regard myself in the mirror. Black hair pulled up into a stick straight pony tail. Hot pink and black bangs forward and straight across. Make-up, subtle but there, with hues of pinks and purples. Lipstick, cherry chocolate. Perfect for my complexion. Earrings - my mini-spikes and I've changed my industrial piercings to my hot pink barbells. Top - low cut, falls off the shoulder, exposing part of my ink with a tank top underneath to hide the bra straps of a red, sexy lace bra and panty set. Pants - black skinny jeans with my fur lined buckle boots. Jewelry - there's plenty of that to go around.

Confidence boosted.

I grab my deep hooded jacket, my messenger bag and turn out the lights just as there is a knock on the door. "Coming," I shout and finish grabbing everything I think I need. I grab everything except my courage to actually do this. The moment I open the door, all bets are off.

Dex is standing there with his hands on the door's frame and he is staring at me. Courage recovered. "Wow," he breathes as if he expected me to be dressed in a frumpy housedress. Though a dress did cross my mind, but it's not really my style. I figure if I'm hanging out with rock gods all day, I might as well look the part.

"Breathe, Dex," I tell him and he smiles.

"I can't help it, you're gorgeous."

I know I blush as red as a cherry and he lights up.

"We need to talk," he says softly.

"We don't have time. I need to stop in and say hi to Addison and..."

"Tonight?"

I shrug. "We'll see." I slide out of my room under his arm.

"You're killing me, smalls," he whispers.

I stop and turn to look at him. His eyes are alight with some excitement and a little bit of desire. "You can handle a little payback," I tell him and his eyes widen a fraction and then narrow at me.

"Payback? For what?"

"For being an assholian."

He snorts, "A what?"

"An assholian - it's a religion for assholes."

He crosses his arms over his chest, the muscles in them bulging, my mouth waters, wanting to lick along the bluish veins popping out. "So you think I'm an asshole?" There is a playfulness in his eyes that I've never seen before, and well, I kind of like it.

"No, Dex, I don't think, I know." With that, I turn and walk away, walking toward Addison's room just as Talon comes out and we nearly collide.

"Shit, Raine, sorry," he says with a small smile.

"No problem how is she?"

His shoulders slump. "Not much of a change, she's sleeping now."

"Should I..."

He just shakes his head. "You're coming with us, right?" he asks and I nod. "Okay, then we should probably get going." I nod again and Beck, Mills, and Rusty come out of a room near the elevator decked out in black cargo pants, with guns secured in gun holsters and black t-shirts. They actually look very scary and intimidating when they're like this. "We're ready," Talon tells them and we all head toward the elevator.

Dex is bringing up the rear behind me. He leans closer to me and whispers in my ear, "You're right, I am an assholian. But I still want to talk."

I shiver at the breath that washes over my neck as he whispers but I don't reply. I know what he wants to talk about and I don't want to discuss it. It was easy to tell Tori because I didn't exactly tell her, she just kind of knew. But Dex, I have a feeling I'm going to have to spell that one out and I don't know if I can do that again. But the caveat to that is the fact that telling him could make or break any future plans he may have for me. Some men can handle the pain and trauma that comes with a rape victim, but many can't. It's hard to sleep next to someone who wakes up screaming in the middle of the night because something has triggered the nightmare in the first place. Michael was an exception, though. He never complained, but I also never told him why either. I guess that was our first mistake.

When we arrive at the studio, I sit back to enjoy the show as they get set up for Dex to lay a drum track on the original song Talon had written. It's performed on stage as an acoustic duet, but the change in adding a drum is to enhance the experience for radio, taking away the sound of a live performance and making it something else entirely.

I watch as Dex tirelessly practices his part. It was only written recently and he hadn't had a chance to work on it yet. I'm blown away by how his demeanor changes when he sits down behind his drums. Gone is the asshole and sitting in his place is a man of music, creativity and sexy hot rock god drummer. It's like flipping a switch with him and I have to tell you, it is the sexiest thing I think I have ever seen.

"Go easy on him." I turn to Talon who's joined me in the mixing room.

"I don't know what you're talking about," I tell him but then I can't help but let my eyes drift back to watching Dex on the drums. I can't hear him play; I can only hear the faint sounds coming through the headphones in the room.

Talon snorts a laugh. "Really?"

I look back to him and he's smiling slightly. "We've gotten off on the wrong foot," I tell him.

"I know." My eyes widen a fraction. Talon takes a seat next to me, leaning forward on his elbows. The last twenty four hours have really taken a toll on him and it's physically showing now. "But I also know that when Dex wants something, he won't stop until he has it."

"I don't want to be just another girl."

"That's not what happened Sunday night. At least I'm gathering that you had no inhibitions about where things would go from there," he tells me quietly.

"I was fueled by fantasy and alcohol. I knew then that it would probably be best to just let him get it out of his system; at least it might have made it easier for us to work together. But instead, it turned disastrous and it's making it more difficult. I only pulled Beck into the room because I needed a sense of security. I was pretty certain that Dex would have torn me to shreds if we'd been alone," I share quietly and it's true. My gut instinct had told me that I could decipher the difference between fucking Dex and wanting something more if someone else was in the room. That it would make the situation less intimate, but instead, it only heightened the intimacy. An intimacy that I suspect was brought on by jealousy.

"He more than likely would have. That's how he operates. Never getting close to anyone he sleeps with. Then again, he never really sleeps with anyone either. He's a complex person, Raine, very difficult to figure out and even more difficult to tame. But I do know that he's into you, like really into you. More than I've ever seen him act before." Talon's voice is gentle. "But, if you give him a chance, you need to know that there is a better chance that he will fuck up."

"What's that supposed to mean?"

He chuckles a little bit and looks at me. "When Addison, Kyle and I first got together, I asked Addison for patience and understanding because I was going to fuck up and I have." I look at him, shocked. "Not in the sense that I'm sure is running through your mind, but in the sense that relationships are a new thing for me. Just like they would be for Dex. I'd never even thought about wanting to be in a relationship until I was in one up to my eyeballs with the two of them. But I quickly realized that loving them was easier than I thought. Then I realized that because I love them so much that everything else is trivial. Nothing else matters if we can work through things together." He scrubs his face. "But now...now I don't know what's going to happen."

"Still no word from him?"

He gives me a very sad smile. "No, and now it's to the point that I fight the urge every minute to call him, to go find him. If for nothing else, answers, closure, anything. I just need to know so that I can reassure Addie. So that I can tell her that it will all be all right, but I can't and that is what hurts the most." He stands up, scrubbing his face again. I notice now that his hair is disheveled and his beard is growing longer and more unruly than his normal scruff. "I think the only thing that's keeping me sane is Thursday." I raise an eyebrow at him. "Our next show. Kyle has never missed a show, no matter what. No matter how drunk, how high, or how far away he may have been, he has always made it to the next show."

"So you think he'll just show up at the show?"

He nods and I look through the glass into the studio, watching Dex beat away on the drums. It's the same beat he's been playing for the last forty-five minutes, each time getting faster and more refined. It's impressive.

"If he doesn't show up, that's when the cops will get involved. That..." his voice drops to a whisper, "that's when I know something is very wrong."

"I wish there was something I could do," I mutter.

"You're doing it." He gives me that sad broken smile again and my heart breaks for him and Addison.

In an attempt to change the subject, I bring up the baby, but it doesn't work, he just says that everything is fine. I can tell, just by the look in his eyes when I brought it up, that it's something he hasn't quite come to terms with yet.

"You do realize that everything happens for a reason, right?" I tell him and he looks at me.

"Addison says the same thing."

"It's very true, you know. It's how I ended up here; it's how you ended up here, on tour, doing something that you love. There is a reason behind it and maybe yours is Addison or Kyle, or both." I give him a smile. "Everything, in the end, will be how it was meant to be."

"You honestly believe that?" He raises an eyebrow at me.

"Absolutely. We all have our secrets, our own demons, our highs and lows, the good and the bad, but in the end, there's a reason behind it all. An answer to the millions of unasked questions, reasonable explanations for which we will likely never know the why, but when we come to accept that there is a logical explanation, we come to better understand ourselves and who we are and what we wish to accomplish."

"That's a pretty profound statement."

"It is, but if you stop and think about it, it's true."

He doesn't respond to that, instead he goes back to watching Dex through the glass as he plays through the song one more time. Then he stops, hops out from behind the drum set and pulls off his shirt causing me to involuntarily drool all over myself as I watch him wipe down the sweat pouring from him. His back is to me as he drinks down about a half-gallon of water from the jug he'd brought in with him.

It is in this moment, this unguarded, drooling like an idiot moment that I realize, in the end; I am going to give in. I am going to talk to him, I am going to give him what he wants. Whether it's a one-night stand or something more. And I know that I'm the one who is going to get hurt.

chapter
22
raine

About six hours later, we're wrapping up at the studio and I'm feverishly typing out an email to Cami in response to some of the issues she's having back at the office. I'd spent a good part of the day tweeting and interacting on behalf of 69 Bottles, telling fans about being in the studio and the upcoming shows here in New York.

While watching the guys work, I decided that tonight I would go out and do what I'd wanted to do last night. I discussed it with Rusty at one point and he's going to have Casey or Troy shadow me. He had insisted that it be him, but I told him he'd worked enough for one day.

Last night, when I left my suite, I only went downstairs to grab a bite to eat. I was too emotionally wrung out and too claustrophobic sitting in my room so Rusty had escorted me downstairs. I felt awful about it and tried to convince him that I wasn't going to go anywhere but there.

Ironically enough, he'd kind of disappeared part way through my meal, which I ate while reading the latest book by one of my favorite authors.

"Can I take you out to dinner?" Dex asks me as we arrive back at the hotel.

A part of me is screaming on the inside, say yes, damn it don't miss this opportunity, but there is another part, equally as insistent, telling myself to make him work for it. "Not tonight."

"I asked you to talk to me." He's actually a little hurt by my turning him down. Once we're in the lobby I turn on him, facing him.

"Yeah, and we will. I know that one of the probably thousands of questions in your brain right now is about what happened last night. You deserve answers, and I promise you, I will give them to you, but not tonight." I touch his shoulder and he looks at my hand and back to me. There's desire burning in his eyes. My attempt to make him work for it is working better than I'd planned. Without really thinking about it, I move my hand from his shoulder to his cheek. His eyes close at the contact and he leans into it, sending my heart soaring and my blood burning. My breath hitches and if I didn't know better, it's almost as if he's purring.

"We can talk about other stuff," he finally says softly.

"Dex, I have no doubt that we can fill an entire evening with conversation about everything but that. But what that is, is something that I need to tell you and you need to decide for yourself what happens afterward."

"It doesn't matter what it is, it won't..."

I put my fingers to his lips. "Please don't say that. Please don't say that unless you really know what it is I need to tell you and you need to hear it from me. So please, give

153

me a day or two. Show me that the conversation is truly what you want to happen, and it will." I pull my hand away from his lips. He takes my hand in his. "Good night, Dex," I tell him and he kisses my knuckles.

"Good night, Raine," he says sweetly to me and I head for the elevator. He doesn't follow me, but Rusty does.

After several hours of wandering around New York City, Casey and I finally return to the hotel.

That's when I see it, or rather him, sitting on the same semi-circle of couches as the other night and not much has changed. Except Mouse and Peacock are still with him and there are no less than six girls between them, one of which is sitting on Dex's lap, running her fingers through his hair, smiling and talking animatedly with him. Everything else in the word fades away when she looks up at me, waves at me and then she plants her lips on his. I watch as his arms wrap around her, holding her to him, and he kisses her back, all the while she's looking at me.

Beck, unbeknownst to him that I'm watching, sidesteps in front of the two, blocking them from my view. Giving me my chance to escape into the elevator and up to my room.

That rat-fucking bastard. One minute he's sweet talking me, the next minute he's making out with some chick on the couch in a bar, seventeen floors below a room that he can take her into and have his way with her.

My skin crawls. My heart breaks.

dex

"Right here, sweetheart." I point toward my door.

"Oh," she squeaks and giggles like an idiot. I will never understand why women think that's attractive, but then again, I'm the idiot that brought her to my room. She hasn't stopped touching me since we left the bar and she does so now as my drunken ass tries to unlock the door.

Just as I slide the card inside the slot, I hear a door open down the hall. I don't look, assuming it's one of the guys. I usher her inside. No, I don't know her name, don't ask. She's all right in the face, nice body and she's someplace to bury my cock for an hour.

Right as she walks in the door, past me, I catch a glimpse of who opened their door and I freeze. Standing against the frame of her door is Raine. Her arms are folded and a completely crushed look is etched on her face. I look from her to the chick who's checking out my room and back to her again.

She pushes away from the wall and I think she's going to come down here, but instead she says, "I should've known." Then she goes into her room, lets the door slam shut and I hear the click of the deadbolt followed by the slamming of the chain.

The woman I brought up to the room with me comes up, runs her hand along my now limp cock and she rubs it. "What's taking you so long, big man?" she purrs in my ear. I slip inside and let the door close behind me.

chapter
23
raine

Knock, knock, knock.

I debate on not answering the door. In fact, I probably shouldn't because whoever is out there will have to deal with whatever wrath rolls off of me.

Knock, knock, knock.

I'm standing naked about to get in the shower, trying to wash off the creepy fucking crawlies from seeing Dex with that other woman. *Should I open the door?*
Oh fuck it.
I grab the fluffy white robe off of the back of the door, put it on and cinch it at the waist.
I flip the chain, unlock the deadbolt and pull open the door.
"What?" I snap.
"Easy."

I look up at him, he's still clothed, looking delicious as always, but I can't dwell on it. Not now, not anymore. "What do you want?" I say with an attitude.

"We need to talk."

"Like hell we do." I try to shut the door and he stops me.

"Yes, we do," he says a little more sternly. "Can I please come in?"

"What happened to your bimbo?" I ask as I realize there wasn't anywhere near enough time for them to have done anything.

"I threw her out."

"Why?" I breathe.

"Because..." I watch as he looks down the hall toward his room. I peek my head out the door, expecting to see her and instead I see Casey.

"Just making sure everything's all right," Casey says with a smile. "Dex asked me to come."

I smile a little and nod at him. "It's all right." Then I look up at Dex, my heart is pounding in my chest, and my body is coming alive from the look of desire in his eyes.

"Because I lost my head for a minute. Seeing you brought me back. I was angry that you turned me down for dinner, I was...fuck, Raine, I don't know what the hell is happening. One minute all I want to do is talk to you, the next minute you infuriate me to the point of what I nearly did tonight."

"Do what you want, Dex." I have no control over him or what he does and I don't even know why I let the fact that he brought some random chick to his room bother me, but it does. It fucking stings everywhere.

"Can I please come in? I really don't want to stand in the hallway and talk."

"I don't know what else there is to say," I tell him and try to shut the door again.

"Damn it, please let me explain, let me come in." His eyes are pleading with me, desperate to talk, to what? I don't really know.

My hesitation is in my eyes and he can see it. "I will be a perfect gentleman, I swear." He makes an X over his heart and my resolve falters, cracks off and dissolves away at the sweetness in his voice, his eyes.

I look over to Casey and I nod. He smiles and turns back toward the other end of the hallway and I open the door for Dex to step inside. As he passes me, he leans over and kisses me on the forehead and the last little bit I was holding on to waltzes out the door behind Casey. I must stay strong. Do not let him seduce you. I repeat the mantra over and over in my head as I close the door. Effectively locking us into a tight space.

When I look at him, the air charges between us. The tension is as thick as frozen butter. "Talk," I say softly as I cross my arms and lean against the wall.

"I think I need to explain Sunday night first." I freeze up.

"I don't know what you need to explain. I'm the one that left, remember?"

"You left because I fucked up," he says and walks further into the room and he takes a seat on the foot of my bed. I slide along the wall so that I can see him and he can see me. "I lost my head."

"Again with the head," I grumble.

"I lost it because watching what Beck was doing to you made me jealous." He looks at me, eyes serious.

I nearly expire from shock at his confession.

"I didn't like what he was doing to you, it bothered me. Which," his eyes dart to the floor, "is why I stayed back, trying to stay out of it, honestly trying to look away from it. But yet I couldn't. I couldn't because…because you were so fucking beautiful, laid out for him like that. Almost as beautiful as you were when I had my mouth on you. Then you called me over and I didn't have a choice, well, I did, but I was desperate for you, your touch. I needed it like nothing I've ever felt before." He's still looking at the floor as he continues his speech. "When I came, I had every intention of taking Beck's place … it got to be too much, I was overwhelmed by what I was feeling, what was running through my head and for the first fucking time in my life, I went soft in front of a woman I was desperate to be with because I'd let my head run the show. Then you freaked out and you left. I kicked Beck out almost immediately afterward, I was a fucking mess. I'm still a fucking mess."

Finally his sad steel grey eyes meet my tear filled blue ones. He stands and closes the gap between us. His hands cup my cheeks while his fingers slide into my hair. "When I fucking look at you, nothing matters. Nothing else exists but you. I froze because I realized that something as precious and beautiful as you are deserves far better than I can give you. I'm a manwhore, I've been a manwhore and I will always be a manwhore and you deserve much better than that."

With his declaration the tears streak down my cheeks hard and fast. The calloused pads of his thumbs gently wipe them away. "I don't believe you will always be a manwhore." That's all I manage to say.

"Oh how I wish that were true," he says in a rush of air filled with longing and loss. "I wish it were true so then maybe, just maybe, I'd be good enough for you."

With that, he slants his lips over mine in a soft, gentle, passion filled kiss that has my insides quivering. His lips are warm, soft and gentle against mine. The slight stubble of growth tickles against my lips. I kiss him back, bringing my hands up to mirror his hands on my face. His open mouth kisses are met with mine. No exchange of tongues, just passion and desire. I lick along his bottom lip and he groans. His body melts against mine. His erection forms against my belly and I'm hot, ready, wanting. I lick his upper lip, then his bottom one, until finally I find his tongue and I begin licking and stroking mine against his.

I whimper and he swallows my cries as his hands move down my neck to my shoulders, coming to rest on the collar of my bathrobe. "You're so fucking sexy in this thing," he murmurs and goes back to kissing me. My heart flutters with joy and hope that maybe, just maybe, all my years of fantasy might be coming true.

Desperately wanting this fantasy to come true.

His hands tug slowly on my robe, bringing it down my shoulders. "I'm not..."

"Do you want me to stop?" he asks. There is some concern in his voice, but it seems truly genuine.

"No," I assure him and capture his mouth once again, throwing my arms around his neck and pulling him into me. He's so much taller than I am that I pull him down so far his body pulls away from mine and I shiver. My nipples harden into tight, painful peaks. I release him so that he can stand up more and bring his body back against mine.

His fingers trace lightly along my neck and the hollow between my neck and shoulder, leaving goosebumps in their wake. I shiver again. "You're going to shatter me," I say quietly.

He stills.

Our eyes meet.

"You're right," he agrees. The words are not hard or cold, they're just simply the truth. "You deserve far better than this, Raine. I do not deserve you." With that he rights my robe and steps back. "I can't control myself when I'm around you. I think I should go."

I'm momentarily frozen by his words and he kisses my forehead again as he slides past me toward the door. I finally come unfrozen as his hand reaches the door. "Dex?"

"Yeah, sweet girl?" He turns back toward me. His eyes are locked on mine. He looks haunted and afraid.

With that look, I see all I need to see as I let the robe slip from my shoulders and it flutters silently to the floor. His eyes travel down, taking in the sight of me, naked, before him. "One night. I will give you one night," I whisper. I watch as he turns.

All his resolve to leave washes away. He's happy yet scared, concerned and excited. I watch as the idea of what I'm offering him overwhelms him and he falls to his knees before me.

chapter
24
raine

His hands fall to his sides, but his eyes never leave mine. "You're so fucking beautiful," he breathes. I take a step forward, toward him. "If you keep coming closer to me, I won't be able to hold back," he warns me. His eyes are wild with fire and I can see his hands twitching with a need to touch. I step forward again.

"I can't stop," I say softly and his eyes meet mine. "I need this, I need to know."

He cocks his head at me. "Know what?"

"I need to know whether this is real." Another step forward. "Or if this is just lust." I need to take two more steps and then he can touch me. Two more steps and I can be in his arms. "I have to know." One step...two. "I'll give you one night," I repeat.

His arms come around me, holding my naked body to him, his head resting against my stomach. The sharp stubble of three days of growth scrapes near my belly button. I run my hand through his hair and the tension in his body starts to fade away. I pull back from him slightly and he looks up at me. I gently grab his arms, pushing them off of me. His eyes go wide in fear that I've changed my mind. His vulnerability is evident. He's afraid.

I lower myself onto my knees. "Show me you want this, even if it's only half as much as I do. Just show me," I breathe and he claims my head in his hands and my lips are on his with gusto. He wastes no time in prying at my lips with his tongue, desperate to be inside me anywhere he can be and I let him in, moaning into his mouth.

My hands go to his shoulders and down along his sides, going for the hem of his shirt. When I get there, I start to tug upward and he smiles against my lips. "Eager much?"

"There's something that I've been dying to do to you," I whisper and he pulls back, allowing me the access I need to pull off his shirt. He lifts his arms over his head and I quickly toss it aside.

"I'm all yours," he says in a rush and I start first at his shoulder, licking and kissing and sucking my way to his arm and down the tight skin of his bicep. Finding those little blue veins and licking and kissing them until I'm even with his chest, I kiss my way across, careful to capture his nipple with my tongue and when I do, he groans. Spurring me on, I suck it into my mouth and nip at it gently with my teeth. He hisses and a rush of fluid drips from my sex. "I can smell that sweet cunt," he breathes against my ear and I shiver. "You're getting wet for me, aren't you?"

I nod my head and continue licking and sucking my way along until I find the other nipple, licking it first then sucking it into my mouth. I feel him tense up, anticipating the nip but I lavish it with my tongue and he relaxes.

As soon as I know he's distracted, I bite again and he growls at me. The sound is so intoxicating and erotic that I shiver with need and my nipples burn to be touched, to be licked and sucked into his mouth. He moves to reach for my pussy and I hold him back with a gentle shake of my head and he whines. I move off of his nipple and onto his other bicep, repeating the process until I reach his neck where I keep kissing my way to his jawline.

The sharp pricks of his growing beard bite into my tongue and I tremble again. Gently rubbing my lips against the grain, feeling it, tasting it until I find his lips once more. His hands are instantly in my hair, holding me to him, sucking my tongue into his mouth and I moan. His hands tighten into fists in my hair, pulling and tugging me backwards and I release his lips and I'm trembling with an urgent need to come. "You like that, don't you, princess?" I nod and smile seductively at him.

He adjusts his hands to take more of my hair in one hand. When he's settled, he wraps it around his hand and tugs my head back so that I'm looking up at him. He's so much bigger and taller than I am that my head back is the only way he can truly claim my mouth with his and he does. Fire ignites across my skin, sending sparks of pleasure straight to my core. "Ahh," I cry out and his mouth goes to my jaw and down my neck, leaving a blazing trail in his path as he makes his way further south. Finally, he's almost there. My nipples ache. I can feel every inch of the barbell running between them. "Please," I beg.

"Please, what?" he says with a commanding tone in his voice that makes me shiver again.

"Please, suck." I can't say anything else. On the verge of completely losing control.

He obliges my request by sliding a fat wet tongue from the bottom of my areola to the top, his hand tightens in my hair as he does. I whimper. He blows across my nipple in the sweetest torture of warm and cold I've ever experienced in my life. "Ah fuck," I cry out.

"Oh yeah," he moans, releasing my hair and he pulls away from me completely.

"No," I whimper.

I hear him stand and slowly I open my eyes. The perfect height. I reach for the button of his jeans and he pushes my hands away with a shake of his head. I pout prettily at him, giving him the saddest puppy dog eyes I can manage. He leans down and whispers, "Your begging, while sexy as fuck, isn't going to work. I owe you an orgasm or three."

"Please," I beg. He smiles and shakes his head. I sulk.

He laughs. "Come here, sweet girl." He holds out his hand for me to take. His nickname of sweet girl is enough to send my heart soaring onto another planet. The other night he called me names like sweetheart and baby and I wonder idly why he isn't calling me those names tonight. I take his hand and he pulls me up before leaning down for another kiss on my forehead. "Bed," he commands and I find myself turning into the bed. I decide that two can play at this game so I climb onto the bed and stick my ass in the air as I do.

That's when I feel a playful smack on my ass. "On your back, princess." I smile to myself and roll over.

Somewhere along the way and my playful teasing as I climbed onto the bed, he's shed his pants. He's standing at the foot of the bed gloriously naked and I moan in pleasure at the glorious sight. His cock really is as big as I thought it was. Pushing close to 9 or even ten inches but it's also wide at the base and tapered to the tip. I can't stop staring and he knows it. He takes his cock in his hand and he starts to stroke it. I moan and writhe on the bed, my hand immediately diving into my folds and finding my clit.

I'm so slick that I can barely find purchase against it, frustrating me, but I do my best not to show it.

"Whatever you do, do not come," he says, once again the authority is back in his voice. "Your orgasms are mine for tonight," he growls as he continues to stroke his cock.

I shiver, my legs start to twitch, desperate to defy his request and desperate to come, I don't know if I will be able to stop.

"Shit," I moan as my orgasm crests. "Fuck, Dex. I. Can't. Stop. It's too. Fucking. Good."

With that he's on the bed in a flash, his mouth even with my sex. "Move your hand," he says with a look in his eyes that promises exquisite punishment if I come without him, but my hand moves and his tongue immediately replaces my fingers and he starts licking and sucking at my clit. My orgasm is right there, ready to explode.

"Ahh. Fuck!" I cry out. Then he stops completely, pulling away from me, right there. I look at him, probably a murderous glare on my face, and he slinks back slightly. "Why did you stop?" I whine. "I was right there."

"I know." He gives me a knowing smirk.

"Assholian," I grumble and bring my hand back to my pussy, but he smacks it away with a smile on his face.

"Oh no, you don't." That's when I see it in his hand. A black foil packet and I moan watching him put it between his teeth and ripping it open.

I writhe, trying to scissor my legs, desperate for relief, but he's there, in my way. I watch as his long fingers quickly slide the condom on. "I fucking hate those things," I groan.

"Sorry, sweetheart, but..."

I nod, understanding. Though I wish he wouldn't, I see the condom as his own little barrier of protection, keeping me in line with all the others. Briefly a moment of shame washes through me as I catch one of his old nicknames. Then realizing and understanding the significance behind the condom. It's his separation, his way of detaching himself from me so that I can be that one-night stand. So that when he's satisfied and done, he can walk away. I'd resolved myself to that fate, to being able to let this happen for one night, indulge in the fantasy and then just let it go. I was willing to suffer the emotional consequences of my decision because I knew an opportunity like this would never present itself again. Take it, run away with it, indulge, purge and move on. You can do this, Raine.

Vowing to let my temperamental mood drop, I watch him as he's looking at me, absently stroking his cock. "Stop torturing me," I whine and he leans down. "Just go slow," I say softly. He's fucking huge. He's going to tear me apart and the look in his eyes tells me that it won't just be physical. He's checked out in some way, detached himself from the situation, confirming what I suspected. "Dex?"

He doesn't answer. He's kind of frozen in place. I watch him carefully, and I slowly watch the fog fade from his eyes and he returns to me. Though he's still distant and likely unaware of what I can actually see in his eyes. I feel him run the head of his rubber covered cock against my sex. Spreading my juices along my entrance, allowing the condom to be coated. Then he lines himself up and slides inside of me, slowly, but there is a warmth, a desire that spreads over me immediately. Unlike anything I've ever felt before. A sensation that I can only describe as being earth shattering and soul crushing at the same time.

When he's found his way inside as far as he can go, he adjusts me so that my legs are higher, bringing my ass into the air, changing the angle, making him slide in just a little deeper and I moan as his head rubs against that special ball of nerves inside. "Ahh, fuck," I cry out and close my eyes. Men have the wonderful pleasure of hiding behind a rubber barrier, separating themselves from their sexual partner, women on the other hand have no choice but to be speared, spread wide open both emotionally and physically.

He pushes in a little harder, a little deeper, the thickest part of his shaft toward the base is pressing inside and I feel a burning sensation that doesn't last, but it's enough to know that he's stretching me beyond limits I knew I was capable of. "Don't stop," I cry out and he starts to slide in and out faster. I close my eyes, concentrating on the overwhelming feeling, trying to block out the act itself. It doesn't work. I open my eyes and meet the closed eyes of Dex Harris, drummer and fantasy man. I moan again. My orgasm is simmering just below the surface. I writhe. My back arches, shifting the direction and angle just enough that he slips in further. A small stab of pain and my legs lock down, my body explodes and my mind soars into orgasm.

My own cries are matched by Dex as he grunts and grinds out his orgasm.

Slowly my breathing returns to normal. Dex doesn't extract himself immediately and that's okay. My fear and shame rattle around in my veins. I reach up to touch his cheek and as soon as my fingers make contact he blurts out, "I can't."

He backs off, slipping out of me. "Wait, what?"

"I can't do this." He slides off of the bed, pulling the condom from his still rock hard erection, tying it off and throwing it in the trash can.

"What the fuck?" I'm so embarrassed, sitting here completely naked having given myself to him and he's completely shut down. I get the impression that this, for Dex, is normal. I grab a pillow and hold it in front of me, holding it to me like a barrier, a lifeline. I sit cross-legged on the bed. "What did I do?" I ask in a whisper.

"I fucked up. I shouldn't be here, I shouldn't be..." He doesn't look at me as he pulls his pants back on.

"Dex, stop."

"I have to go."

"Dex, don't."

"Too late."

"Don't walk out that door. I can't promise to..."

"I don't need promises from you, doll face. I don't need promises from anyone. I don't fucking deserve this or you. I fucked up," he says as he storms out of my room, slamming the door behind him. I start crying into the pillow I'm wrapped around.

chapter
25
raine

After he left, I somehow managed to get myself under the covers, not caring, not giving a shit about what just happened. Fuck him. I knew when I agreed to this that I was never going to be able to detach myself enough and I convinced myself that what happened wasn't going to hurt like a bitch. It does.

I wanted to indulge in the fantasy and I got my chance and it was glorious. But what I didn't expect was the aftermath of feeling wholly and completely rejected. I don't know what it was that I was expecting when he'd gotten off, but it certainly wasn't him running out the door like a scared cat.

I punch the pillow next to me. I shake my head. So fucking stupid.

As I lay there, in a piss poor attempt to fall asleep, I come to a decision. I've done it, I got what I've wanted for years, a night with a rock star and with that, I resolve myself to going about my job. Doing what it is that I need to do in order to do the best possible job I can do, regardless of the obstacles in my way.

About two hours later, I woke up, it was really early in the morning, and the sun hadn't even come up yet. I decided that I needed to get out of my room, clear my head a little bit, but short of going wandering around NYC with a security detail, I could only think of one place to go. Rusty nearly had a heart attack when I told him where I was going and that no one was to go with me. I convinced him only because it was the roof and there wouldn't really be anyone up there when I climbed up the ladder to sit atop the stairwell and watch the sunrise.

While I was up there, I made several decisions for myself. One of which is that Dex, though a force to be reckoned with, at some point was just going to have to slide out of my system. No pun intended of course. I needed to put on my professional hat, like I've done many times regardless of what was bothering me, and do the best job I can do while I'm here in New York. Once I can get back to California, away from him, away from the band, I know that I can better deal with this.

In just a few days, we will be so busy with appearances and appointments that thinking about anything other than what's going on at that moment will be nearly impossible to do and I take comfort in that. I decide then and there that I will take as much stuff off of Addison's plate as I can and allow her the time she needs to grieve.

Inevitably my thoughts always wander back to Dex. You know, all assholes have a past, and it's usually pretty haunting. A reason for why they are the way that they are and I wonder idly if I ever found out that reason, if it would change the way I see him. Yes, he's a dick, an assholian, king assholian if you want the truth of it, but there has to be a damn good reason why. Unfortunately, there is no way for me to find out, without asking the assholian himself and that is a task no woman wants to undertake voluntarily.

While I stew around in my head, I curl up and watch the sun rise over the city and listen to the sounds of the street below. The hustle and bustle of New York City never slows, but in this case, it certainly picks up.

dex

Walking out on a woman I've just slept with has never been harder than that just was. I knew I was losing my grip on myself, especially when it comes to her. I knew that in order for me to snap the strings clean off I had to walk away and not look back.

So why the fuck do I feel so shitty about it?

I've walked away from countless women after getting myself off and I've never, ever, thought about them again. Except maybe in an unguarded, stroking my cock moment. Some girls' eyes just never leave you, but their names, faces, those are things that never go away. I've been haunted by Raine's eyes for two fucking days now and I can't seem to shake them off.

You know her name, that's your fucking problem, asshole. If you hadn't bothered to learn it, you wouldn't be tripping about it. I finally get into my room, strip off my clothes and climb into the shower. I can still smell her

172

cherry chocolate scent on my skin and I don't want to wash it away. I want to bathe in it, enjoy it, and who the fuck knows, but it's so sweet and... stop it, you fucking pansy ass.

I grab my body wash and scrub it away. Scrub her away. Though I wish all it took was some body wash to scrub her out of my fucking mind.

When I'm done, I fall into bed, or on top of it rather, and pass out.

I'm getting ready to leave the bar area downstairs after grabbing a late breakfast when my phone vibrates in my pocket.

"What's up, T-man?"

"Dex, Addison's in the hospital."

"Shit! What happened?"

"All the shit with Kyle, she hasn't been eating and I've been shit at making sure she does. They're keeping her overnight, giving her fluids and all that good stuff."

"Damn, man, what about the babies?"

"They're fine from what we can tell, nothing indicates otherwise."

'Okay, good, want us to come down?"

"No, no. Stay put, I don't want to draw a bigger crowd. Listen, can you let the rest of the guys know? Mills, Tori and Rusty are taking shifts at the hospital, so if you go out, you'll need to work with what you got. And...have you heard from Kyle?"

"No, T-man, I'm sorry I haven't."

"I called him around ten, when they were taking her to the hospital, but I haven't heard back. He wouldn't do this to her. I'm worried that something's happened. Or about to happen." I watch as Raine approaches looking fucking gorgeous in a pair of jeans and a cute t-shirt that just says rock 'n roll in bold font across her chest. My insides tighten. I don't know what to say to her, not after last night. But Talon has given me the out I need.

"I'll try calling him. We have a show tomorrow anyway. I'll find out what the hell is going on."

"Thanks, D. Call my cell if you need me, I won't leave her."

"Right."

He hangs up. "Sorry, sweet girl, I've got some business to attend to."

"What's going on, Dex?" she asks me.

"Uh…" Shit, does she know? Fuck. "Just some stuff with Talon, no biggy."

"Doesn't sound like something that's not a big deal, Dex. What's going on?"

Fuck…I can't deny this woman anything. "Addison's being kept overnight at the hospital."

"Babies?" She overheard that? Where the hell was she?

"Uh, you might want to talk to them about that," I say and walk out of the hotel bar.

I flip through my phone, find K's number and hit send. It rings once, twice, then finally he answers…

"Dex, I need help…"

Thirty minutes later…

"Did you do it?" I point to the baggie of coke on the table in front of him.

"No, I… I can't bring myself to open it."

"Good. Come on, let's get you cleaned up. Your girl needs you."

"I failed her."

"You screw someone else?"

"Fuck no!"

"So you fucking got drunk."

"For like, three fucking days. I've failed her so bad. She's in the fucking hospital because of me and instead of going to her, I fucking bought coke."

"You haven't failed her. Not yet, you haven't. Come on. Shower, now." Fuck, this hotel is the shittiest of the shitty. I know he can afford better, but I get why he came here.

I go into the bathroom and start the shower. I'm going to have to fucking undress him. Ugh. "I'm going to strip you out of your clothes, fuck, do you have more clothes?"

"No."

"All right…"

"Take that shit off."

I pull my phone out. "Beck."

"Such a jack ass as always…I need your discretion and more than anything, this stays between us."

"What do you need, Dex?"

"I've got K."

"Shit, where?"

"Relax, brotha. He's drunk, he's been essentially homeless for three days and he bought a teenie."

"Fuck."

"Relax, he's clean. He chickened out, but listen, he smells like ass, I need clothes. Can you get some and bring them?"

"Of course."

"And, Beck?"

"Yeah?"

"You call anyone, I'll have your balls for breakfast."

"No one."

"All right." I proceed with filling him in on where Kyle and I are and when I'm done, he quickly hangs up.

I turn around and Kyle is fucking naked as a jaybird. "All right, let's go."

I drag him into the bathroom and throw him into the shower. "Oh FUCK!" he shouts. "THAT'S FUCKING COLD!"

I slap his chest. "Sober up, big man!"

chapter
26
raine

"Hi Raine." Cami's sweet voice comes over the line.

"Hi Cami."

"What's wrong?" Her tone immediately shifts, compliments of my own.

"We have a problem."

"With?"

I know I can't beat around the bush with her. "Addison collapsed at the studio this morning."

"She what? What's wrong? Is she all right? Is she hurt?"

"Relax. She's fine, she's been admitted to Bellevue for the night for observation."

"What caused her to collapse?"

"Low blood sugar. I was calling to let you know, hopefully before the studio got a hold of you. You know how they are."

"Oh boy, let me guess, they didn't get the song done today?"

"No, they didn't. She passed out before they even got started," I tell her.

"I didn't know she had blood sugar problems," she says quizzically as if trying to wrack her brain for something she might know about Addison.

"I don't think she does, I think the fact that she's pregnant..."

"What?" she practically squeals into the phone.

"I'm sorry that I'm the one telling you. I do know that Addison wanted to, she just didn't quite know how and from what little I know of the situation, they're not talking to anyone about it really."

"Well, I would imagine not, considering..." She trails off, probably thinking the same thing I did after talking to Mills and forcing as much information from him as I could. No doubt he's not happy with me. Personal issues are just that, personal, but I explained to him that I needed to be able to deal with the studio among other things, and I needed as much information as he could give me. Which confirmed what Dex had let slip, she's having twins, but I withhold that detail from Cami.

"No, she's not very far along. But there's more to this mess."

"Oh lord, all right, fill me in."

I fill her in on the details of Kyle's disappearing act and what little I know at this point about him being found. Which extends only to Dex running off to go rescue Kyle. She is shocked at first, but there are some demons in Cami's own closet, so I can imagine what's going through her head about why Kyle left.

"Look, I've already sent out an email. I will be on the plane in a couple of hours. I will be there tonight. I will probably bring Tristan with me. I'll email you the flight details, but we'll have a car arranged, so don't worry about picking us up or anything."

"I don't think you need to…"

'Well, I'm looking at it this way, she's cornered, in a hospital room, nowhere to run. I can get the answers I need from her while she's there. I hate to force her into telling me anything, but you know, probably more than anyone, that I'm not your normal boss. Besides, I need to spend some time in the New York office anyway. So I might as well come out there now."

"Am I in trouble?"

"Oh, good heavens, no. Why would you be in trouble?"

"Just making sure. You don't usually go jetting off when a client is in trouble, or an employee for that matter."

She laughs into the phone. "You're right, I don't. But Addison's a little different. One, she's handling a very big band and up until I sent you out there, she was doing it alone and doing a damn fine job of it. Now she has you and I would have never known anything was wrong. Between the two of you, you guys have everything under control. I am not going to step up, step in, or start making changes unless something completely disastrous happens and I don't see that happening." I can tell she's smiling on the other end of the phone. "You're doing great, Raine, don't let this be a downer for you. It's a bump in the road and if Kyle's back, maybe things will right themselves. If I know Addison, things will be back to normal in a few days."

I smile. "Thank you, Cami."

"Absolutely. But her pregnancy does change a few things."

"Like?" I ask her and she launches into the numerous contracts sitting there waiting for her to decide on and sign.

She doesn't dive too much into it, but there will be quite a bit of negotiating involved should Addison decide to sign on. I love it when Cami gets on work related tangents. They can be quite comical. I lean back against the hallway wall. As much as I would rather be in my room, I wanted to be out here in case anyone came back.

Fifteen minutes later, the plan is hashed out and no sooner than we hang up do I have Cami's flight itinerary and scheduling changes. Though I am no longer her assistant, this isn't the first or last thing I will no doubt receive from her. I've received a few online projects from her as well. Those emails were fun to read because she said she doesn't like my semi-replacement as much as me. I replied to one of them telling her that when I got back, I would handle both her and Addison for a while.

That was when I got this response....

If you're agreeable, available and capable, I'm sending you on the road with Addison. Let me know as soon as possible.

My gut reaction was to reply with a resounding yes, but then I thought of Dex. What would my staying mean? It's not about what he thinks really, it's more about my handling being around him if he reverts back to his old ways. If he goes back to seducing women, how is that going to make me feel in the long run? Then again, watching him seduce another woman may just be the nail in the coffin I need to bring myself out of this rut where it comes to him.

My cell phone vibrates. A text.

Talon: Addison is settled in. Mills said he filled you in on everything. I'm sorry I didn't think to do it myself. Addison is resting comfortably and will be okay. Have you seen Dex? He's not answering his phone. Thnx - T

Raine: Glad Addison is okay. Mills was reluctant to say the least, but I had to tell Cami before the studio called her. She's talking 2 them now, hoping to reschedule session ASAP and negotiation of fines. Cami said she'd cover fines. Dex? No, I was with him when you called, he took off to do whatever Dex does. Will check around with the guys, see if NE1 has talked to him. YW - Raine

No sign of Dex? What the hell? I'd chalked up his silence to dealing with Kyle, but it's obvious Dex isn't answering Talon, so what exactly is going on?

dex

"Jesus, he's a mess," Beck says when he finally arrives at the hotel.

"What took so long?"

"Fuck off. You said you didn't want anyone to know, well, I had to get to the floor so that I could go into the suite and pull some of his shit." He drops a black duffle bag on the bed. Kyle, meanwhile, is slouched over on the other bed with his head in his hands and a skimpy ass towel half wrapped around his waist.

"All right, brother. Let's do this, yeah?" I say to Kyle who nods and stands up. I grab the bag off of the bed and walk it over to him. "Go get dressed and we'll get you some food and get you to Addison."

181

Kyle is a walking zombie, minus the nasty black circles. No wait, he has those too. My phone vibrates again in my pocket. I pull it out.

Talon: Anything from K?
Dex: nah man, still trying. Sorry.
Talon: Fucker.

I shrug off the exchange, he ain't pissed at me and I know that.

I point to the table. "Dump it." The fluffy white powder has been taunting me since the moment I walked through the door. Though this time, my resistance was much easier than it was back in Phoenix and I think I have Raine to thank for that, though I'm not sure it can stop the next piece from happening.

"That bad?" Beck asks me.

"Not Phoenix bad, but yeah, it fucking sucks."

"We sure he didn't do any of it?"

I shake my head. "Not unless teenies have gotten bigger in the last five years." Beck nods and walks over to the table, grabbing the bag and pocketing it. Then grabbing the beer bottles, alcohol bottles and other trash that litters the room. "Fuck it, leave it, man. This place is a dump. Those were probably here before Kyle showed up."

Beck snorts a laugh.

"Just make sure you dump it," I tell him and step outside to light up a smoke. Letting it fill my lungs and curb that appetite.

Fifteen minutes later, Kyle's semi put back together and I watch Beck dump perfectly good coke into the toilet and flush it. I would have never been able to do it and he knows it. My phone vibrates again.

Unknown: don't be mad at Casey, but you never gave me your number. PS now you have mine too. How's K? Talon is flipping out - he texted, wanted to know if I'd heard from you. Said no, but didn't tell him you had K either. Didn't want to raise hopes if, well you know. Addie ok 2. In case you're wondering. - Raine

Unknown: PS. We should talk.

Dex: Not mad, happy you conned my number from C. Thnx4 not telling T. K is sobering. Going to feed him, take him to Hosp. Glad Addie's Ok. Talk? About?

I know that I cannot and do not want to wipe the Cheshire grin off my face as we walk into a deli near Bellevue. As Kyle consumes his food, he sobers more and more. He's finally starting to talk, though more beating himself up, talking himself into showing up at the hospital than actually to Beck or I.

When he's done, Beck calls Mills and lets him know we're coming.

When we arrive at the hospital, Mills is standing outside waiting for us as we pull up in the rented SUV. Kyle turns to me.

"Thank you," he says softly.

"That's what brothers are for, man. You'd have done the same for me."

He smiles slightly. "Yeah, I would have, in a second."

"Then quit thanking me, you need to go and see your girl." He nods and the small smile fades. I've suspected for some time now that this isn't a two against one situation between Kyle, Talon and Addison. I'm pretty certain that it's a three-way street with them. "Talon too." I wink at him. Letting him know that it's cool. Totally not my cup of fucking tea, but then again… nope, not at all.

When Kyle climbs out of the truck, I follow after him. I'm gonna ride up front with Beck on the way back. Mills wraps Kyle up in a hug.

"Welcome home," Mills says with a smile.

"How is she?"

Mills' smile doesn't fade. "She'll be better now." He turns to me. "Thank you." We grab arms at the elbows and bump chests.

"Anytime." I pat Kyle on the back. "If things don't go so well up there, call me. Don't run. She ain't the only one you ran away from and you know damn well that I will always take care of my family."

"I won't run. I can't promise to stay, but I won't run," he says somberly.

"I have it on good authority that you mean more to that girl than you realize. Talon too. And I'm pretty sure you aren't going anywhere." I smile at him and climb into the front seat of the SUV. "Hey Kyle?"

"Yeah?"

"Come here." He walks over to stand at my window. "That chick is pretty special. She has a way of bringing out the best in all of us. Just keep that in mind. Take your punishment like a big man, but know that it won't be easy."

"I'll do whatever I have to do," He states firmly.

"Good. Now go." I nod toward Mills and the door and Kyle takes his leave of us. "Hi ho silver - away," I joke and Beck laughs as he throws the SUV into drive and we take off.

I pull my phone out.

Dex: Kyle delivered safely to hospital. What happens next is totally up to him. On my way back with Beck. Hungry?

Raine: Thank you. Not hungry, not at hotel. Glad K is safe & where he belongs.

Dex: Where are you?

While I wait for her response I wonder why I asked, why I even sent that damn message in the first place, but can't change it now.

Raine: Out.

That's the only response I get from her and it irritates me, but I let it go. I have no rhyme or reason to give a shit about what she's doing but the fact that she's not at the hotel has me a little bummed.

"What are we doing tonight?" Beck asks as we continue toward our hotel.

"Going out," I say simply.

"Anywhere in particular?" He looks over at me briefly.

"Anywhere but the hotel."

He nods and drives on.

When we return to the hotel, I knock on Mouse and Peacock's door. Mouse answers. "What's up?"

"Kyle's home," I tell him.

"No shit." He smiles and turns into the room. "Yo Eric, Kyle's home."

"Fucking A, about fucking time." He comes to stand in the doorway with Mouse.

"Yeah, Addison's in the hospital."

"Whoa, what? What the fuck, dude?" Mouse says as he and Peacock come out into the hallway.

"Yeah, she collapsed this morning, which in turn is how I ended up calling him. It wasn't pretty," I tell them and they both nod absently, like they know what I'm talking about without having to ask the question. "So, I'm going out, want to join me?"

"Yeah, man, let's go," Peacock says with enthusiasm. Great.

chapter
27
raine

"Hey Mills." I answer my phone.

"Hi, everything all right?"

I scowl at nothing in particular. "Yeah, why?"

"Just making sure, you ditched your detail." His tone is accusatory, but I shrug it off.

"You guys have enough going on. You don't need to worry about me too."

"I will argue that with you later, but can you at least tell me where you are and if you're all right?" His tone softens.

'I'm perfectly fine. I'm at the Crown Plaza down the street and I'm with Cami and Tristan."

"Oh, I didn't know they were coming to town."

"They just got here a little while ago. I needed to get out, so I came over here. Cami plans on stopping by the hospital in the morning. Speaking of which, how is she?"

"She's much better now that Kyle's back, but they're still keeping her overnight. I sent Tori and Rusty back to the hotel for some sleep. They'll be back up in a few hours."

"Good, keep me posted if anything changes?"

"Absolutely. Please call if you need a ride back to the hotel."

"Got it covered, Tyson is here too."

"Good," he says. "Tell him hello."

"Will do. Thanks."

He hangs up.

"Everything all right?" Cami asks.

I nod. "I just ditched my detail, Mills was a little rattled."

I get a raised eyebrow from Cami. "Why'd you ditch the detail?"

"Because it's ridiculous and completely unnecessary for me to have one. No one knows who I am, where I am or that I have anything to do with the band." I shrug. "Besides, I just needed to get out of there."

"That bad?" she asks for the second time today.

"No, it's just," I sigh, "I made a bad decision last night and I needed to kind of clear my head."

"Please, don't tell me you…" I nod my head. "Who?" she asks me in a way that makes her more of a best friend than a boss and I smile with no intention of telling who. She shakes her head and laughs. "As long as you keep working, I don't give a rat's ass what ya do, just don't let it affect the job you were sent here to do."

"Food's here," Tristan says as he comes out of the other room with Jayden on his hip. I'd have never pegged him to be the daddy type, but he and Jayden are two peas in a freakin' pod and I love watching the two of them together.

"Great, I'm starving." Cami walks over and Jayden jumps in Tristan's arms. Cami takes him and tosses him into the air and he laughs. "You hungry, big man?" She sets him down and he grabs hold of her pant leg. He's still pretty unsteady on his feet, but he's figuring out this whole walking thing. He can manage a few steps on his own before he gives up and starts to crawl.

"Come here, Jayden," I coo and bend down, hoping he will find the courage to take some more steps on his own. He smiles at me, but doesn't seem sure.

"Go get her," Cami says and Jayden looks from her to me.

"Come on, big man. You can do it," I encourage and he steadies himself. I watch as he eventually lets go of Cami's pants and takes a step. The shock registers on his face when he realizes he's standing up. "Come here," I say again and he giggles as he takes one step, then another. Then as I suspected, he plops down on his butt and immediately crawls over to me. "Good job." I pick him up and settle him on my hip.

We have our own little private conversation while Tristan and Cami set the table in their suite. Once they're done, Tristan comes over and takes Jayden from me. "You all right, kid?" he asks me.

I shrug. "Yeah, I think so."

Tristan smiles, "Whoever it was, don't let them bring you down. We Hollywood types are jerks, but eventually we either come around or we don't and we let you know." He winks at me.

"Not all of Hollywood are jerks," I tease him. "You turned out all right."

He snorts a laugh. "But look at what I had to go through to get there."

I shake my head. "You've always been humble. Sure, you've had your demons to deal with, but look at you now." I smile at Jayden and Tristan lights up.

"Come on, let's eat," Cami says.

I join them for dinner. We talk shop, but when she finally gets around to asking the dreaded question, my blood runs cold. "So, what do you think about going on tour?"

"I think it's an opportunity I'd be stupid to pass up," I say softly.

"But it's an opportunity that will come again. This isn't the only time I see you going on the road. At least, not if Addison agrees. You guys seem to be getting along pretty good."

I smile. "For what little we've interacted, I think we do. But with what happened with Kyle being gone. Jeez Cami, I felt so bad for her."

I watch as sadness creeps into Tristan's features. I remember a time not so long ago when Cami had bailed on him and I remember what that was like too. It was awful. "She's been a mess from what I understand," Cami says softly.

I nod. "I've only seen her a handful of times and that was usually just to check on her while Talon was at the studio." The comment allows me to turn things onto a new subject. Things between Cami and Tristan are amazing now, but I know that time still haunts them both. "Speaking of the studio…"

"Oh, yes, it's rescheduled for Saturday morning. They're not going to fine us because of the circumstances behind what happened, considering it was Addison they were recording. If it had been Talon or someone else, they wouldn't have made the exception. They're opening the studio specifically for them. I emailed you the details from the plane."

"Sorry, I haven't checked my email."

"No worries," she smiles. "So, what have you decided?" she asks as she takes a bite.

"I'll go."

"Good."

"What about the office?"

She sighs, "We'll get there, it's just going to take some time. I never realized how much you did and how efficient you were at it until you were gone."

Tristan snorts a laugh. "Don't let her fool you, she's been a wreck."

"Tristan," she scolds and laughs. She looks at me, and I know I have concern in my eyes. "Don't you worry about it. I just see now why my father hired you and I see now why you will be missed around there. As long as this remains something you want to do, you'll continue to do it. I doubt I will find a replacement anywhere near as good as you, but eventually, I won't need you anymore." She winks at me and we finish our meal.

When we're done, I leave them to their evening. If there is one thing that Cami is known for, it's being there for her family at night, regardless of what's going on or if she ends up back at the office after Jayden has gone to bed. I've always admired her for that, considering her father wasn't as available when she was growing up.

I take a cab back to the hotel and when I enter the lobby, I detour into the bar. I have no desire to go back upstairs, at least not right now. Considering that it's Wednesday, it's pretty crowded in here. It isn't until I see the couches occupied, not by band members, but by other patrons that I realize that maybe I should have gone to the rooftop bar instead. I quickly scan the room and there is no sign of 69 Bottles anywhere. Thank god.

I grab a seat at the bar, facing the entrance from the lobby, hoping to not be caught unaware and giving me an escape through the outside entrance to the bar if I need one. I have no intention of sticking around if they show up. I refuse to watch Dex work some other woman over.

Agreeing to go on tour is going to be fraught with more heartache than I can bear. This is confirmed for me when I see Mouse enter the bar with a woman, Peacock enter with a woman and finally bringing up the rear, Dex. But he is alone.

I try to slink out and away, but it isn't long before he catches me and looks me square in the eyes. I fight the urge to smile over him being alone. I wonder if he struck out, or if his lack of companion is by choice. I shake my head. I shouldn't be making assumptions, but the fact that Mouse and Peacock each seem to have someone on their arms and Dex is alone sends a thrill through me. But then again, she could be in the restroom for all I know.

Just a few minutes ago, the couches they'd been using all week emptied, giving them their spot to sit. They do and the waitress I'd paid to pour Crown all over Dex's head is there to greet them. That's when a leggy, tall, narrow waist brunette walks into the bar. She goes straight for the couches where Dex and the guys are sitting and she sits down right next to Dex whose arm is sprawled over the back of the couch. The waitress leans over, giving me a view of her ass and Dex a shot right down her low cut shirt.

I knew it was too good to be true. I see the chance to make my escape since I know he can't see me and I know the other guys don't know I'm here. I'd thought that I would just walk around the building and into the lobby, sneak onto the elevator and finally up to the safety of my room, but instead of turning right, I turn left and walk right in to Times Square. The lights are bright, the signs are dancing and I just stand there, soaking it all up.

I'm not even gone for ten minutes when my cell phone rings in my back pocket. Pulling it free, I see that it's Casey. I press the button, just once so that it rings on his end and silences on mine. When the call is done, I put it back in my pocket and start walking.

There are several people milling about outside when I come up on the first theater. It must be intermission. I walk through the cloud of smoke and politely excuse myself when I almost run into someone. I just keep walking, letting the anger and frustration well inside me. I have absolutely no one to blame for this but myself. I gave in. I told myself that I could do it and I knew damn well that I couldn't. But seeing what I saw tonight is going to give me the fuel I need to move past it. To move on from it. It only takes me a few more steps before I realize that I'm crying. Before I realize that the idea of giving up on him, giving up on the idea of him, hurts more than what he just did, again.

When I come to a street that I can't cross yet, I pull out my phone to see if Casey left me a voicemail. "What the fuck?"

I have eight missed calls. It's only been five fucking minutes. There are no voicemails. Five calls are from Casey, one is from Troy, one from Tori - who is supposed to be sleeping- and the last call, less than a minute ago is from Mills. "Shit," I sputter just as my phone starts to ring again.

"Hello?" I say tentatively into the phone.

"Where the hell are you?"

"Dex?"

"Answer me," he says, his voice is harsh and commanding.

"Fuck off," I snap and hang up. That felt pretty good actually.

My phone starts to vibrate in my hands once again and this time, it's Mills and I know it will really be him since he's at the hospital and not with the guys.

"Hello?"

"Raine, are you all right?"

"Perfectly fine. Is there a problem?"

"I just got a call saying you'd walked back out of the hotel and that no one could find you."

"Oh, I just went up to the rooftop," I lie.

"So you're fine?"

"Perfectly fine."

"Okay, thanks for taking my call."

"Anytime." I smirk and hang up. Fuckers.

I don't wander far, just around Times Square. Popping in and out of some of the shops, people watching. Despite the cold night, the Naked Cowboy is playing on the streets, naked as ever. You know he's not really naked, right? So disappointing.

I finally head back toward the hotel with the theater crowd as the shows close up for the night. Though this is the city that never sleeps, the streets become quieter after the shows are done. At least at first glance. During the summer months the sidewalks are narrowed by delis and restaurants that offer outside seating and window walls move, opening up the bars to the elements. I pass by a couple and debate on going inside but I decide against it. It's approaching midnight and I have to be up early in the morning. Cami is meeting me at the hospital before talking to Addison. I get the impression that it's going to be a very long day.

I go through the main entrance of the hotel, not wanting to see Dex with his groupie or the rest of the guys, but I can't stop my eyes from looking in that direction when I walk past the bar and immediately I wish I hadn't. Mouse and Peacock are still there with their girls. Dex, of course, is gone, so is the girl he was sitting with. Assholian.

As I ride the elevator up to the seventeenth floor, I realize just how exhausted I am. When the doors open, I am greeted by Tori, Rusty, Beck and lastly, Dex. They all just stare at me. "Hello gentlemen, Tori," I say and step off of the elevator. I feel daggers being shot at me. "What?" I say exasperated.

"You lied to Mills?" Beck says.

"About what?"

"Where you were," he retorts, his tone is clipped.

"Not at the time I talked to him." Okay, I did, but that's moot.

"Where did you go?" Dex asks.

"I don't really think that's any of your business," I snap.

"It might not be his, but it is ours," Beck says.

I roll my eyes. "Look, I'm fine, all in one piece. See." I lift my arms and turn around. "Now if you'll excuse me." I try and sidestep Beck, who doesn't move for a minute before eventually moving aside.

I don't expect the next wall as I collide with Dex, who grabs me at my elbows and on instinct, or maybe because I'm just that pissed at him, my knee flies up, nailing him square in the balls.

"Oomph," he groans and doubles over.

"Oh shit," Myself and three other people say. "Stay away from my elbows," I snap and walk around him, fighting the urge to laugh at Dex's shocked expression and pain. He's turning red as a fucking cherry and...

"I warned you, dumb ass," I hear Beck say.

"Fuck. Off," Dex growls. "Fuck, this hurts."

That's when I hear the roar of laughter and I can't help but join in. I should feel bad, but I don't.

chapter
28
dex

Fuck, this shit hurts like a bitch. "What the fuck did I do?" I ask out loud but I don't expect an honest response. Though when Tori hunches down next to my head, I have a feeling I'm going to get one.

"Stay away from her elbows," she says pointedly.

"No shit, Sherlock, but what the fuck else was I supposed to do, she was gonna fall." I blink a few times, the pain is starting to subside, but it's going to hurt tomorrow.

She just shrugs and then holds out her hand to help me up. "Maybe get out of her way next time."

"I wanted answers," I grumble as I get up. New pains shoot through me but I crack my neck in an attempt to get rid of the aches elsewhere. It doesn't work. "Fuck," I groan. It's been ten years since I've been kneed in the fucking junk and of all the people to do it to me, it had to be her and it had to be here.

"Answers to what? Where she was?" Tori asks me.

"Yeah."

"Why do you care?" she replies.

She has a fucking point and I hate her for it. "I don't fucking know." I start to limp my way to my room but when I reach the door, I straighten slightly and change my course.

"What are you going to do about her?" Beck asks from behind me and I know he's not talking about Raine.

"Get rid of her. Or do her yourself," I groan and start walking toward Raine's room.

"Oh no you don't, slick." Rusty steps in front of me. "She doesn't need you knocking down her door."

"Seriously? Move."

"Nope. Come on, Beck will dump the chick in your room. You can come to mine if you want while he does. But leave Raine alone."

"I want an apology," I state.

There are a few snorts from behind me. "I don't think you're going to get one.

"Can I at least make her kiss it and make it better?" I smirk and Rusty rolls his eyes at me. "What? Can't fault a man for trying. All right, lead on." I make a half-ass attempt to point toward his door. I have an ulterior motive for agreeing to go to his room. I have to walk right past Raine's.

No matter, I follow Rusty dutifully until I get to her door and before he or anyone else can stop me, I pound on the door.

"Go away, Dex," she shouts from the other side. "I'm not apologizing."

I pound on the door again. "Open it up."

"For-get-it." This time she's standing at the door.

"Come on, please?" I whine.

"Dude, drop it. Don't keep pushing or you're going to be in a world of hurt," Rusty whispers.

"Come on, Rusty is here. Please open the door," I plead at the door and bump my head against it.

I know I'm winning when I hear the creak of her chain and it doesn't bump against the door. I smile, probably a little too sadistically. Then comes the deadbolt. She's a smart girl. We have keys.

Finally the door handle clicks as she turns it, opening it up. She's standing there, one arm on the frame, one on the door, not defensive in the least. She's changed into pajama pants and a t-shirt and she fucking looks sexy as hell. "You look like shit," she snarks.

"He he he. Thanks so much."

"Have a good evening?" The sarcasm dripping from her voice is evident.

"I was, until about twenty minutes ago when my nuts got a nice introduction to your knee, thank you very much."

She stands up a little straighter. "You're welcome."

That's when I go for it. I grab both her arms and bring them up over her head and I push her into the wall just inside her door. My cock hardens and I fight the urge to let it show on my face as I press my body against hers. "Tell me you're sorry," I whisper sweetly.

"Never."

I slant my lips over hers and she groans, melting into me and me into her. I can hear Rusty getting huffy, but she's not fighting me so he won't stop me.

"Apologize," I breathe against her lips.

"You wish." I press into her a little harder, making sure she feels my erection and my body pinning her down. She moans and I slide my tongue along hers.

"Tell me you're sorry."

"You can't seduce an apology out of me." She nips at my chin.

'No, but I'm sure I can fuck one out of you."

"It still works?" She snorts a laugh and I press into her hands harder, adjusting them so that I can hold her with one hand as the door clicks closed.

"Oh, it works all right, sweetheart. It will work just fine," I growl as I gently wrap my hand around her neck, then slide it up and into her hair. She moans and I take her mouth, sliding my tongue along hers. Taking her, possessing her. She spreads her legs a little wider and I slide mine between hers. I can feel her rubbing against me, seeking, demanding relief. She moans again. I can barely breathe. Her body is flush against mine, and it's stealing any resolve I may have had to coax an apology from her. "Tell me you're sorry," I whisper.

"I will never apologize for defending myself." Her breathing is ragged and it takes longer for her to say the words.

"I would never hurt you." I release her hair and gently trail a finger down her cheek.

"It was a knee jerk reaction," she snickers.

I smile. "I know. But I'd still like to hear you say I'm sorry."

"Not going to happen. No matter what you do to me." She nips again at my chin and then she licks at the stubble of my half-ass beard with the tip of her tongue.

"Oh, I bet I can make you apologize."

"Is that a challenge, Mr. Harris?"

"You bet your ass, sweetheart."

She freezes on me for reasons I don't understand. I release her, afraid I've said something that's made her freeze up. "What?" I finally say.

"Get out," She whispers.

"Not until you tell me what I've done."

"If you don't know, then it's not worth the effort to tell you." She finally looks at me. Her eyes are vacant, like she's checked out on me. "Please leave."

She walks into her room, rounding the corner to where her bed and her chair are.

I head for the door. I open it and then slam it shut without stepping outside. What I did strikes me like lightning and I immediately understand her reaction and I want to beat myself over it. The nickname. I called her sweetheart. The term I use with the women I want to fuck.

"Asshole, cocksucker, motherfucker," I hear her say. I didn't leave. I couldn't. She's a fucking princess and doesn't deserve my bullshit. I fucked up, I reverted right back to my old way by detaching myself. "What the fuck just happened?" I hear her ask out loud.

If it wasn't for the fact that I'm so torn up about this, I'd laugh. I can hear her moving around. My cover, my guise, my weakness for her is going to be revealed and I have no way out without her knowing I'm still in the room listening to her rant. If she goes anywhere other than her bed, she will see me.

I hear her sob.

I turn around in time to see a pillow flying across the room and hitting the wall next to her dresser. "Argh!" she cries out in frustration. 'Why? Why do I fucking do this to myself?"

I hear her shifting again, then I hear feet stomping across the floor. Just before she screams.

She looks at me, looks at the bed, the pillows, then back at me. "Get out," she shouts at me.

"I can't," I admit softly.

"You were so eager to get out of here five minutes ago, but yet there you stand. Listening to my rant, watching me throw pillows. Are you enjoying the show?"

I shake my head.

"What the fuck just happened?" she asks.

"You freaked out."

"No shit, Sherlock. Tell me something I don't already know."

"Because I called you sweetheart?"

She raises an eyebrow at me. "So? I shouldn't expect anything different from you, yet here I am, pissed the fuck off because...well, because I guess I did."

"I saw you warring with yourself, and it wasn't until I was about to leave that it hit me, why you froze. You caught onto my terms, but when I said it just now it wasn't..." I can't believe I'm telling her all this. I could have just been the complete and total asshole that I am and left. Left her to suffer not knowing until another time, but I'd know, I knew what I did wrong. "I was ashamed. It made me realize how much I don't deserve what you were offering me." I take a deep breath. "Raine, I've slept with more women than I can count. In fact, I've never counted. If it wasn't sex, it was a blowjob or..."

"Shut up," she snaps, putting her head in her hands.

"I'm sorry," I tell her. "I'll go, I wanted to, but I just couldn't leave."

"Why?"

"Because I was hoping to give you an explanation, then you started ranting and well, here we are."

"Well, if it makes you feel better, I'm sorry I kneed you in the nuts." She smirks. "Better?" She cocks her head at me.

"Only if you mean it."

"Ask me again tomorrow and maybe I'll feel a little guilty about it. But I wouldn't hold your breath."

"I don't want your apology, Raine. I don't need it. I fucked up, I know your elbows are some kind of a trigger for you. I wish I knew why. But it was either that or you would fall, in which case I might have gotten a foot instead of a knee." I give her a half smile.

"Probably." She chuckles. "Next time, just get out of my way." She raises an eyebrow at me.

"I wanted answers."

"To what?" she asks.

"Where were you tonight?" I ask her back.

"Around." I give her a 'you're-full-of-shit' look and she shrugs. "You're not my keeper, Dex," she says deadpan. "I was done in the bar, so I went for a walk. Big fucking deal." She's getting testy again and I'm getting hard. Painfully hard.

"No, I'm not your keeper," I tell her. "Good night," I say and open the door. She's right, so was Tori. I don't understand why I care so much about her, where she is or what she's doing, but I do and it pisses me off.

"Night, Dex," she says and I leave her room. Rusty never ventured far as he's standing outside Raine's door. "She gone?" I ask and he nods. I need a fucking shower, and my bed.

You know, had she been anyone else, I'd be fucking furious over the fact that she kicked me in the junk, but fuck me, all I want to do is fuck her senseless. We get about ten feet away from her door and it opens. "Dex?"

"Yeah?" I turn around. She's leaning against the frame, looking sexier than ever.

"I'm sorry," she says sincerely with a small smile.

I smile back. "Apology accepted. Good night, princess." She lights up at the nickname I'd inadvertently given her, but it fits her to a T.

"Good night," she says as she steps back into her room, before closing her door, dead bolting it and flipping the chain.

"Princess?" Rusty raises an eyebrow at me.

"Don't you fucking start too."

He laughs, much harder than he probably should at my discomfort with the subject. I shoulder check him. "Keep your pie hole shut, will ya? I don't need the rest of the guys to know."

"Yeah, all right." I tell Rusty good night and slip into my room, shed my clothes and climb into the shower, still hard as a fucking rock and my balls hurt. I take comfort in the pain. The pain that washes away what happened with Kyle today, the pain that washes away the fact that I am left to fuck my own hand instead of her. Raine is the star of tonight's fantasy.

chapter
29
raine

I can't dwell on what happened with Dex. I was kind enough to apologize for kneeing him in the nuts, but I can't even begin to analyze his reaction. I expected more of a fight out of him. Instead, he slams me up against a wall and kisses me. And he was hard as stone when he did it.

A shiver of disgust creeps over me. Jesus, for all I know he fucked that chick downstairs before making out with me. I should shower first before going to sleep but I'm too tired to give a shit.

When morning dawns, I get up early, shower and have breakfast delivered so that I don't have to go downstairs to eat. Casey is all set to take me to the hospital where I am meeting Cami and I just need to meet him in the hallway when I'm ready. I finish up with ten minutes to spare if I hope to make it on time and I step out of my room. Beck,

Casey, and Troy are in the hallway. They're talking in hushed tones but whatever it is sounds urgent. "What's going on, guys?" I ask as I get closer to them.

Beck turns around and eyes me up and down. I want to roll my eyes. You've been there once, buddy, won't happen again. At least that's all I can manage to think. "Nothing," Beck says.

"Really, because it sounds like something is up. If it's band related, with Addison out of commission, I need to know what's going on."

Beck rolls his eyes. "One of our buses was in an accident."

"Oh shit, was anyone hurt?"

Beck and Casey both shake their heads at me. "There were a few roadies on board when it happened, but everyone is perfectly fine. Equipment might be another story."

"How so?" I raise an eyebrow. I know they have two buses here. One is the band's and the other is the crew's. "It wasn't the band's bus, was it?" I ask.

"No, it was the crew's. But on that bus is a trailer and the trailer took the brunt of the damage."

"What's in the trailer?" I ask them.

Troy answers, "Suitcases, amps, and Dex's set." I cover my mouth in shock as a door opens just behind me. "Well shit," I hear Dex say. I want to roll my eyes. "Mills is bringing Talon to the venue now. Beck and I are going to take Dex so there are more hands to help out. Bruce is getting dressed and will take over the hall watch for now, and Leroy is off rotation. So if you go to the hospital, you will need to stay until Addison is either discharged or someone is free to bring you back. Kyle may be joining us at the venue shortly."

"Okay, so equipment damage, trailer totaled?" I raise an eyebrow and three heads nod. "What about the show tonight?"

That's when Dex speaks up. "We won't know until I can examine the set. Drums are finicky, if there's even so much as a pin sized dent, it won't sound right. Which means in order for tonight to happen, I'll need a new set."

"What can I do?" I ask softly, still looking at Dex.

Beck is the one who answers. "Go to the hospital. Take care of what you need to there. Hang out with Addison because Talon's already gone and I wouldn't be surprised if Kyle is too when you get there. Just keep her company, if you don't mind. Help her get back to the hotel and then we will go from there."

"Do we know if she'll be able to perform tonight?" Dex asks the same question I was thinking and all three of the guys shrug. The elevator dings and Bruce walks off and into the hallway. His hulking size seems like a waste to be sitting around in the hallway and frankly I haven't seen him a whole lot since I've been here. Seems like he could be better used at the venue.

"For now, let's plan on a no for Addison," I say, better to assume no. "I'll take care of that side of things as soon as I know," I tell them and Casey looks at his watch. "Yeah, we need to go." I look at Troy, who's like my safe haven between Beck and Dex. "Call me if you guys need anything."

Troy nods and Casey and I step into the elevator and descend to the parking garage.

"Are you staying at the hospital?" I ask him.

"Yeah, until Kyle leaves. I'll go with him, or if he's gone, I'll stay until replaced or Addison is discharged." I notice that Casey, like Beck, is looking me up and down and I want to roll my damn eyes.

"What is it with you guys?" I ask exasperated.

"What do you mean?" Casey asks, completely unashamed.

"You, Beck, Troy? Don't you guys have girlfriends or something?"

Casey lets out a humorless laugh. "No. We don't have time for that sort of thing." He crosses his arms over his chest. Not bad, if you're into the wiry ones. But he's not my type.

"Did you guys do this with Addison when she showed up?"

"Uhm." I catch a glimpse of him as he turns red and then casually watches the descent of numbers. I know we're almost there. "No."

"I don't know if that's insulting or flattering," I tease him.

"I'm going to go with flattering." Casey smiles. "Look, it's just, well, you're gorgeous, just get used to it and remember that we're a bunch of horny bastards that barely get a chance to look for a girlfriend, let alone..." He drifts off in embarrassment.

"A one-night stand?"

"Yeah, that," he says shyly.

Finally our descent is over and the doors open. Casey ushers me to an SUV and opens the back door. "I don't need a chauffeur. I can ride up front."

Casey rolls his eyes and shuts the back door. "As you wish," he says as he opens the front passenger door.

"Thanks," I say as I climb in.

We don't talk anymore on the drive so I take to checking emails and messages, scanning the inter-webs for any sign that the accident is making headlines. There's only one small thing. Then my phone rings.

"Raine," I answer.

"Raine, this is Mitch Aarons from the LA Times." My heart skips a few beats. "Cami forwarded me your number. I'm calling in regards to a rumor that 69 Bottles was in an accident this morning."

Shit, what do I say to this?

"I'm wondering if you'd like to clarify for me."

"The band was not in an accident this morning. One of their buses was in an accident. However, there are no injuries and aside from some damage to the bus, everything is fine."

"Great, do you know what happened?"

"No, I haven't been given the details at this time."

"Will the show be cancelled for tonight?"

I try not to laugh. "We're still assessing the situation at this time, however, we are confident that everything will go as planned and on time."

"We understand that Addison was taken to the hospital this morning following the accident, can you elaborate on that?"

"I'm sorry?" Where the hell is this coming from?

"Was Addison injured in the accident this morning and taken to the hospital?"

"No, she was not on the bus this morning."

"So she's in the hospital?" he counters.

"No, I'm sorry, I don't know what you're referring to."

"So she's not in the hospital?"

Shit! "Not that I'm aware of."

"Okay, thank you, Raine."

"No problem," I say and he disconnects.

"What was that all about?" Casey asks.

"A reporter, looking for dirt on the accident this morning, but he brought up something interesting. I thought Addison's hospital stay was confidential?"

"It absolutely is."

"Then why was he probing for more information about her being in the hospital? Though he played it off like she was on the bus this morning and then taken to the hospital after. Of course I told him there were no injuries."

"Fucking reporters." I watch as Casey grips the steering wheel a little harder than necessary and I can feel the tension. There's more to this reporter thing with him than he lets on. But it's none of my business, so I don't press it.

"They're just doing their job. But what surprises me is the fact that Cami sent him to me. I realize Addison is out of commission but..." I let the thought fade away. Cami is notorious for throwing curveballs at people just to see how well they handle things. For all I know, she set Mitch up. Baited him or even called in a favor.

dex

"Man, I'm sorry," Talon tells me.

"Nah, don't stress it. If we were anywhere but here, this would be a major issue," I tell him as I've just hung up with a local retailer. I need four drums replaced and my crash too. Dents in that aren't a big deal, but it's practically folded in half. "We'll get 'em picked up and get them set up. Stop stressing over it." I grab Talon's shoulder.

"I don't mean to, it's just; fuck, so much shit going on right now."

I nod. "I know, brother, but it will all work out. She's doing better, Kyle's back, things will be fine. I promise." I give him a smile.

"Yeah, I just, I'd convinced myself he wasn't coming back."

"So you don't want him back?"

"Oh fuck that, I'm glad he's back, it's just… well, fuck. I don't even know anymore. Addison was so kind and so forgiving of him. I don't know if I can be that forgiving," he says sadly.

"Give it time."

He eyes me suspiciously. "Look at you, giving relationship advice, what the fuck happened to you these last few days? I know I haven't been around, but damn."

"Knock it off, I'm still the same dick as always."

"Bullshit," he states.

I scrub my face. "Honestly, I don't fucking have a clue."

"Get laid," he tells me, which is usually his way of telling me to take a fucking chill pill.

"I'm fucking trying." And that ain't a fucking joke. Last night, Jesus, I was so fucking glad that the detail was freaking out about Raine. Despite my reassurances that she'd come back eventually, they were still worried. Regardless, it gave me the out I needed to avoid sleeping with that chick.

God, when I'd walked into the bar last night, she'd been sitting there, alone. It was rather depressing to see it, but when she realized I was alone, she lit up a little bit. I'm sure she had a few choice words for me since she disappeared after the brunette sat down. She'd gone to the bathroom on our way in, but the moment I saw Raine sitting there, I immediately regretted the idea of having her walk in behind me. I hoped the brunette would take her chance and bail on me. No such fucking luck as it was.

"What do you mean, you're trying? Since when do you have a problem getting a piece of ass?" Talon asks me with a smirk on his face.

"I don't. That's certainly not the problem." No, it's the fact that I can't get a black haired, ice blue eyed beauty out of my head long enough to focus on someone else.

"Then stick it and get over it."

I stuck it and can't get over it. "Yeah, tonight should be better. Amped after the show usually helps." He shoulder checks me.

Shortly after that, Kyle showed up with an update on Addison. He said that Raine and Cami were over at the hospital and for the briefest of moments, I entertained the idea that Raine would be stuck at the hotel tonight with Addison, just so I wouldn't have to look into her eyes while someone else threw herself at me. Then again I cant seem to get my dick into anything else with or without her around, maybe it's a sign that she needs to be the last notch in my bedpost for a while, or at least I need to make it a full dent and finish what we've started.

No such fucking luck. Addison and Raine showed up at the venue some time later, after we'd gone and gotten the new set and set it up. The heads were tight and I broke three sets of sticks trying to break them in. "I fucking hate new drums," I grumble as I wipe sweat off my face and throw the used sticks in the box. For some reason, the girls go crazy over my sticks and they usually get handed out backstage after the show.

I'm standing around with the guys when the back door opens, letting in a flood of sunlight, momentarily blinding me. Walking in the back door, leading the way is Addison, followed by Talon, Kyle and Raine. My heart skips a beat when I see her.

Eric and Calvin head straight for Addison and I can't help but go straight for Raine.

"Hang on, guys," Addison says and the next thing I know someone, Addison, is grabbing me by the ear and pulling me back, away from Raine. "Down boy."

"Hey, come on, stop cockblocking me."

"She's my assistant," she says as she lets my ear go. I look down at her. She's much taller than Raine is, but still short compared to my six three. "She's not for you to schmooze."

I snort. "Schmooze? What are you, five?" I laugh. "And I'm not schmoozing, I'm working it." I give her a look like, knock it off.

She shakes her head. "I hope she plays hard to get."

"She already is," I growl in frustration.

"Good, but she doesn't need to be another notch in your bedpost, Dex."

I lean down and tell her, "I want her to be the last notch in my bedpost."

She looks a little shocked but she grins and whispers, "Prove it."

"I'm trying," I growl again. "Now stop blocking me."

Addison bursts out laughing and I throw my arms around her, picking her up. "I'm so glad you're back. Fucking missed ya, little mama." She rolls her eyes at me. I don't blame her, I sound like an idiot.

"Thanks for bringing him back." She hugs me back and I squeeze her a little tighter.

"Anytime, now let me go. I got schmoozing to do," I laugh and she punches my shoulder.

I just barely get to Raine when I hear the guys macking on Addison. I look over and something is a little bit different today about Mouse and Peacock. I shrug it off and turn to Raine, giving her my best smile. I watch as she quivers slightly, and not in a bad way.

"Tell Mouse, what?" I hear Talon ask.

I look over just as Peacock says, "That I'm gay."

"About fucking time you admitted it, brother," I say. There is a look exchanged between Peacock and Addison. Whatever, I shrug it off. I watch as Talon hugs Peacock.

"I know, Eric," Talon says as he taps him on the chest. "But you know what?" Peacock shakes his head. "I'm glad you finally told me."

We've all suspected Peacock to be gay, or at the very least bisexual since he doesn't seem to have issues with women. I've seen him in action, but Talon's right, he's never actually come out and said it to anyone. I chalked it up to either being wrong, or letting him come out when he was ready.

"It doesn't bother you?" Eric asks.

That's when what I've been waiting weeks for actually happens. Talon grabs Kyle by the neck and kisses him. I can see Kyle's face from where I'm standing and he's momentarily taken aback. His eyes widen and I watch as he softens and melts into what Talon is doing to him. Raine pushes my jaw back together. "I have no room in my heart to judge you. You're my brother, you're my friend," Talon says to Eric and they grab arms the way we all do.

"Oh crap" I hear Addison groan and I bite my tongue to stop from laughing as she scurries her way to the garbage can to hurl. I turn my attention back to Raine.

"Still mad at me?" I ask her and she scowls.

"I was never...well, okay, maybe I was." She smiles. "Not at the moment," she tells me and I stroke her cheek.

I walk over to Eric. "Just because you've finally come out, doesn't mean it changes anything." I smirk. "I will still tease you, I will still rib you, and I will do my best to keep it strictly to girl ribbing."

"You're a dick, dude." I laugh with him.

"No, you need a dick," I tell him.

"I think it might be you who needs one."

I grab my dick through my jeans. "Got one right here." We both laugh.

chapter
30
raine

My breathing is ragged and my head is getting dizzy.

You'd think he was kissing me, but no. Instead I am standing backstage while 69 Bottles performs an amazing show. I can't take my eyes off of Dex. Jesus, he's so fucking gorgeous. Watching him move, watching his hands fly across his drums, his legs bouncing, fuck me, he's so fucking gorgeous.

"Pretty epic, isn't it?" Addison asks from behind me. Kyle is behind her and I step back so that we can talk a little easier.

"I've never...I don't have words," I say, flushed. Addison gives me a knowing little chuckle.

She leans into me. "Are we talking about the band or Dex?" she asks me and I flush scarlet. "That's what I thought. The man is a fucking machine. I've never seen anyone play the way that he does."

"That makes two of us."

I go back to watching. He's glistening in the lights. Sweat has matted down his hair. He's still quite possibly the sexiest thing I've ever seen and I realize now that I was stupid to think that I could do this job without letting my feelings get too attached. Yup, we aren't even on the road yet and I'm already drooling all over him. I should go, I should leave before he comes off stage, but I don't think I can move.

I don't get a chance to make an escape because they're coming for Addison with her mic. She still has her duet with Talon to do, the new one, 'To Be Free'. It's the song they were recording on Tuesday. Because they added the drum in the studio, I wonder if they will do it here. As they wrap up their current song, the lights dim out, covering the guys and leaving Talon the focus of everyone's attention. The next thing I notice is Peacock and Mouse are coming off the stage, followed by Dex, then Kyle is kissing Addison and jealousy rockets through me. I want to be here, though not with Kyle. No, I want to be here with Dex.

I want to be the girl he kisses before shows. I want to be the one he walks off stage to during their break, I want to be the one who he goes to bed with at night. It's stupid of me to want something that I know is impossible to have.

The guys high-five each other and Kyle and I watch, just leaning back, keeping to the shadows, hoping to just be nosy and eavesdrop and not be noticed.

I watch as Dex grabs a fresh, cold bottle of water from the bucket. He downs it in two gulps. His body is covered in sweat and I wonder why the shirt, why not go shirtless. But no matter, the view has my blood heating. When that bottle is gone, he grabs another one, doing the same. By the third, he's slowing down.

Talon and Addison have just now begun their performance and the guys all turn toward the stage to watch. I immediately see why Cami is so interested in her. Sure, I've seen the videos. Boy, have I ever seen those videos, but there nothing compared to what it's like to watch her onstage. There is a deep connection between her and Talon and it shows. Her voice is positively amazing and her stage presence, through the progression of videos, has gotten better with each performance.

I feel eyes on me. I look around to find Dex staring at me. He's got a small smile on his face and I wonder what it is that he's thinking about while he watches me. I know I've probably turned his head tonight. In fact, it's what I was going for. I'm wearing my torn up jeans, my own version of shit kickers and an old sweatshirt, cut up and hanging off my shoulder, exposing part of my tattoo, the ugly part, well, not really but that's what's there. Under the sweatshirt is just a purple a-shirt tank top. It's nothing special, but the jeans hug my curves and the sweatshirt is short so my ass is on full display.

I look back to the stage and watch Addison and Talon sing their song. Thinking about what Cami had told me today. She told me to go shopping, buy some more clothes for going on the road. I told her that it would be cheaper for me to fly back to California, pack my clothes and then fly back. She told me to shut up and go shopping. So I'm planning on doing just that.

I can still feel Dex watching me and my nipples harden. My attraction to him has got to stop. I was supposed to purge him from my system. Realize what an assholian he really is and move on, but yet all I can think about is wrapping my legs around him while he slides into me. My mouth goes slack and my breathing falters. "If you want another round, all you have to do is ask."

I jump. Too caught up in my own thoughts to realize that he'd moved in behind me. "No, thank you," I state.

"Then stop thinking about me between your legs." I whip my head around to look at him. "Years of being a manwhore have taught me one thing, sweetheart." There's that word again and my blood runs cold. Amped up libido wiped out. "I can read women better than they can read themselves."

"I doubt that," I retort.

"Oh really?"

"Yes, because if you can read women, you'd know that you were a few short seconds away from another round with my knee."

He growls in my ear and backs off. I turn and walk toward the back door of the arena the moment that Talon and Addison wrap up. Giving him absolutely no time to follow after me.

"Raine," he shouts, and I ignore him. Then I hear it, his feet hitting the concrete of the floor. "I won't grab you, so please, stop," He calls after me. I stop. With my back still to him, he slides up right behind me. "I have less than thirty seconds, but I'm going to tell you this. Do not leave."

"Give me one reason to stay."

"We need to talk," he breathes and I feel his presence leave mine as he goes back toward the stage. I turn around just in time to see him step back onto the stage for the last little bit of their set. I turn back and crash through the door. Once I'm clear, I put my hands on my knees, breathing heavily.

Why does he do this to me? How does he do this to me? One minute it's sweet, the next minute I want to knee him in the balls. Why am I so offended by 'sweetheart'? It's a term of endearment, but coming off of his lips, he makes it sound like sweetheart means hooker, whore or prostitute and I hate it so much. I shouldn't have let it bother me, especially when you consider the fact that he was talking about being a manwhore. I'd detach myself too. I've got to stop acting like this when it comes to him.

My phone vibrates with an incoming unknown caller.

"Hello?"

"About fucking time you answer my call."

"Excuse me? Who is this?" I look again at the phone, but it still says unknown caller.

There is an exasperated huff on the other end of the line. "We need to talk." The man is gritting his teeth, but it's not Dex. "I'm on my way over."

"Who the hell is this?" I say again, not understanding who this person might be, but oddly familiar.

"Stop playing games with me, teddy bear."

I nearly drop my phone. "How did you get this number, Michael?"

"I have my sources. Answer your fucking door," he growls into the phone. I hang up. My hands are shaking.

"Raine?" I look up to see Rusty coming toward me. "Raine, what's wrong?" He comes to stand close to me. I shake my head. "You're as white as a ghost," he tells me and I nearly collapse.

"Um, I..." I hand him my phone. "I need to call the police. In Los Angeles."

"What? Why?"

"Someone...someone is at my door to my apartment and..." My voice is shaking so hard. "He...I don't know what he'll do if I don't answer."

"Why didn't you tell him you weren't home?"

Why didn't I tell him... "Because he isn't supposed to have this number." The numb fog is fading. "I changed my number, the only thing I haven't been able to do is move. I was afraid he wouldn't believe me." My hands are still shaking.

Rusty withdraws his phone from his pocket and talks to someone through his headset. "I've got her now. We're outside. Can you get me her address?" He pauses. "No, text. The California address." There is another pause and his hands come to rub along my arms, comforting me. "Great, thanks." Just then his phone chimes. "Raine?" I look up at him. "Let's get you inside, all right?" I nod and he helps me inside. He takes me into one of the dressing rooms where he sits me down on the couch.

He goes to his phone, and pulls up a number. "Ryan, hey, it's Rusty...not much, listen, I need a huge favor...no, I'm in New York. Look, one of my girls...no, now stop, I'm being serious...yeah yeah, look, she's got someone who's pounding on her door there in LA, she's here with me. The guy's a nut job." He can say that again. "We're not sure what he'll do when she doesn't answer the door and she didn't tell him that she was out of town." There's a long pause filled in only with 'yes' and 'mmhmm' on Rusty's end of the phone call. "Thanks, Ryan. Let me know?...Great, thanks." Rusty ends his call and I can hear the band wrapping up their set. I cross my fingers for an encore to buy me a little bit more time, a chance to escape.

There's a knock on the door and Rusty answers it. Mills is standing on the other side and the crowd noise comes through as they shout for more. Mills steps inside and shuts the door, shutting out the noise. "You okay?" he asks me.

"Yeah, it's all so stupid."

"Nothing is ever stupid. Never hesitate to tell us anything, we will do anything we can from wherever we are," Mills says as he kneels down in front of me. "Can you tell me about this guy?" he asks sweetly.

I nod and fill him in on Michael, what little I know. He's never acted like this. I tell him about our relationship, how it ended and then finally my last run in with him outside the bar the night of Kansas City. "I don't think he'd really do anything, but I'm really not there to stop him."

Mills smiles, "I would hope that even had you been there, you would have called the police."

"I would have. I was going to; Rusty just beat me to it. Though I don't know if they would have listened to me or acted in enough time."

"No, they wouldn't have," Mills states matter of fact. "Is there someone in LA that can watch over your house, stay there or..."

"No one to stay there, I won't subject anyone else to him. But I can have the house checked on every couple of days," I tell him, thinking about Erica. "I can call her right now." I look at my watch, it's nearly eleven here, but not yet eight out there.

"Do that," Rusty says. "Make sure she stays away from the house tonight."

I nod and grab my phone. It starts to ring again. Unknown number. "It's him." I look up to Rusty and Mills, terrified. I reject the call.

"Call Erica, then we're going to call and have your number changed."

I groan. I'd just gotten everything updated. Rusty chuckles. "You're right," I finally agree and I pull up Erica's name and press the phone icon. After three rings, she answers the phone.

"What is up, buttercup?"

"You'll kill me when I tell you where I am." I smirk.

"Where?" she says excitedly.

"Back stage at a 69 Bottles concert."

She screams so loud I have to pull the phone away from my ear. Mills and Rusty both laugh. "You bitch," she says.

I roll my eyes. "Look, there is actually a purpose for my call."

"You can't tell me something like that and then not tell me details," she says.

"I know, but I don't have a lot of time before I need to get going and I need a really huge favor."

"For backstage access to 69 Bottles, you can have my first born."

"Deal. But instead, I need you to check on my apartment for me."

"Why?"

"Because I am going on the road with the band."

"You bitch," she says again.

"Look, Michael is causing me some problems. He's supposedly pounding down my door at the apartment. We've called the cops to go over there tonight, but honestly, Erica, I don't know what he's capable of."

"That fucking moron," she says into the phone. "I can do that. I have your other key, do you want me to check inside too?"

Mills and Rusty shake their heads because they can hear her. "No, not really. Just swing by, take a look from the outside, if anything looks off, let me know. Don't stop by every day or anything. I don't want him to see you and catch on either. But if you see him lurking around, call the cops."

"I'll hook her up with Ryan's information," Rusty whispers.

"Reeka - I'll send you a phone number, a contact the security guys here have. You can call him rather than nine-one-one."

"All right, you sure you're okay?" she asks me.

"Yeah, baby, I'm perfectly fine. I just don't want anything to happen to my apartment. Listen, I have the majority of my stuff in a fireproof safe in the closet. It's too heavy to move, so leave that, but…"

"You want me to grab some stuff."

"Yeah. I will email you the list tomorrow."

"All right, sweet-cheeks. Anything else?"

"Nah, I'm good for now."

"Don't forget my tickets."

I laugh. "They're in LA in a few weeks, I'll get you passes."

"Ohmygod, Iloveyou," she says in a garbled mess of excitement.

"Gotta run."

"Okay, bye."

We hang up and I take a long deep breath.

chapter
31
dex

Well, fuck. I knew she'd...damn it. I wish she wouldn't have done that. I owe her an apology. It took me all of three seconds to figure out what I did.

"We ready?" Talon says.

We all nod. "Let's do it!" Mouse says and we retake the stage. My arms are burning, my legs are killing me and my hands hurt. But they're calling for it. I step back onto the stage and sit down behind my set. The replacement set turned out to be pretty decent. But they won't last the tour. I'll be lucky if they make it through the three shows here in New York.

I flip the sticks in my hands and start to tap out the next song and the roar of the crowd gets me going a little bit. But not enough. Not until I feel a certain pair of eyes on me. She's been watching me all night. I've felt her all night and I've fed off of the feeling of her watching me. There's something spectacular about knowing that someone is watching you and you alone. Anytime I capture her in my peripheral, it sends a thrill through me and it's fucking driving me mad. I need to get laid. I wonder if I need to stick it in someone else and get over her, but the idea of someone else sends chills up my spine.

When I'm able to, I look over at her and she looks sad, looks like something is bothering her. I wonder what it is. That's when I see Mills and Rusty pretty close by, closer than is normal, at least for them.

Trying to focus on what I'm doing, I turn back toward the crowd and finish out the song. We play one more, this one is a cover song, one that first got us noticed, one that we've played for a few years now. The crowd goes nuts and I'm finally able to draw some energy from it. It's enough for me to finish out the set and the concert.

After Talon says good night to the audience, we finally leave the stage just as the lights in the arena come up. The crowd is still cheering. It makes me smile. I grab three bottles of water out of the tub and head toward the dressing room. Grabbing Raine's hand along the way.

"What are you...where are you taking me?" she protests, but she doesn't stop.

We reach the dressing room that has the shower in it and I open the door for her and she steps inside. I follow her in.

"What's wrong?" she says.

"I should be asking you that question. You look like someone choked your cat."

"I don't have a cat," she says sardonically.

"Well, then what happened?"

"It's nothing. Don't worry about it. That was a great show," she says with a wide smile "You were wonderful."

"Thank you. Stop deflecting. What's wrong, Raine?"

"Why do you care? We slept with each other once, Dex, and you've treated me like shit ever since."

"You said you'd give me one night. That was all." She looks at me, shocked.

"You mean you wanted more? You fucking ran out the door the minute it was over," she says.

She's right, I did walk out right afterward, but for reasons other than the ones she's thinking. I walked out because I freaked out. I knew then that she was different and I knew then that this was going to fuck with my head and it has.

"I did. I did for reasons I'm not ready to discuss."

She nods. "Well, what if I'm not ready to discuss my foul mood?"

I open one of the water bottles, downing it quickly, tossing it away and then open the next one. I offer the third one to her and she takes it, opening it up and drinking down a good portion of it. "We're going out tonight. Come with us."

"I'm not going to be very good company. I'm really not in the mood."

"Then let me help you get in the mood." I take a step toward her, she doesn't move, so I take another step forward, and finally another one, closing the gap. I run my finger down her cheek and she leans into my touch. When my finger touched her skin, there was a connection there that I never noticed before.

"If you want me in the mood to watch you pick up some bimbo, I'm not going." she says, acid in her voice.

"So is that was this is about? You being upset?"

She shakes her head. "No, I think the knee to the nuts cured that last night." She winks and steps away. "Why are we in here?"

"I need to take a shower. Want to join me?" I raise an eyebrow at her. She stops, her jaw goes slack and I can feel the shift in mood. She's gone from angry to horny in a nanosecond.

She recovers rather quickly. "I don't think that's a good idea," she says in a rushed whisper.

"Why not?"

"Because...because..." I smile at her. She can't come up with a logical reason to not sleep with me. "Because you will fuck me in the shower and go out with the guys and find someone else to get your rocks off with later. I gave you one night, you took it, took what I gave you and you ran away as soon as you could. You had your chance, Dex."

I can't argue with her logic and reasoning. I don't want to get into the reasons for my leaving that night. She either wouldn't understand or she won't care. Either way, it is what it is. I pull off my t-shirt and start toward the bathroom. I stop next to her briefly, trying to build up the courage to tell her, but saying it out loud to her means that I'm admitting my own shame. My own indecision and I can't do that.

I go on to the bathroom, leaving the door open, hoping that she'll take me up on my offer to join me, but the longer I stand there, the less likely I think she will climb inside with me.

Once I'm completely naked, I turn into the shower to turn it on and something catches my eye and I turn toward the door. She's standing there, completely naked. I straighten and my semi-hard cock hardens to stone in a second. There is still a sweet ache in my balls from where she kneed me, but I let the pain radiate outward, consuming me briefly before I reach in, testing the water.

raine

I can't believe I'm standing here naked before him, but I couldn't resist the fact that he was offering another chance. Then another part of me tried in vain to tell me that this was a colossal mistake, but I couldn't stop my hands from undoing my clothes. I think a part of me wants to see if his reaction is the same as last time.

When he's satisfied that it's warm enough, he offers his hand so that I can step inside. Once inside, under the spray, he joins me, pinning me against the cool tile. His chest to my back. His chin brushes along the top of my head with a kiss and his hands slide down my shoulders, capturing my arms and lifting them over my head. Pinning me to the wall. "Spread your legs."

I do as he commands, the water shifts from off me and I hear the ripping of the condom packet as he holds my hands up with one of his. Excitement and anticipation rock through me. I'm desperate to have him inside me. The next thing I know, he is sliding up into me. Warmth, desire, need, and reverence wash through me in a tidal wave as he holds me against the wall. "So fucking perfect," he growls into my ear. Fear creeps into my veins as I realize that this man is inadvertently stealing my heart and running away with my soul.

They say there's one person for everyone. That your soul is only half to a whole and right now, I feel like my soul is becoming whole, becoming fuller with each thrust into my body. "Dex," I cry out as overwhelming emotion takes over. Fighting back tears, I let him consume me. Mind, body and soul.

He doesn't bolt out the door the minute he's done. Though he did make sure I came before he did, I give him credit for that one. But in the end, I feel dirty for giving myself over to a man like Dex for the first time, let alone a second time. I stay in the shower a little while longer. I really should just get dressed and go back to the hotel, but something tells me that I should go out with the guys. Get to know them a little better.

I have a really bad feeling about this.

"I have to go," he says softly. "They're expecting me in the greenroom." I nod, trying to hide the war I'm playing with myself. "Come out with us tonight, please?" he asks me again and I nod again. Unable to answer him with words. He kisses my forehead before leaving the room. This time I make sure he's actually left before I completely break down.

What pisses me off the most about this is that I have no one else to blame but myself. I gave in to my weakness for him yet again and now I'm left alone, in a random dressing room in some arena in the middle of New York City.

I've never felt so used before, well, maybe a little with Michael or at least after that disaster was over. But that was for obvious reasons. Why do I do this to myself?

It's a question I cannot answer.

I get dressed again and make myself presentable before leaving the dressing room. He ran last time, maybe I should run this time. But I'm a glutton for punishment. I guess I should test the waters, and really see where we stand before I make any final decision on the whole cut and run.

chapter
32
raine

It took me some time to get myself together enough to be presentable. When I finally adventure out of the dressing room, Casey is standing by and he gives me a small smile. I make my way to the greenroom. The fans have dwindled down and there are just a few milling about, some flirting with Dex, Mouse and Peacock, but surprisingly, Dex looks over at me and smiles.

I ask Bruce, who's standing next to me, "Where's Addison?"

"She and Kyle went back to the hotel. She was pretty wiped out."

"Oh." I'd been counting on Addison as a buffer between me and Dex, between me and the guys, but now she's gone and my desire to flee increases.

Talon comes over to me. "You okay?" he asks, I nod. "Mills filled me in on what happened earlier."

I look at him with wide eyes. "I'm sorry," I say softly.

"Don't be. But I hope it proves to you that these guys, though bulky and intimidating, are really just trying to help." I nod. "So maybe you'll stop running away from them?" He raises an eyebrow at me.

"Is there anything you don't know?" I ask, though my intended sarcasm is lost.

"Not really, no. Just like them, I care. I care about the people that are a part of this crew, whether they've been with us for ten years like some of our roadies, or they've been with us for four days." I nod my understanding and give him a small smile. "It's also my understanding that you will be joining the tour?"

"I, shit, um..." I fluster a little, "It was Cami's idea, she thought that Addison could use the help. After...well, you know. She wants Addison to be able to have less stress to deal with and if I can do that for her, then..."

He smiles. "I think it's a brilliant idea and I was thinking of suggesting it myself. The last few days have proven that you're a valuable asset and that Addison can benefit from you being around."

"Good." I smile hesitantly.

"Are you coming out with us tonight?" he asks. My resolve to ditch falters since it isn't just Dex that wants me to come out. "Come, have a few drinks, maybe we can chat some more."

"All right," I say before I let my emotions win out and send me running for the hills.

"Good." He smiles and goes back to the guys. Dex doesn't ever say anything to me in the greenroom but I catch his eyes wandering over to me from time to time.

Shortly after that, we leave for the bar. Piled into different cars, they escort us over there. I end up with most of the security detail. How aptly appropriate. The help, with the help. I roll my eyes at myself. I don't know why all of a sudden I'm so self-conscious about what I'm feeling. Okay, I really do know why. It's because of Dex. He's tearing me apart whether he means to or not.

Once we get to the bar, I head straight for the bartender and pound back two shots of Crown. Might as well enjoy myself.

Again I catch Dex staring at me from time to time, but I let it go. He and Talon are talking and laughing and having a good time. I'm almost envious of whatever they're discussing, wishing I was a part of it.

I watch woman after woman approach the guys. Peacock and Mouse seem to be sticking to themselves, but occasionally talk to a few of the girls. After the revelation this afternoon, I'm not really sure what to make of it anymore, but Mouse and Peacock seem to be getting along the same as ever.

Though Dex is watching me, he doesn't hide the fact that he is talking to women as they approach him. He even signs a few autographs and Talon does too. I notice that Talon seems to be off the market and while the girls talk to him, they make no show of advancement, unlike with Dex. Every once in a while, his eyes meet mine in a 'see, I can behave' kind of way. But it seems superficial.

After my fourth Cosmo and another shot, I'm really drunk, exactly where I wanted and needed to be. Numb. At some point I'd turned my phone off because Michael kept calling; the private number wasn't something I could block. Rusty was my source of information, but he went back to the hotel with Addison and Kyle.

Bruce stays close to me, which actually makes me feel better. Almost like he knew what happened in the dressing room with Dex, and he's protecting me from his antics.

"Talon's leaving," Bruce tells me.

"Good, I'm going to go too."

I slide off of the stool and Bruce catches me as I nearly fall over. "Yup, I'm drunk," I mutter and try to find my footing. Casey comes over and helps my drunken ass get out the door and into the car. Talon joins me, but I just close my eyes.

I'm pretty sure I kind of passed out because the next thing I know, I am getting off the elevator on the seventeenth floor. Though I'm upright, the last however long just doesn't exist. I see Rusty standing near us and Talon gives him a friendly fist to the shoulder as he passes. When he gets to their suite door, he turns back to me, standing near Rusty. "You good?" he asks and I nod. "Good, night," he says and steps inside to find Addison and Kyle. I smile. I'm so happy they're back together. They really do make the best couple or triad I think I've ever seen, though I've never seen a triad and I blew my chance at fulfilling a fantasy to have two men at once.

"Any news?" I ask Rusty. My head is still spinning.

"He was arrested a couple of hours ago. I got a call shortly after we left. Neighbors had called the cops because of his pounding and yelling, so it made the situation a little more dire than originally thought."

"I didn't think he'd get arrested, I just wanted him gone." I feel bad, but only momentarily.

"Apparently they'd told him that you weren't home and when they told him that, he lost his shit and took a swing at Ryan."

"Oh fuck." My hand comes to my mouth. "Jesus, I'm so sorry," I say apologetically.

Rusty laughs, "No worries, Ryan thought it was funny and it was entertaining to say the least. It also gave him the grounds he needed to take him in. Disturbing the peace isn't exactly an arrest-able offense." He smirks. "His hearing isn't scheduled until tomorrow afternoon. So if you can get Erica to get your stuff, I'd suggest she does it as soon as possible. There's no telling what he's going to do once he's released. Ryan promised to keep me posted."

"I don't know how to thank you."

He smiles. "Just doing my job." He nods down the hall toward my room. "Get some sleep."

"Pfft."

I'm about halfway down the hall when the elevator door opens again and I hear voices, some deep and some distinctly female. My blood runs cold. I refuse to look back and I walk a little faster.

"See you guys tomorrow," I hear Dex say and there's some random responses and some more giggling.

As I reach for my door and slide the key card in, I'm a glutton for punishment so I look out of the corner of my eye and catch a brief glimpse of Dex at his own door. I can't hide the smile that spreads across my lips when I realize that Dex is the only one in the hallway. And he's alone.

chapter
33
raine

Avoidance becomes the name of the game over the next few days. The band, along with Addison, have a photoshoot today and I don't go. Addison tells me it's unnecessary and I also know that Cami is taking her to lunch before Addison becomes the center of attention at the shoot.

Instead, I lock myself in my room. I go through emails, adjust some of the schedules for the next few days and then finally email the changes to Mills, who promptly replies with a thank you. I learned quickly that a lot of what I'm doing now is stuff that Kyle usually handled and I wonder if I'm just taking over without permission.

I email the information to Kyle as well, and he responds back with a very positive yes and thank you. So apparently I am doing something right.

I have a detail outside, well, waiting for my call should I want to go anywhere and I decide that maybe it's time to get out of the hotel room for a little while. The weather looks decent outside, the sun is shining. Though it is New York, so looks can be deceiving.

Casey, bless his patient soul, escorts me anywhere I want to go. Which includes SoHo where I do some shopping. Finding a few outfits to bring along for the road, and a pair of new shoes and a couple of knock-off bags, which I don't put on my Bold credit card. I didn't think that would be appropriate and I got my first paycheck with my raise. Allowing me the chance to splurge.

One of my conditions for going on the road was that Bold, namely Cami, would cover the cost of my rent while I was away. Since I'm not there to enjoy the fruits of what I'm paying for.

Finally, I end up at the Apple store near Times Square. I've had a company laptop for a really long time, but it's crap and Cami insisted that I go buy a new machine, plus an iPad for going on the road. When I asked her about programming it to Bold's specifications she said to bring it by the New York office Saturday morning and the tech would meet me to program it with the necessary apps and programs I'd need to do Bold related business.

By the time I'm done in Apple, I'm starving and it's just after seven in the evening. Casey needs to switch with someone and rather than having a detail placed on me, I ask him, "What if I eat upstairs?"

"You don't need to eat in your room," he tells me.

"No, I mean in the restaurant on the top. Do you guys have to follow me around?"

"Apparently you have a knack for ditching us, so yes."

"If I promise to go eat and then go to my room or come get one of you, can I please eat in peace? Without eyes on me?"

He snorts. "I doubt you've ever eaten a meal without eyes on you, but I suppose we can make an acceptation."

"Good."

Before going to Apple, we'd taken the car back to the hotel and had the concierge take my stuff to the room and we walked to the Apple store. So Casey, being a gentleman, carried my shopping haul for me. When I protested, I got the look. That look, like don't even try it. I don't argue with him as we walk back to the hotel. The band has another show tonight and when I talked to Addison earlier she said there was no need for me to be there when I shared my reluctance to go. She understood why and didn't argue with me.

As we're walking toward my door, my cell phone rings. It's Erica.

"Hi buttercup," I greet her as I answer.

"Hi there, I got your stuff."

"Oh my god, thank you, sweetheart. Are you all right?"

"Yeah, totally good, just getting ready to head out of the office." I look at my watch, it's only four-thirty in California.

"I really appreciate you doing that. I just don't know what he's going to do."

"No, I totally understand. I've got your stuff in my car, I'll keep it with me until you get back."

"You're the best, Reeka." I open my door and take my bags from Casey.

"I know, sweet-cheeks. I'll call you tomorrow?" she says.

"Absolutely," I tell her and we hang up. I turn to Casey, "Thank you for putting up with me today."

"I don't put up with you, you're good company." He smiles.

"Thanks," I grumble and he laughs.

"Behave yourself. Troy is here tonight. I'm going to bed. Don't make him wake me up."

I laugh. "I won't." I hold up the bags. "I have new toys."

With that, he leaves me to it.

Before coming upstairs to the restaurant, I unpacked my new laptop and emailed Cami from my phone letting her know that I'd gotten it and the iPad. I need to be at the office by ten tomorrow morning. She also said that she and Tristan would be heading home tomorrow.

At ten after eight, I get a text.

Dex: where r u?

I sigh. Do I respond? Yes, I probably should.

Raine: at the hotel, having dinner. Y?
Dex: Y R U not here?
Raine: had other business to attend to.
Dex: Come now.

Why is it so important that I go to the show? That's the only question I can think of. It doesn't make any sense.

Raine: Going on road, will c many more.
Dex: Please
Raine: Tell me y.
Dex: I like having you here.

What in the world is so special about my being there? It's not like I've been to dozens of shows. Last night was my first.

The clock rolls over to eight-thirty and it's not worth the effort to text him back, he's on stage.

While I eat my BLT and French fries, I ponder the meaning behind his texts.

He wants me at the show - why? I can't come up with a logical reason for why it is that I should be there. Other than to help Addison, but she insisted it wasn't important for me to be there.

Does this mean he actually wants to see me, to talk to me, or does he just want another quick dressing room fuck? If that's the case, he can find some other bimbo to bang. My heart wrenches into a knot at the idea of him sticking his dick into someone else. Is that what I need to do, in order to keep him from his manwhore ways? Sleep with him every night? I shudder at the thought of being his new receptacle.

Then again, he's had sex, or at least orgasms, with me three times and I imagine that's the most he's ever had with any one partner. Then again, I get a feeling he isn't a one hit wonder, so maybe three is nothing for him.

I send a text to Rusty.

Raine: Are they going out tonight?

It takes him a few minutes, so I finish up my meal, sign the room charge and then check my phone again.

Rusty: Yes, going to a club near the hotel.
Raine: Forward the information to Troy? I'd like to join them.

Rusty: Done. See you later.

I leave the upstairs restaurant to find Troy standing guard. "Casey's coming for you after the show," he tells me as I step off the elevator.

"Great, thanks." I hand him his sandwich.

"Oh, thank you," he says sweetly and with a smile that could light up Manhattan.

"You're welcome. Anyone else here?"

"Nope, just me and you."

"All right, I'm going to go get dressed. What time is he coming?"

"Probably around eleven, eleven thirty."

"Okay, great, thank you." I head toward my room.

Once inside I contemplate changing my mind, but I might as well. Just because I'm trying to avoid Dex, doesn't mean I have to avoid everyone else.

Around ten thirty, after a shower and a change of clothes, I get a text from Addison.

Addison: You're coming out tonight?

Raine: Is that okay?

Addison: Absolutely. Would love to see you.

Raine: Can't wait. Don't tell Dex.

Addison: my lips are sealed. See you in a bit.

I finish up my make-up with purple eye shadow, darker colored lips and a new outfit I bought today.

All in all, the ensemble is complete. I'm not entirely sure what it is that I'm going for here, but regardless, I think I look fucking hot. Eat your heart out, Dex Harris.

I tuck my ID and credit card into my bra, not wanting to carry a purse and then finally I clip my phone on my skirt just as Casey knocks on the door.

chapter 34
dex

Be still my fucking heart. I tap Mouse on the shoulder and point to the beauty that just walked in the door. She's wearing one of those black tutu skirts over those sexy as shit leggings and a pair of flats. Her back is to me, but her hair is up in a semi-messy ponytail. She's skinny but curvy at the same time. My dick gets hard in my jeans. "Not bad," Mouse says as he watches her with me. She's walking toward the bar, there are more than a few guys smiling, nodding and then watching her as she walks past them. Eventually my view is obstructed.

I shrug her off and start talking with the guys. Addison makes her way toward the bar and Talon and Kyle watch over her until she disappears, but Rusty, ever the chameleon, is watching her dutifully. I quickly lose sight of her and the guys go back to talking to each other. With Addison gone, the girls approach in waves. Jesus, she's not that intimidating. But regardless, there are more than a few honeys coming this way and finally my eyes land on one gorgeous chick. She's got strawberry blond hair, a beautiful rack and a decent set of hips. She comes over and sits down next to me and we start to talk.

raine

"Hey." I turn to see Addison approaching me. "What are you doing over here?" she asks.

"Just getting some liquid courage."

She laughs, "Oh, I miss those days."

"How'd it go tonight?" I ask.

"Great. Wish you would have come."

"I know, I just needed to get some stuff taken care of."

"You mean you were avoiding him." She leans against the bar. I just shrug. "You'll be on board a tour bus with him in less than a week. What will you do then?"

Her voice is soft, genuine concern can be heard. I shrug. "I'm hoping I'll get over him by then."

She just smiles as if she knows more than I do about Dex. Which is totally okay. "How'd your day go, with the shoot and stuff?" I ask, trying to change the subject away from Dex.

"It was amazing. I wish you'd have been there," she tells me sadly. Then she shows me her left hand. "The guys proposed."

"Holy shit." I smile wide and look up at her. "Holy shit, Addison that's awesome." I hug her. "Now I wish I would have come."

"Oh, there's video and a whole array of pictures. I'm surprised no one told you." She laughs. "Everyone else seemed to know but me." She blushes.

"Well, as long as you're happy, that's all that matters," I tell her and the bartender finally brings me my drinks. I down the shot of Crown, throw the glass back on the bar and grab my Cosmo.

"Come on," she says and she leads me back to where the guys are. She's in front of me and since I'm wearing flats, I can't see past her. She's taller than I am.

She finally finds a break in the wall of people, it's Friday in New York after all, but when she moves out of my line of sight I damn near drop my drink when I stop dead in my tracks. Someone bumps into me and I slosh my drink all over me and look up just in time to see Dex pull his mouth away from the lips of some strawberry blonde chick sitting on his lap. He has a semi-satisfied smile on his face and his eyes lazily open, then they land on me and his smile fades away.

"Shit," I hear him say, but I turn on my heel and duck back into the crowd of people, heading for the door. I down my drink and place the glass on someone's table. They're shouting after me because I just dumped it there. I nearly slam into Casey.

"Where's the fire?" he asks.

"Move. I'm leaving," I tell him and I skirt around him, headed for the coat check. When I get there, I hand them my ticket and throw my thigh length pea coat over my shoulders and the hood over my head. Hoping like hell that it's hiding my outfit and making me less recognizable.

I step out into the street, catch my bearings quickly and turn left as I slide my arms into the sleeves of my jacket, buttoning it up and walking back to the hotel. Casey is hot on my heels, I can feel him. I stop, turn toward him. "Leave me alone," I snap.

"I can't. It's my job."

"Not anymore, it's not. I quit," I snap and turn back around.

dex

"What the fuck is wrong with you?" Addison scolds me.

"What the fuck did I do?"

"You must seriously be kidding. You can't possibly be that stupid, Dex."

The strawberry blonde that I was making out with quickly makes herself scarce and I don't blame her. I'm so fucking furious. "I didn't know she was coming," I say in my defense but it's weak and feeble at best.

"That doesn't fucking matter. If she meant anything to you at all, it wouldn't matter if she was coming or not."

I put my head in my hands. She's fucking right. Not four hours ago, I was actually missing her, I wanted her at the show and she refused to come. Now, sitting in a bar, I grab on to the first thing that walks up and don't even think twice about it.

"Well, go after her," Addison tells me.

"What's the point? She's pissed."

"She'll be more pissed off if you don't go after her," Addison says matter of fact. "Trust me."

I stand up, and all eyes are on me. "What?" I snap. They all just shake their heads. I take two steps forward and I'm met with the wall of Casey and Rusty.

"Where you going?" Rusty asks me as Beck joins them.

"I'm going to go find Raine. Wait, why aren't you with her?" I look at Casey.

He shrugs.

"Is she still here?" That's the only logical explanation I can come up with so I start to look around, hoping to see her, to spot her in the crowd, but it's futile.

"No, she's gone."

"Then what the fuck, Casey."

"I told him to let her go," Mills says from behind me. "She's not our responsibility anymore. She quit and Cami told us to back off."

"She what?" Addison says from behind me. "What do you mean she quit?"

Mills just shrugs.

Addison pounces on me like white on fucking rice. "I warned you about this shit when I climbed on board the bus. Now you've...Ugh! I can't even talk to you right now." She looks past me to Rusty. "Take me back."

"Addison, wait," Kyle says. "Maybe we should give her a chance to cool down."

"She'll be on her way to the airport," Addison says.

"You don't know that, baby girl."

"This is my fuck up, let me fix it," I say firmly. I turn to Beck. "Take me back." Beck hesitates but nods. Mills lets us go and it takes us all of a few minutes to get out of the club and on the street. We walk back to the hotel, it's only two blocks away.

We head straight for the elevator and wait impatiently for it to show up. When it does, we climb in and I nervously watch the numbers tick by until we reach the seventeenth floor. The doors open and Troy is standing there. "How long ago?"

Troy scowls at me. "For what?"

"Since Raine came through here."

Troy shakes his head. "She hasn't been up here, not since she left with Casey. You mean she's gone again?"

"She quit," I tell him. "Mills made Casey back off. We assumed she came straight here."

"No, she hasn't come up here."

"Fuck."

raine

Sometime before I managed to get falling down drunk, Casey found me and Cami convinced me to stay. Why, I haven't a fucking clue. Though there may have been job threats involved. Cami has always said it's fine until a job suffers because of it and frankly, I really didn't want to quit. I'm not here for Dex. I'm here for my fucking job.

I threatened bodily harm to Casey if he told Dex that he'd found me. He agreed to let it drop, but not before telling me that Dex was freaking out. Good, the bastard deserves it.

Finally the elevator reaches the seventeenth floor, it dings and the doors open. I'm fascinated by their movements and annoyed at what I see down the hall. Beck is on duty and he gives me a look. It looks like concern but with Beck you just never know. I smile sweetly at him and momentarily entertain the idea of taking Beck to bed, just to piss off Dex.

That's when I see him, down the hall, leaning against the wall by my door. He looks like he's passed out.

I put my finger to my lips and 'shh' Beck who rolls his eyes as I stumble my way down the hall. When I come up on him, I hear him snoring softly. I very carefully step over him, hanging on to the wall so that I don't fall. When I get to the other side, I look at Beck who's shaking his head back and forth more in annoyance than anything. I shrug and slide my keycard into the door, turn the knob quickly and slip inside, slamming the door shut behind me.

dex

Slam.

I bolt awake, sitting upright and I can hear someone, Beck. I look down the hall. He's laughing and I realize quickly the source of the noise. She fucking snuck past me. God damn it. I scowl at Beck who slinks back into his chair. He doesn't want a fight and neither do I.

I pound on her door. That's when I hear the deadbolt engage and the chain flips home. "We need to talk," I say through the door.

"I've got nothing to say." Her words come back jumbled and almost incomprehensible. She's drunk.

"But I do."

"Forget it, Dex. You had your chance, you fucking blew it. Go to bed."

She says from a little further into the room.

I fucked up royally tonight. I was stupid to think that Raine wouldn't show up. I was stupid to even entertain the idea of another woman and it was fucked up for me to see her the first time, get a hard-on and not even realize that it was her I was drooling over. Though Mouse had no fucking clue either. He was equally as intrigued.

I pound on the door again. "Open up, Raine."

I hear the chain and the deadbolt. I'm winning, she's going to open the door for me.

What a stupid fucking thing to think.

She opens the door. She's naked as a jaybird, and my cock hardens instantly. She steals my breath away. "I'm sorry," I breathe out.

"You forgot these a few days ago." She throws something in my face, blinding me, and the door slams shut once again. I pull whatever it is off of my head. It's my fucking underwear. Fuck.

I bang my head against the door.

"If you were truly sorry, Dex, it wouldn't have happened in the first place," she says through the door. "If you were truly sorry, truly wanting what it is that you're apologizing for, you wouldn't need to apologize because there wouldn't be anything to say. I told you to prove it and all you've done is break my fucking heart, one tiny piece at a time."

"I told you I was a manwhore. You've known that from the beginning."

"And I was stupid enough to think that maybe, just maybe, I might have been enough for you. Good night, Dex."

"You are enough," I say softly against the door. So quietly that I don't know if she can even hear me. But I word vomited and I can't take it back. I puked them out and I realize that it's true. She is enough. She's what I want, what I need. I can't keep doing this to her. "I will," I say aloud as I decide right then and there that I intend to prove to her that I need her, that I need to be with her.

I pound on the door one more time. Hoping that maybe she might let me in. That's when I hear music coming from her room. It's a softer piece. It doesn't take me but a minute to recognize the song. It's a song that defines my life and me. It's a song that she is listening to because of me. I fall to my knees.

chapter
35
raine

Saturday dawns, and I'm exhausted. I didn't sleep for shit last night. I kept having visions of Dex sleeping outside my door. With Saturday comes a nasty as hell hangover which I deserve like nobody's business. I manage to get myself together enough to risk the walk down the hall.

Hoping like hell that Dex is still passed out, I make my way with Troy to the office.

I'm there for just over an hour and leave with a programmed laptop and iPad.

When I return back to the hotel, I order room service and climb into my comfy as hell pajamas and curl up on the bed. Working with my laptop to get everything set up and in working condition.

I also woke up this morning with a new resolve. I will do my job. I will go about my life, and I will not let Dex Harris stand in my way anymore.

I know it's a load of crap and I've said it a dozen times already, so I guess we will see how this goes.

I decided earlier in the day that I wouldn't go to the concert tonight. I don't need the reminders, I don't need to have Dex in my face. After his whispered words at my door last night, I know that something is shifting in him but I can't put myself on that path, not anymore, and not until he really decides that's what he wants to do.

Knock, Knock, Knock.
I climb off of the bed and call, "Who is it?"
"Addie."
"Oh," I squeak and open the door.
Her face falls as she takes in my attire. "You're not coming?" She actually pouts.
"No, do you need me to?"
"No, I guess not, but...I was hoping you would."
"I..."
"Can I come in?" she asks. I open the door, she steps inside and I close the door behind her.
"What's up?" I say once she's inside.
"Can I be honest with you?"
"I'd hope you'd be honest with me about anything," I tell her. She takes a seat in the chair and I sit on the bed.
"I think you should give Dex some time," she states. Though I can tell she's concerned about bringing this up.
"Just when I finally decide to let it go," I mumble and she laughs.
"I can see that. I'd let it go too, but I think there is more going on with him when it comes to you than he's letting on."
"It's hard when he's texting you one minute, begging you to come to the show, then you show up at the bar and

he's making out with some chick. I can't handle the mixed signals from him. One minute he wants me, the next minute he's running out the door," I say bitterly. "It's very confusing. It's very draining."

"I don't know much, as far as Dex's history is concerned, but..." she pauses and bites her lip, "he's been going crazy all day today."

"So is this why you want me at the show? Because if it is, I'm sorry, I just can't."

"No, that's not why I want you at the show. I want you there because you genuinely look like you're having a good time while you're there." I don't need to mention that my good time is compliments of watching Dex behind his set. "But I won't push you to do something you don't want to do." She gives me a half smile.

"What do you mean he's been going crazy?" I finally manage to ask.

She snorts a laugh. "He's been in my suite most of the day, talking to Talon and Kyle."

I blink at her, trying to understand why he would be talking to them, what he would be talking to them about. So I ask her, "About?"

"You."

"What about me?"

She gives me a full megawatt smile. "How he can fix what he's fucked up." The air in my lungs leaves in a rush and I lean forward, putting my elbows to my knees. "I'd love to give him some pointers." She laughs. "Have any for him? He's still in my room."

I shake my head. "I think he needs to figure this out on his own, Addison, really I do."

She smiles wide and stands up. "Yes, he does." She comes to stand by me. "Get dressed. I'll leave Casey behind for you. Come to the show tonight. If I'm going to

253

offer you any piece of advice, it's this." I look up at her, righting myself. "Don't give up, not yet. I know you don't want to hear that. I know you want me to tell you to just walk away from it all, but I can't do that. Being with Talon and Kyle has been the best time of my life. I wouldn't deny anyone the happiness I feel when I'm with them. I know it's there, between you and Dex. Just give him some time."

"I can't handle a cheater. I won't do it again."

She smiles at me then. "He's kissed a woman, maybe two."

"Try three," I interrupt.

She frowns, "But I know for a fact that he hasn't slept with anyone but you since getting to New York."

Her words wash over me in a bath of warm light. "Kissing, looking, touching, it's still the same as cheating in my eyes."

"In mine too, but," she hesitates, like she shouldn't be telling me this, "every time he had one in his sights, you did something to destroy it. You'd show up, you'd disappear, you'd do something that would put you in the center of his world."

I let her words slide over me once again. "He's going to shatter me."

"I doubt that. But I learned something since getting together with Talon and Kyle. If we hold back, if we don't give into our longings, don't give in to allowing ourselves to be hurt, we will never have anything we want in this lifetime. If you run away from this before it's even had a chance to begin, you will regret it."

"I know," I breathe.

She gives me a sad smile. "Come tonight?"

"If you don't tell him I'm coming, yes." I need to be able to see it for myself. I need to see that he's ready for what I have to offer him and if he's really that torn up about it, then this will change everything between us.

"I won't say a word," she promises as she takes her leave of my room.

I rush straight to my closet.

Undeniable and gorgeous. That's what I'm going for tonight and I think, somehow, I've completely managed it.

Bright red peep toe, fuck me pumps. Skinny leather pants, an open back, tapered three-quarter sleeve t-shirt with a skull on the front, though faded, the shoulders are exposed, and though it's opened backed, it's held together by being shredded. Make-up, jewelry, hair - pinup girl style. High in the front, pulled into a ponytail.

I glance at the clock - seven-thirty. I text Casey to let him know I'm ready.

There's a knock on the door. I know Dex is at the arena, Addison texted me, so I don't hesitate to open the door. "Fuck me," Casey says in a very unguarded moment. I smile wide. "Sorry," he mutters.

"Don't be. Thanks for being my unsuspecting test subject." I smile at him.

"Anytime. Can you walk in those things?" I laugh and step into the hallway.

"Yes. Are we under the radar?" I ask him and he gives me a knowing smirk.

"I will bet you a hundred dollars that he will fuck up when he sees you." I smile wide.

"That's the idea."

He just shakes his head and escorts me down the hall and into the elevator.

chapter
36
dex

I crack my knuckles, pop my neck and take my seat behind my drums. I'm finding it increasingly difficult to get into the right frame of mind tonight. I really wanted her to be here. I hate that I drove her to the point of ignoring me, hiding in her room, not wanting to really be around anyone.

When Addison had returned to their room, I was hopeful, but she said that Raine wouldn't be here tonight and I resolved myself to finding other ways of making it up to her. We would be back on the road Thursday night, and she would be confined to a bus with me. She can't avoid me forever and I am determined to prove it to her, prove that I need her, that I need her to help me. But I'm not worthy of what she has to offer. She's offered more times since she got here than I deserve. Tonight just proves that my head is falling out of my ass just a little too late.

Talon gives me the signal and I count it off. Mouse and Peacock hit their notes at the same time as I do, creating

257

the loud and intense sound that is 69 Bottles. A sound that took us years to perfect but only seconds to recognize.

We continue through our opening and then finally Talon starts to sing. We open the show with one of our most popular songs. It's usually a good crowd starter. They get even more excited.

We've been playing the song for years, the drums roar under my sticks and the band rocks.

I'm just starting to warm up when that song ends and Talon talks to the crowd while I casually beat on the drums and the guys play their guitars. It's soft, but the subtle strains of our next song has the crowd getting a little more wound up. When Talon is done, we fly effortlessly into the next song.

We're about halfway through the second song when I see her, she's here, backstage. One of my sticks pops from my hand, causing me to miss a crash. I get a sideways glance from Mouse and a smirk as he realizes I've popped a stick. No, I fucking dropped a stick.

I recover quickly with a spare from the pouch that's tied to my stool. She, on the other hand, has the widest, wickedest grin on her face. She's done this on purpose, the little fucking minx. Jesus, she's fucking gorgeous. I can't keep looking at her, I'm going to fucking lose my place. I go back to concentrating on what I'm doing with a Cheshire grin on my face.

She's shown up just in time.

raine

I'm not sure what has me more excited, the fact that he dropped a stick, or the fact that I owe Casey a hundred dollars. I watch him, and he's watching me, whether he intends to or not. He's angled himself in such a way that he can keep stealing glances in my direction. Before the song finishes, I move out of his line of sight and walk around the back of the stage. His drums actually face the opposite way, well, they're angled that way. By moving to the other side, he can look and play at the same time.

I watch the slow sexy smile that spreads across his face when I fall into his normal line of sight and he keeps playing. Though we don't retain eye contact, I can tell he's always looking at me.

When that songs ends, the atmosphere shifts and Mouse takes over on the guitar.

It's the very familiar chords of the song I played on repeat last night. I cover my mouth and fight tears.

The crowd is going insane and Dex...he's staring hard, searching my eyes. Conveying that he'd heard it, there's sadness in his eyes too and I finally get it.

I point to him and he nods, I point to me and he nods. I can't stop the slow smile that spreads across my face as Talon starts to sing 'Broken' by Seether.

When the song finishes up, they cut right into one of their faster songs and I wipe tears away from my eyes. Addison makes eye contact with me across the stage. She holds up her phone and I pull mine out.

Addison: You look amazing. Thank you for coming.
Raine: him dropping a stick made it all worth it.
Addison: Casey's on cloud 9.

I look at her and chuckle lightly and go back to enjoying the show on the stage in front of me. Addison gets hooked up to her mic for the second time and I escape back behind the stage to the other side because I know Dex will come off stage shortly and I want to be there when he does.

They finish up the song and my heart starts to flutter. Dex makes eye contact with me. His steel grey eyes penetrate me and cause me to shiver and my already heated sex to fire up. The little ball of nerves is on fire as he narrows his eyes at me. He's on a rampage, but he's not angry. He charges off of the stage first and Addison giggles as she passes him.

Excitement, terror and pure lust course hotly through my veins. I back up toward the wall, trying to put some distance between us before he crushes me. But I have no outlet, nowhere to go. Fuck, he knows this. I put my hands up in self-defense, but he smirks. Grabbing my wrists, he spreads my arms wide and then over my head, pinning me to the wall.

His lips crash hard onto mine. He smells like Dex, heady and sweaty, but it's fucking sexy as hell. He steals my breath away the moment his tongue slides inside, seeking mine.

He abruptly pulls back, he is breathing heavy. "You." Kiss. "Made." Kiss. "Me." Kiss. "Pop my stick." Lick across my lips. "You made me lose my place." He kisses me again. "You made me screw up." I give him a wicked chuckle. "You naughty girl."

"Think about what you just said." I'm still laughing.

"Well, that is how fucking gorgeous you look tonight."

"Shut up," I tell him.

He pulls back.

"Shut up and fucking kiss me, you idiot."

He smiles wider than I've ever seen him smile before and he presses his lips and sweaty body against mine and I'm completely and totally lost in his kiss. His lips, his tongue, his body pressed against me. His knee slides between my legs and I writhe against him and he groans. After a few more beats, he breaks the kiss. "We need to talk," he whispers.

"Yeah, we do."

"Stay?"

"Yes," I breathe.

"Promise?"

"I promise."

He slowly lets me go, like he knew I was going to be unsteady on my feet and he doesn't want me to fall. Once I'm situated, he goes and grabs three bottles of water. He tucks one under his arm, then hands me one. I smile as we both open our bottles. He downs his in two swallows and immediately goes for the other one and downs that one equally as fast. I take a big pull off of mine and hand it over to him.

He smirks, takes it and drinks it.

"Gotta go," he breathes. "Get back on the other side of the stage," he says as a command.

'Yes, sir." He scowls at me, but then smiles and goes back on stage.

When Addison comes off the stage, she's a little sweaty, but she's all smiles. Then she comes to me and teases, "No wonder he dropped his sticks." She winks and takes Kyle's offered bottle of water. I escape to the other side of the stage to watch him perform the rest of the concert.

As soon as the guys were done on stage and with their encore, Dex disappeared into the dressing room so he could shower. He was a sweaty gross mess, but still sexy as fucking hell. He kissed me chastely on the forehead and he told me where he was going, but I felt disappointed that he didn't ask me to come along.

What was really funny about this night is that Dex never once advanced on me beyond kissing. In fact he never even made a move to try and take me back to the hotel. He was just content to have me next to him.

When he'd asked about going out after the show, I'd said that I had enough to drink the night before and that I wanted to just go back. He escorted me back to the hotel and kissed me on my doorstep, for lack of a better term. It was ridiculously sweet. But that was all she wrote. When I asked if he wanted to come in, he respectfully declined.

Gone was the assholian, and here arrived the gentleman.

We didn't talk that night, in fact we didn't talk Sunday, Monday, Tuesday or Wednesday as we were swamped with band appearances and then it came time to board the bus late Thursday. I dreaded it, I really did, but as the week progressed, Dex remained ever the gentlemen and even when I wasn't with him, he behaved. Even on the one night that I showed up, just to watch. Think of me what you will, but I couldn't help myself. I needed to know that he was really trying to prove himself and so far, it seemed to be working.

We travelled from New York to DC on Thursday night for our show on Saturday.

We arrived in DC around eight and got checked in. The bus collectively decided that we would just stay in DC until late Wednesday when we would head to Greensboro for the next show.

It's nearly midnight when there's a knock on my door. I no longer dread answering the door, in fact, when I do and see Dex standing on the other side, relief washes through me. He holds up a bottle of Crown. "Can we talk?" he asks.

I smile at him and open the door. He kisses the top of my forehead as he passes me and steps into the room. This one has a little sitting room between the bed and the patio. I go to the counter near the bathroom and grab two tumblers and fill them with ice and join him in the sitting area. There are two couches, one on either side of the room with a table between them. I set the glasses down on the table, drinking in his long fingers as he opens the bottle and pours us both a glass. He slides one over to me. I sit back and smile. I don't say anything, this is his talk. It's up to him to make the first move.

chapter
37
dex

She's so gorgeous, even kinda mussed up and tired. I can see it in her eyes and I wonder if she's been sleeping well.

I took the ground less traveled after our last New York show. Yes, it took everything I had to not drag her into that dressing room, but I figured I had a lot of making up to do first. Though it's been a few days, I don't feel fully redeemed, not yet. She was the star of my fantasies every day and every day it's becoming harder and harder to stay away from her. I can't do it anymore.

"I am drawn to you like a magnet. When I'm not around you, I miss you. When I'm near you, all I do is fuck shit up. I keep making an ass out of myself and one of these times you're going to kick me to the curb."

"You deserve it," she says, putting her hands down.

"I do. You shouldn't want to be with me. I'm dangerous. I'll fuck you up the way I fuck up everything else in my life."

"Why is it so easy for you to detach yourself, but impossible for you to see what's really in front of you?"

264

I look at her. She's right of course. "I do see what's in front of me. You, beautiful, forgiving, sexy." I give her a smile.

"You really think I'm beautiful?" I nod. "Sexy?" I smile. "I wouldn't say forgiving, not yet anyway." She sighs. "Dex?"

"Hmm?"

"Call me sweetheart or baby again and I won't be so forgiving." I give her a raised eyebrow. "I see it in your eyes, I watch you war with yourself when you drop those terms on me. I was there, in that room that Sunday night, and I saw firsthand how you process things. You drop those names and it's like flipping a light switch off. You detach, you disappear. I wanted to believe the moment you called me sweet girl or princess, that you were changing your tune with me. Whether it was a play to get laid, or a reality, I've yet to figure it out. I'd like to go with reality, but I'm not sure anymore."

"It's reality."

"I know because you tried to walk away, or run rather," she says with a small smile playing on her lips.

I stand up and take a step toward her. She puts her hand up to stop me. I can see the war in her eyes. But I don't have to guess. "I don't know whether to forgive you or kick you out."

"I'd like forgiveness. I've never done this before, Raine. I've never felt like this before." I sigh. "I'm a dick because it's the only way I know how to guard myself or even to process all of this."

"Well, I need you to drop your assholian beliefs, because I can tell you three things." She pauses and I nod in encouragement for her to continue. "One, I'm not one of them. That Sunday night I was indulging in a fantasy of being with the ultimate rock god. Yes, I was willing to give it one night, but Beck being there was meant to be a buffer for me and my normal reaction to sleeping with someone. But Beck wasn't the man I wanted to sleep with." She runs her hands through her hair. "Two, I don't know why you push people away or keep them at arm's length. I would honestly like to know because it will help me to better understand you and it will ultimately help me to stop you from self-destruction when you're around me. And lastly, I'm not asking for a long term commitment from you, in fact I don't even know what it is that I want from you. But I know, after all this angst and frustration, that if I sleep with you again, it will tear me to shreds."

I take a step toward her. I can't believe I am about to say what I'm going to say, but frankly it's the fucking truth. "I know you're not one of them. I can never clump you into that group of women. You're so much better than that and I don't deserve your compassion, I don't deserve your forgiveness and more than anything, I do not deserve anything you have to offer me." I take two more steps and bend down before her.

She eyes me warily and I slam back the glass of Crown in my hand. I need the liquid courage to get me through this.

I take a moment to feel the Crown burning in my stomach and making its way out into my limbs. Stalling is the name of this game. I stand back up and move back to the other couch and take a seat. I know I can't stall any longer. "My parents were killed when I was seventeen."

She gasps and covers her mouth. I can't look at her because I don't need to see sadness. "You need to know that I've never told anyone this before. At least not someone that I want to be intimate with. The guys know, for obvious reasons. When you spend as much time together, it's hard not to." I take a deep breath. "I'm sure what's running through your mind is something to the effect of me being seventeen, being older. Well, you're right. Being older made it easier for me to emancipate myself and avoid going into the system for seven months. But it also means that I spent sixteen years in a loveless household. They fought constantly. They ignored me whenever it suited them. I was making myself dinner at nine because I was starving. I was making school lunches at seven, and by twelve I was grocery shopping, smoking, drinking and never getting in trouble because nobody cared." I scrub my hand over my face. "My father had a fast fist and an even deadlier belt. My mother had indifference."

I get up and grab some more ice off the alcove. I didn't even hear her get up, but she comes up behind me, wrapping her arms around my waist and I slouch.

"Your touch obliterates everything I grew up knowing about love, compassion, forgiveness. When you touch me, nothing else matters," I admit and she holds me tighter. I put my hand on top of hers. She puts her head against my back and I set the glass down and turn in her arms. "Looking at you, I realize that I want so much more than a receptacle. That I need it and I wonder how I've lived this long without it," I tell her and she smiles sadly at me.

"I'm not a cure-all, Dex. As much as I want to be that for you, I don't know how to do that. I'm not strong enough to deal with your mood swings. It will break me."

"I never want to break you." I kiss her forehead.

"I'm afraid that you will and not just physically." She wiggles her hips and he stirs again.

"You sweet dirty girl." I kiss her forehead again. "But I'm not done."

"Then I need a drink." She pulls back and I step out from in front of the fridge and she goes straight for the ice bucket before she walks back to the couch. She puts a few more cubes in her glass and tops it off with more Crown.

"A girl after my own heart." I smile at her as she downs the glass. I smirk at a memory. "Your love of Crown the other night."

"That was such a waste of good booze." She smirks as she gets back up off of the couch and goes into the fridge for a bottle of water.

"No, it wasn't," I say seriously. "It brought us together, though in a rather fucked up way." She smiles as she passes me again on the way back to the couch. I watch her curl up, but she doesn't take much care with how her shirt slips off of her shoulder. A little further and she'd be hanging completely out. I notice now that there is no tank top and no bra strap. Her comfort level makes me smile. I try not to stare. I have another idea and staring will give me away.

"When they died, I was pissed. Not because they were gone, but because my parents were loaded." She gasps. "I know, it sounds like a poor man's story, but in reality, it was the opposite. I was pissed because they were dead, and I was thrown out of my house and onto the streets, or friends' couches as was the case for the first three months while everything was locked up in the estate. Their will specifically stated that the property was to be sold and yada yada, you don't need the gory details of that. But with my time on the streets and on couches, I discovered cocaine, crack and heroine. I always told myself that I was lucid. I could function, I could hold down a job, but as soon as the sun went down, it was another story." She's listening intently. I walk over in her direction, toward the window. I stand there for a minute. "That's also where I discovered my love, if you want to call it that, of sex and I found rich women, mostly that my parents used to know and who would feel sorry for me. I'd seduce them into giving me money to feed my habit."

"While you were still a minor?"

I snort a laugh. "Ironically, with no money, no solid place to live, I managed to emancipate myself, making me a legal adult. Though if anyone pushed the issue, it was technically illegal, but no one did. Once my parents' estate freed up, I found a shit apartment, paid for two years of rent in advance, banked and safe deposited access to the majority of my money. That's when I went on a ten day bender. No longer needing to work, I blew through more than thirty thousand dollars in drugs."

She gasps and I look at her. "I can't even... I've never even seen that much money at once, let alone..."

I cock my head at her, then I walk around behind the couch and bend down, resting my elbows against the back of it. "I didn't even know I'd spent that much money until about six years later. Though by that time, my spending had jumped into the hundreds of thousands of dollars. Then I was forced to relive my parents' death all over again when a lawyer found me. I was thrilled when I walked out of the first lawyer's office with the amount of money that I did. I was young, didn't know and certainly didn't care. I had enough to live on and not work. I could play drums when I wanted to. Panhandle on the street with a pickle bucket, it didn't matter, I could do it all. I was invincible. Then everything started to unravel. I was a complete mess. I stopped being careful with my money, with my spending and with my body. I got arrested. Spent three days in jail and when I got home, sober for the first time in years, I found a letter from an attorney. The letter basically stated that I'd reached the term of a trust that had been established by my parents."

"More money?"

I nod. "I knew that I had to claim it, but because I was sober, I knew that I would have to claim it and get clean. I made an appointment with the attorney, and then called Betty Ford in California, made an intake appointment for that same day. I walked into the attorney's office and I gave him all the information he needed to get the money to me and I walked out of there and into Betty Ford." I can't stop my hand from pursuing its destination. She brought it on by letting her shirt slip down her arm. I slide my hand down her shoulder and I gently cup her breast. I roll her nipple between my finger and she moans.

"Dex," she breathes.

"Sorry, princess, I couldn't resist." I slowly pull my hand away and she shivers but stops my retreat. In fact, she pulls my hand back down in an invitation to continue what I was doing. I won't deny her that. I can't help it. I love the feel of her pierced nipples beneath my fingers. I love feeling the warm flesh rolling and hardening at my touch.

"What happened after rehab?" she says huskily.

"I enrolled in college. Met Kyle, Calvin and Eric. Eventually we found Talon and 69 Bottles was born."

She lets out a hot rushed breath at my continued touch. I slide my other hand down the other side. Cupping both her breasts in my palms and fingering her nipples. She writhes and shudders. Her legs start to twitch with need.

She doesn't say anything, but I slow my playing. I want to keep talking even though I am slowly building up a case of blue balls but it reminds me of what I deserve. I don't deserve her. She's too perfect. Too pure. A true princess.

In my silence, she feels the need to fill the space, I guess it's because I've been so open with her. "I was raped," she says and I freeze.

chapter
38
raine

The words tumbled from my mouth before I could stop them. His disclosure of his story combined with the shot gave me the little boost of confidence that I needed to blurt it out. What I didn't expect was his reaction. "Dex, can you let go?" I say softly. When he froze on me, he had a pretty good grip on my nipples and he hasn't let up. It's not uncomfortable, but it starting to hurt. Slowly he releases my nipples and he pulls his hands back.

No, no, no. "That... that's why I didn't want to tell you," I say as I stand up and go lean against the counter by the fridge.

"What happened?" he asks in a voice so low I can barely hear him.

"I don't know that you want to hear this. Not tonight, not while you're so...exposed," I say.

"Sweet girl," his eyes meet mine, "now is the time to tell me."

His eyes are soft yet serious.

"Typical really."

He growls, "Nothing about rape is typical, Raine, try again."

"I was at a party with a group of friends. I was barely eighteen, naive. I was drinking, like everyone else at the party. Dancing and having a good time with my friends. Somewhere along the line I'd caught the eye of a guy. I was drunk, probably for the first time in my life and I flirted with him. Dancing provocatively with my girlfriends, you know the type." I shrug but he's unamused and I don't blame him. "Somehow, I don't remember how, we ended up across the street, walking through the park. He came on to me, attacked me. I managed to knee him in the balls and I ran away." I watch him flinch at the memory of our own little knee to balls encounter last week, but the story is coming out automatically. I'm not really seeing Dex, the room or anything else but that night.

"What happened after you ran away?" he asks softly. He can tell I've checked out on him.

"He caught up to me. Grabbed me by the elbow so hard he activated a pressure point." I grab my elbow to show him and recognition and awareness alights in his eyes. "I fell to my knees under the pain of his grip and he hit me with something, I don't know what, but it was right across the side of my head." My hand instinctively goes into my hair to rub the three scars I have. "I don't remember much of what happened after that."

He doesn't say anything. He just looks at me.

"I spent nearly four weeks in the hospital recovering from head trauma, a broken leg, I had to have surgery to fix two tears, down there…" I stop talking. I don't talk about the last bit, ever.

"What else?" he says quizzically.

I shake my head. He stands up and walks toward me. My whole body starts to tremble and tears well in my eyes. I momentarily think that he's going to walk away, walk past me and out the door, but he doesn't. He comes to stand in front of me. "Tell me," he implores.

"I can't."

"Please?" he whispers.

I lean into him with my head, pressing it against his chest. He gently brings his hand into my hair and strokes it, comforting me. "I didn't have a choice. Not that I could have made it anyway because there were too many factors involved. In order for them to repair the internal damage, I had to have an abortion…" I can't control the sobs that pour out of me.

"Shh. It's all right," he says trying to lift my chin up. After a couple of taps I give in, raising my tear soaked eyes to his. "You did nothing wrong," he tells me softly. "And anyone who tells you otherwise is a fool." He leans down and kisses my cheek, kissing away my tears then he moves to the other cheek, repeating the process. "It doesn't change." I feel his hands slide down my body and up under my shirt. I shiver as his hands touch skin and all my nerves are on fire, desire building once again. "It doesn't change a thing about how I feel about you." His lips land on mine the moment his fingers brush across my nipple, forcing me to open my mouth and he steals my moan with his tongue. The kiss doesn't last. "If anything, it makes what I feel right now a thousand times stronger. We both have scars. Scars we're required to live with."

He kisses me again, this time the passion is almost more than I can bear. I pull on the bottom of my shirt, and he breaks the kiss only long enough for me to rid myself of my shirt and toss it to the floor. He pulls off his t-shirt too. "If you tell me to stop, I will stop. If you tell me to leave, I'll go." He lays a gentle kiss against my forehead. "If you tell me to stay, I will stay. I am not doing this out of guilt for what you've told me, or for what I've told you. I'm doing this because I have to be inside you. I can't take it anymore."

"Don't stop," I breathe and his hands come up to cup my cheeks and his lips are back on mine once more. I place my hands against his chest, my fingers trailing down over his nipples, down his washboard abs to the button on his jeans. His tongue slides in against mine and I slide mine along his. Soaking him in, savoring the taste that is distinctively Dex.

My head starts to spin as I slide his zipper down. Hooking my thumbs under his boxers, I push them down, freeing his cock and I take it quickly into my hands. His breathing hitches and he moans into my mouth. My head is spinning and I pull back, attempting to catch my breath, but he grabs my shoulders and guides me towards the bed.

Once my knees back up against it, he gently pushes me down on the edge. "Don't move," he says softly and I obey, waiting patiently while he gets out of his jeans and goes into his pocket. "I...I don't want to use this," he says in a rush as he pulls a condom from his pocket. "But I owe it to you to get tested first." He looks me in the eye; I try hard to hide my panic. "I get tested regularly. I was tested right before the tour, but..." I shake my head.

"I'd appreciate it if you got tested. Then you can ditch the condoms."

"I've never not worn one." I can't hide my surprise. "I was more afraid of other things than...fuck, should we really be having this conversation?"

I smile at his flustered expression. "Probably not, but I have an IUD. It's highly effective." He smiles then. "I was never going to let that happen again, not until I'm truly ready." He nods his understanding and tosses the condom on the bed. "Come here," I tell him, desperate to have him touching me again.

He comes over to me on his knees, and I cup his cheeks and kiss him. He doesn't linger there before he starts kissing along my jaw, down my neck, across my shoulder, kissing the points of my wings as he goes. He swaps licks, nibbles and kisses down my chest, avoiding the one place I desperately need him. I groan in frustration and he smiles like a Cheshire cat. "What do you want, princess?"

I grab my aching breasts in my hands and watch as his face lights up at the overflowing swell of them and he gently sucks a nipple into his mouth. Licking, flicking and sucking on it like his life depends on it. His other hand comes up to play with the other nipple and I moan.

He kisses across the swell to my other nipple and sucks it into his mouth, teasing me. "You're torturing me," I whisper and he smiles as he bites my nipple. I yelp and start laughing. I fall back on the bed.

"Now that's a beautiful sight," he says as he lifts my legs over his shoulders and before I can balance on my elbows, his tongue swipes against my sex.

"Ahh, fuck," I groan and put my hand in his hair, holding him to me, grinding my pussy against his face and he doesn't stop. He's licking, circling, sucking and then I feel him slide a finger inside me. He quickly finds the spot that lights me up like nothing else and my legs start to shake.

His mouth comes away, but his finger doesn't stop. He slides another one inside and I begin to fuck his fingers. "It is my goal to make you come like last time, as many times as humanly possible," he breathes. His hot breath is caressing my sex; my clit is a ball of overwhelming sensation.

"Please," I whine and his mouth is back on me in a second. He doesn't let up licking and sucking on my clit. Occasionally his teeth graze my stiff nub and I writhe. My orgasm is building, simmering just below the surface. "Fuck. Dex..." I practically scream as my orgasm overtakes me. My body shakes with the release he so desperately wanted. The warm rush of fluid slides past his fingers and he groans into my pussy. He slows his motions, letting me ride out the rest of my orgasm.

When I finally settle, he pulls back. His lips are wet, glistening with my juices and somehow I find the strength to sit up; he extracts his fingers as I do. I lick at his lips, tasting him and me combined into one seriously hot aphrodisiac. He's the first to start to lose control. "Take me," I whisper against his lips and I kiss him once more. I slide up on to the bed and lie down, spreading myself out for him. My hand lands on the condom he threw up here and I put it between my teeth, ripping the foil and pulling out the barrier he needs. "Come here." I give him my own command and he dutifully obeys me. I sit up slightly and line up the condom and roll it down his shaft as quickly as I can.

I look up at him. He's concerned.

"Don't stop. I need this. I need you." I take the head of his cock and run it along the seam of my sex and he groans. I smile, satisfied and lie back down. "Just be gentle with me, big boy, you'll tear me in two." I wink at him and he becomes animated and the lust is back in his eyes.

A massive hurdle overcome, now for the next one.

chapter
39
dex

Her pussy is so fucking wet, scorching hot. It takes all the willpower I can muster to slide slowly into her. I remember when Beck slammed into her; it was the moment that everything changed in the room. It was like she'd disappeared and now, knowing what I know, I wonder if that was the start of what set her off. "Tell me something, please?" I ask.

"Anything," she says.

"Sunday...when-" I can't even ask the question.

"He triggered me," she says softly.

My heart sinks into my stomach. "I'm sorry, he...we..." Her finger comes to my lips and she hushes me.

"Later."

I nod, understanding, thankful for the reprieve and the distraction. The last thing I want to do is come before I'm buried inside her. Though it probably wasn't the best topic, I needed to know.

I push into her softly and she moans. Satisfied with her reaction to my pace, I push in more, and a little more. "Fuck, you're so tight," I mumble. My ability to form coherent sentences is gone. My dick is leading the cavalry now. He's desperate, and I'm going out of my fucking mind. "You feel amazing." I notice that she blushes for probably the first time since I've known her. I lean down and plant my lips on hers and she wraps her arms around my neck. I feel her feet come around my waist. I notice now that she's pushing me into her, guiding me and I move a little faster.

Her tight little muscles are like a vice grip on my dick as the pleasure takes hold of her, causing me to pull back and growl. "So. Fucking. Tight," I grunt out as I bottom out inside her. Impressed that she's taken so much of me inside of her. She writhes, thrusting her hips up toward me and back down, encouraging me to move. I do. Slowly pulling out, almost to the point that I fall out.

"Ahh." I watch as her eyes roll up into her head and I kiss down along her neck until I find a nipple and suck it into my mouth. Her tits couldn't be more perfect. When she cupped them and they overflowed her hands, I nearly came unglued in that moment. She moans as my tongue flicks against her nipple and she begins to thrust her hips against mine. "Faster. Please," she begs. "It feels…Gah," she cries out. It feels so fucking good."

I smile against her breast and start to move. Steadying myself on both my hands momentarily until I can rear back on my knees. I look down and watch as my cock disappears into her glistening wet, beautiful pussy and I grunt. Fuck, I'm too close. Too soon. I grab her legs and lean down slightly as I hook her knees on my arms, pushing her ass up. The angle is making her impossibly tight and I lean forward over her, pretzeling her. "Fuck," she cries out as her walls get impossibly tighter. There is a rush of fluid, setting my cock on fire. I need to make her come, I can't without her. I grind my hips into hers. Her legs start to tremble; my balls tighten, sending my orgasm straight into my shaft. "I'm coming," she moans and I slide into her harder and a little faster, pushing her over the edge and she clamps down hard. The glorious orgasm I executed with my tongue is repeated as she squirts all over my cock.

"Fuck!" I cry out as my own orgasm pours out of me.

I rest my forehead against hers while I listen to her breathing return to normal. Her ice blue eyes are closed and I desperately want to look into them. I nuzzle my nose against hers and she smiles. I kiss the tip of her nose and then slowly extract myself. I'm still semi-hard. How could I not be? Jesus, she's fucking perfect. She groans as I pull out and I smile. Teasing her, I push back in and her back arches. She's lighting up again and I want to satisfy her growing desire. "I need a new condom," I say softly. She nods and I tease her a little bit more as I slowly slide out from inside her.

Standing, I pull off the condom, tie it off and throw it in the trash. I go into the bathroom to clean myself up and when I come back out, she's laying on the bed, watching me. I grab a condom from my pocket. My last one. I toss it on the bedside table and climb onto the bed.

I lie down on the bed in a huff, exhausted. I'm trying to bring my breathing back to normal. The next thing I know, she surprises me by sliding her hand across my stomach. I flinch, but she doesn't stop. Then her leg hitches over mine. She brings her head to rest on my shoulder. She holds me to her. "What are you doing?" I ask her.

She looks up at me, she's nervous and I can feel it in her touch as she trembles slightly. "Cuddling," she says hesitantly, the worried expression on her face has me concerned. She starts to pull back and I stop her hand with my free arm.

"Stay," I say with a smile.

She nods her head and looks away from me. I gently kiss her forehead and she squeezes me a little tighter. "You've never cuddled before."

"No."

I can feel her smile against my chest. Her hand on my stomach starts to trace my tattoos and I shiver. I bring my hand, the one under her head, to rest against her back, holding her to me and she snuggles in. "So many tattoos," she murmurs and her fingers continue to trace. "What is this one?"

I lift my head to see which one she's pointing at. I chuckle. "That would be a stupid drunken moment about three years ago. It was supposed to be a snake and it ended up more like a squiggly fucking line." I laugh. "I'm working on covering it up." I rub my hand along her back. "What about this?"

She smiles again. "That is about eighty hours of pure torture."

"I can imagine. It's gorgeous."

"It's unfinished," she says sadly. "It wasn't meant to be left just black lines, and tiny flowers. At least that wasn't my intention when I started it. I just ran out of money." I nod, understanding.

"Why?"

"I wanted wings so I could fly away. So that I could fly away and forget everything that happened that night. So that I could forget the events that followed over the course of the next year or so. The flowers inside the wings were started, in the beginning to be ugly, without actually being ugly. If you look, the flowers trail from simplistic to realistic on my thigh. I took comfort in the pain. "

"I understand that one all too well," I say so softly I'm not sure she hears me.

"I'd started it after I'd moved to California. I'd had a really rough go of it. Wandering from place to place, trying to find a place to call home, permanently. I moved to California on a whim. I thought that if I moved there, I could forget what happened. That I could move on. Finally after about a year, I managed to land the job at Bold. I started as the front desk receptionist. Literally directing calls and people all day. The phones were always so busy and the constant stream of people coming in and out of the office, that was all I had time for." She starts tracing my abs again and I flinch because it tickles and she stills momentarily until I settle. I don't want to interrupt her story.

"Within three months, I'd proven myself time and time again. Despite never having time to help out around the office, I always managed to find a way. They learned quickly that I was a wonderful multi-tasker and they moved me into the office itself. At first I was a secretary to about thirty different staff members. It sounds like a lot, but it was menial work. Shuffling clients in and out for meetings, taking phone calls and messages, making copies of stuff, things like that. It only took me about a month and they moved me up a few floors. Reducing my staff members down to about fifteen and increasing my workload. I stayed there for about eight months or so, but when they moved me into that position I finally got benefits, a significant pay raise and a signing bonus of sorts. That was when I started the tattoo." She keeps trailing over the one tattoo I'm praying she doesn't ask about.

"What's this one?" She breaks her story to ask me the one question I was just hoping she wouldn't ask. I don't need to look up to see which one she's referring to. The skin is still tender. "Is it newer? It feels like it's still healing."

"It is," I say softly, but for some reason, I know I can't *not* tell her. I tap her back. "Sit up for me." She does and I know I have a pained expression on my face, but she needs to see it all as I explain it. "That is a reminder piece. A piece to the whole is added every time I fuck up." I raise my right arm. The one she wasn't lying on and scoot away from her so she can watch as I roll toward her.

"Fuck up, how?"

"Every time I relapse or nearly relapse." I start to roll toward her and her breath hitches. Each block added is defined by white lines separating the pieces, the length of time defined by the subtle fading of color over time. "The ones colored in with anything but black are the ones I actually relapsed on. You'll notice that the latest one is red."

chapter
40
raine

I've never really been able to get a good look at his back, usually too distracted by other things. I noticed that there was something there but couldn't quite focus on it, but as I watch him roll, I can see it, the hundreds of tiny pieces that make up the whole across his back. I gasp at his words. "When?"

I watch as he screws his eyes tight. "Phoenix," he breathes out.

"The story." I let it slip before I can stop myself. He stiffens. "So it was true?"

"Honestly, I don't know. But what happened that day following, I have no doubt." He keeps slowly rolling over and I can finally take in the entire picture.

"It's a dragon," I say and he nods. One wing, the one on top is done, or it has the appearance of being done as it wraps around his left shoulder. The dragon's face is on his other side, though visible from the back, it's primarily under his arm. "When did you start?"

"The day after my parents died. I started with his head. Then once the money came in, I justified a good portion of the body by the hundred plus days I'd been strung out. Then I was too blazed to care, so once I got out of rehab, I started on the wings. Accounting for most of the days that I'd been on something."

I look at the tattoo. As the image pulls away from the body, the pieces get darker.

"I judged how much color would go into the piece by how bad it had been. Whether or not I'd actually used, what I used and how much I used. Each color stands for something different."

I point to a red one. "Red?"

"Cocaine."

"Orange?"

"Crack."

"Yellow?"

"Heroine."

"Green?"

He gives me a 'take a guess look' before answering, "Pot."

"Blue?"

"Meth." I notice now that there are not very many blue ones.

"Purple?" I breathe.

"Anything else or everything, or some combination of drugs"

There are probably more purple ones than any other color throughout the piece.

"Once I went through rehab, I realized that when I would relapse with either the temptation or actually doing it, that putting myself through the pain of being inked would help cure the itch. So I've always made a point to try and get inked as soon as possible afterward. With Phoenix, it was the day the story broke." He sighs. "So you see, I'm all kinds of fucked up."

I run my hand along his back. "We all have scars," I whisper and he rolls back to his side. I look at him. Fighting tears. "My parents disowned me after what happened to me."

"Why in the Sam Hill would they do something like that?"

I wrap my hands around my stomach, seeking comfort within myself. "Because, no matter the circumstances, no matter the reasons, their firm Catholic beliefs rang true. I was no longer a virgin, not that I was when it happened, and I'd had an abortion because I needed to have surgery. It was my life hanging in the balance, but that didn't matter to them. They would have rather lost their own flesh and blood daughter, taking both lives in the process, than for me to have an abortion." By the time I'm done, tears are streaking down my face. "I've never forgiven them and I haven't talked to them in more than ten years. In fact, as far as I'm concerned, I have no family."

Dex sits up, lifting my chin with his finger. "I don't think that's true. Look around you, look at the people here, the people you work with, your friends." I smile.

"You're right and I'm a much better person because of it," I tell him and he wipes the tears away, then he brings his lips to mine. Igniting my nerves and desire for him once again. His lips are soft, tender, and it makes my head spin. I take his face in my hands and hold him to me, trying to find a grip on some balance because I'm going to fall over.

I push him back, keeping our lips dancing as he lays back and I slide on top of him. Straddling him. He moans into my mouth as my pussy brushes along his growing erection. The sensation is overwhelming and I gasp, pulling back from our kiss. "Thank you," I say and kiss him gently once again.

"For?"

"Letting me in," I tell him.

"I don't think I could have not told you. You have a way of making me tell the truth whether I want to or not. But the same can be said to you."

"I had to tell you. I had...It's a big part of who I am, Dex. I've met so many men that are turned off by the fact that I was raped that I needed you to know before we went anywhere with this. I can't not tell you things either. I've told you things tonight that I've never told some of the people closest to me. Honestly, aside from Cami, you are the only person who knows as much as you do."

"Cami? Your boss?" He raises an eyebrow.

"Long story short, I was triggered at work by a client."

I feel his chest rumble as if he's growling at my words. "It wasn't... jeez, that didn't come out right," I mutter. "It was the elbow thing. Only that time I reacted a lot worse, a lot faster and with much more force than what you've seen. It was honestly the first time I'd been triggered, it was unexpected. I'd never had anyone grab my elbow the way that he did and all he was trying to do was stop me from walking into something and I overreacted. Actually, I hit him, right in the eye. It was nearly devastating for my career."

I watch him cringe. "You nailed me in the nuts."

I smirk at him. "That was half because you grabbed my elbow and half because I was just flat out fucking pissed at you."

Dex laughs. "I just can't see you hitting someone."

I give him a playful scowl. "I'll have you know, mister, that I'm trained in self-defense and I train other women too." I give him a smug, 'so there' nod.

He brings his hand up to run a finger along my cheek. "Good." He smiles and I flick my hips, effectively ending that conversation as he groans. "You're going to be the death of me."

I smirk and lean down, licking a nipple and biting down on his peck. His back arches, nearly bucking me off of him, but I hold steady as he groans. "So pain and pleasure seem to be a hot button for you," I say as I flick my hips against his twitching erection.

"Are you a sadist, princess?"

I give him a wicked look as I lower my head to his other nipple. "Maybe." He stiffens, bracing himself for another bite, but instead I lick the flat disc of his nipple. His hand comes into my hair, fisting it and pulling it upward. I come up and away, gasping and shivering as he does. There is an involuntary flick of my hips and his eyes roll up.

"Seems I'm not the only one." He leans up quickly, capturing my mouth with his and my body with his legs as he bends his knees. He releases my lips, and his cock twitches against my sex. I put my hands on his shoulders, steadying myself, but I let my nails dig in just a little bit and his hand in my hair tightens further. There is a hot rush of fluid that seeps from my sex and I moan. I lift myself, finding the head of his cock, and by some act of fate, he twitches at just the right moment and I can feel him lined up perfectly. Before he can stop me, I dig my nails in a little harder and slide down on him quickly.

"Jesus fucking Christ," he growls, falling back and thrusting his hips up and into me. "Fuck, fuck...so good. Too fucking good." His hand relaxes in my hair and I miss the tugging sensation, but it gives me the chance to torture him just a little bit more. I rake my nails down his chest as I rock against his hips.

His hands come up and cup my breasts, his fingers quickly find my now hard nipples and he rolls them firmly between his fingers. I moan.

It becomes a battle of wills, of pain and pleasure. Realizing that we both enjoy something, giving and receiving, it makes me see that maybe, just maybe, after all this time, I've finally found someone who will understand my needs.

I try again to bring my hands up, to run them back down his chest, but he grabs my wrists and pulls them quickly above his head so that my body falls down on his and he slams into me and sparks shoot from behind my eyes. "Easy," I cry out.

He kisses along my jawline. "I'm sorry," he says and I kiss him back. Before I have any comprehension of what's happening, he manages to roll me over as he slips out of me. I whimper at the loss. "I need a condom."

I quickly wrap my legs around him, trapping him. "Please," I say, digging my heels in, begging him to continue.

His look is haunted and tortured. "You've always used one?" He nods. "That was the first time you've ever been inside without one." He nods again. "Your last test?"

"Clean."

"Then please, I hate those things. I've never not used them. I've always... well, when I've had a choice, used them. I want to feel you back inside me like just now. Without the barrier."

With my legs wrapped around him, I have leverage so I slide my pussy along his shaft and he growls. "Fine, but I want to look at that gorgeous ass."

"Deal," I say and release him, flipping over and wiggling my ass against his cock. He smacks my ass with it and I still.

"Give me one hard limit. Something you refuse to do, no matter what?"

"Being shared or sharing someone," I say quickly. "I do not, cannot and will not tolerate cheating," I say softly. No need to bring that up, not now.

"I need another one, a physical hard limit. Something I cannot do to you."

"Ugh, no piss and shit." I make a gagging sound.

"Pain limits?"

"I don't know, I've never-" Just then a hand smacks into my ass, hard. The sound is louder and harder than the bite of pain that accompanies it. I writhe and moan, thrusting forward and back again, just as he finds the entrance of my sex and he slides in hard and fast, but not very deep. "Ahh fuck."

"Again?" he asks, his voice is husky and full of lust.

"Yes," I cry out.

He doesn't disappoint. Another loud smack and stab of pain, only this time on my left cheek. I feel my pussy clamp down hard on his cock and he stills, groaning. "Fuck that's hot," he says. Then I feel him shift. His hands slide down my back, my body arches, sucking him deeper inside of me as his hand slides into my hair.

"Ahh fuck," I cry out as his hand fists in my hair, pulling my head back, the weight of his body and the hand in my hair has me immobile.

"Safe word?" he whispers in my ear.

"Kit kat," I moan, having no clue where that actually came from.

He chuckles. "Mine is sunshine. Because that is what you are, you're sunshine on a cloudy, rainy day." I gasp and he thrusts hard into me. "I will give you your every heart's desire. I will take you to places you've never imagined, on one condition," he growls as he continues thrusting into me.

I cry out as his hand tightens in my hair. "Anything."

"You promise me the same."

"A switch?" I breathe.

"Only for you," he growls, releasing my hair. Pain and pleasure collide when his hands go to my hips, fingers digging in, biting at my flesh as he continues to thrust in and out of me. His confession is heady, the agreement – daunting. The desire sends me over the edge before I even realize the orgasm was there.

chapter
41
raine

The gasp that comes from Dex makes my nipples harden as he continues thrusting into me after my orgasm. "Where'd that come from?" he teases.

"You," I whisper and I hear him chuckle.

His hands let up on my hips, his grip loosening and I help by rocking back into him with each thrust in. Pushing him in to the point of pain, a point that turns that pain into pleasure. His hands begin to gently glide along my ass and up my back as he continues sliding in and out of my dripping pussy. One hand disappears briefly but when it returns, I feel something pressed against the tight ring of my ass. I tense up briefly. "Hard limit?" he asks.

"No, never tried."

"Gah!" he groans and I feel him shiver as he slides to a halt inside me. He's fully sheathed though his girth and length make it impossible for me to take him all the way in. "Never?" he asks softly and I lift myself onto my elbows.

"Never," I confirm.

"Because you don't..."

"No, no one's ever tried."

"So you mean I can claim this for myself?"

I tense.

He chuckles. "Not right now. But..."

I nod my head. "I'd like to try." Then he starts to circle his finger around my entrance. At first it feels weird, foreign, but gradually it starts to feel better. He hasn't moved from inside me. His hand comes away and I'm saddened at the loss of that additional point of contact. Then I feel something wet and warm. "What is that?"

"Just some spit. I want to play." His voice is full of wonder and mischief. I nod.

He goes back to circling me, pressing harder, seeking entrance with his finger.

"Play with yourself, princess," he commands. I obey by reaching down and rubbing my finger along my clit. I feel my pussy clamp down on him as the sensation registers. Ass, pussy and now my clit. I shiver, letting a whimper escape my lips as he pushes into me gently.

"Gah!" I cry out.

"Does it hurt?" he asks as he slowly moves his finger in and out, turning the burning sensation to a warm pleasurable one and my hand goes back to circling my clit.

"No, it's...it's good, just, it's..."

"Different?"

"Mmhmm," I moan.

"Good different?"

"Mmhmm." Coherent thoughts slip away along with the juices of my last orgasm. "Move, I need you to move, Dex," I mumble out and he starts to move in and out in time with his finger. I can tell that with each thrust in, he's going a little deeper and with each pull out the pain subsides and pleasure overtakes me. I start rocking back into him. "I can't..." I pull my hand away. Allowing him to control my sensations, my orgasm. Allowing him to take it from me and giving me the leverage I need to really push back on him.

It doesn't take long before my orgasm simmers, radiating out from my core, liquid fire in my veins. "Jesus," he breathes. "I need it, give it to me, princess."

His hand withdraws from me and one hand goes into my hair, pulling, gripping and pinning me down, forcing me still while the other hand goes to my hip, holding me in place. He pumps once, twice and I explode all over his bare cock. Skin to skin, soul to soul and I'm lost to him the moment I feel his scorching hot cum searing my insides. My orgasm quickly rolls into another one as he grinds into me, growling and milking our orgasms.

After a couple heartbeats, his hand comes out of my hair. His hand loosens up on my hip and my breathing slowly falls to a more normal rhythm.

"Ahh, fuck." I hear something, like a cracking sound. Dex falls out of me fast. "Shit."

"Dex, what's wrong?" I turn to see him vigorously shaking his hand. "Talk to me."

"I...fuck, it hurts. My hand. It's, fuck." He keeps shaking it. Ignoring the fact that our orgasms are now sliding from my body, I stand up and go to him.

"Cramp?" I ask and he nods. "Give me your hand." I don't give him an option and he quickly complies. "Sit." I nod toward the couch I was sitting on earlier and he sits down. I sit on his lap and start to gently massage his hand.

"Fuck, that hurts."

"I know, but give me a minute. Do you trust me?" His steel grey eyes meet mine. Serious and unafraid.

"Yes, I do."

I give him a small smile and go back to his hand. "Take a deep breath. This is going to hurt," I tell him as I find the knot, where his fingers have locked up. I hear him take a deep breath. "Promise not to hate me when I'm done."

"I don't think that's possible," he says softly. Then I use all the strength I have in my thumbs and I push, hard. "Argh! Fuck!" he cries out. I feel the muscles pop under my fingers and finally his hand relaxes and just like that, so does he.

I start to massage that spot and the rest of his hand, working out the kinks gently and he just looks at me. "Hate me?"

He smirks. "Never."

"Good."

After about ten minutes of massaging his hand, I slowly come to a stop. "How's that?"

"Much, much better."

"Does that happen often?" I ask him.

He shakes his head. "No, but I've noticed more tension in my hand since we started the tour. It's the product of playing drums for fifteen years." My own hands are tight from massaging his and I flex my fingers. "My turn it seems." He smiles.

I smile back at him then look over at the clock. It's four thirty in the morning. "Actually, I have a better idea."

"Which is?"

"Take a quick shower with me?"

He chuckles. "I don't think a shower with you can be quick."

"This one will be. I want to show you something."

He cocks his head at me. "What?"

"Can't I surprise you?" I give him puppy dog eyes and I push out my bottom lip in a pout. He leans up and nips my lip with his teeth.

"I told you, puppy dog eyes don't work on me, sweet girl." I smile at the other nickname he's apparently chosen for me. I'm sure I probably blush a little because he says, "You like that nickname, don't you?"

I smile and nod. "It reminds me more of something a Dominant would call his submissive, so yes, I like it." His eyes light up.

"Have you ever?" he asks me.

"Been a sub?" He nods. "No, and I've never been a Dominant either. The lifestyle intrigues me. I'm ridiculously turned on by the idea of being commanded, controlled and just letting everything go. But I also have a Dominant side that likes to take control, be in control and have pleasure bestowed upon me, for my benefit. Let's just say, whips and cuffs excite me." I watch as his eyes widen in shock. "Have you ever?"

I watch as he scrubs his face. "That is a long conversation. Can we just leave it at no and yes. I have some friends, I've seen some scenes, I've participated in some scenes, but I've never found someone with whom I'd like to experience and experiment with. Never found anyone I've trusted enough to turn myself over to and I've never given a woman an ounce of a chance to want to pursue that kind of relationship. But I get the impression that you're going to change that about me."

My heart flutters and my breathing hitches in my throat. "I'd like that," I manage to say past the lump in my throat.

"Give it some time. I'll fuck this up somehow," he says, his tone sad and very matter of fact.

"I don't think you can truly fuck anything up once you put your mind to it." I lean over to kiss him on the cheek and he catches me, turning his head so our lips meet. He leans me into his chest as his hand goes into my hair. His lips are soft, and there is a calming peace that washes over me when he licks at my lips. But he doesn't press.

He pulls back. "I believe you wanted to surprise me."

I smile. "It can wait."

His arms snake under my legs and behind my back. "Nope. I want my surprise." He smirks as he stands up, carrying me with very little effort into the bathroom. He sets me on my feet and reaches into the shower to turn on the water.

chapter
42
raine

"I'm going to run to my room, change into some clean clothes," he says with a sad smile on his face.

"What's wrong?"

"I don't want to leave."

I chuckle a little. "You're only going down the hall, throwing on some clean clothes and by the time you're done, I'll be waiting outside your door." I stand on my tiptoes and kiss him chastely and he wraps his arms around me, picking me up and pressing his lips hard to mine. I pull back. "Seriously, we're going to miss it," I tell him. "Just go. I'll be right behind you."

"All right. Hurry up."

"I'll be there before you're dressed." I give him a smirk. He's only thrown on his jeans, sans boxers which are crumpled up on the floor next to his shoes, and no shirt. Dex topless is a sight to behold, a sight made even better knowing what I know about his ink. I notice now, from the distance, that there are no tiny pieces, only a whole. Though slightly unbalanced and missing a little here and there. Looking at it, I ask him, "What will you do, when you stop having cravings, when you stop giving in?"

He pauses by the door. "Then I will finish it all in black." He turns around and smiles at me. "One day, I hope to be able to do that, but every day is a struggle."

I smile at him and I nod. Secretly hoping that I can give him something else to think about. "See you in a minute," I tell him as I slide into my tennis shoes. He smiles at me and leaves the room. I step into the bathroom to pull my hair up. It's still wet from our shower. It's impossible for me to stand here, looking in the mirror and not see the after effects of his taking me in there. My hand print is still outlined in steam. I shiver at the reminder of his touch, and my hand grazes over the upper swell of my breast. It's tender. He came so hard, he bit me. No blood, but I can see his teeth marks. I smile at the memory of the pain he induced that tipped me over the edge.

I never imagined that I would be able to find an outlet for some of the weirder things that I enjoy, like pain with sex. Now before you go getting all 'is it because?' the answer is no. I've always had a high threshold for pain and as I got older, I found pleasure in the pain I would feel. It makes me feel alive. Reminds me that I am alive, that I am living in reality. So many things in my life have been like a dream or a nightmare, depending on the situation, and sometimes I need to feel the pain in order to remind myself that I am real and alive.

dex

"The walk of shame this time of the morning doesn't suit you." I give Beck a 'fuck you' look. "Hey, just sayin'."

I slide my keycard into the door.

"What the hell is wrong with you, bro?"

I shrug. "A ton of shit, but that's not what you're getting at, is it?" I ask as I hold the door open for him to come in behind me.

"You're acting all weird and shit. Hell, if I didn't know better, I'd say you were acting like Talon."

"Whatever." I'm not sure I'm capable of arguing with him.

I watch as he shrugs. "It's all good, man. Seriously." I look at him, serious. "I mean it. If she wets your whistle, go for it."

"Ahh, speaking of whistle. Sunday night?"

"What about it?"

I shrug. "Forget it. I can't be pissed at you like I want to be, or should be. You didn't know."

"Are you talking about her triggers? She told you?" I nod. "It wasn't intentional."

"I know, that's why I can't be pissed at you, but do me a favor?"

"Anything," he says without hesitation.

"Keep your distance from her. Please."

"That's kind of hard, but if you're referring to that... then no worries. I had my fun," he says smug.

My hands clench into fists and I close my eyes. "You might want to leave before I knock you into the wall," I say through gritted teeth.

He puts his hands up in surrender. "Man, what's crawled up your butt..."

"Her," I say simply.

He smirks, nods and then leaves the room. I change into some jeans, tennis shoes and pull on a t-shirt just as a light knock raps on my door. I smile. It's got to be her.

I rush to the door and swing it open. Seeing her is like seeing her for the first time in days, weeks or even months. She beams up at me. "You might want to grab a jacket," she says and I hold the door open for her. She doesn't come all the way in but stands at the door, holding it open.

"Are you going to tell me where we're going?"

She laughs. "Nope."

I grab my jacket and we leave the room. As soon as we're in the hallway, I wrap my arm around her waist and hold her to me. Rusty is standing near the elevator. He gives both of us a quizzical look. "She's taking me somewhere and won't tell me where," I tell Rusty who rolls his eyes. "You already know?"

Rusty laughs. "The elevator is here." He hits the button and the doors slide open and I escort Raine inside.

We turn around. "You're not coming?" I ask Rusty. He just shakes his head. Odd.

We take the elevator to the second floor and she secrets me through the doors and into the adjacent parking garage where we have a black SUV. A tired looking Casey and Troy are there waiting for us.

"Did you really have to wake them?" I ask her, skeptical.

"Rusty wouldn't let us go alone." She shrugs and Troy holds open the door for her, she climbs in and I follow behind her.

"Where are we going?" I ask.

"Have you ever been to DC before?"

I shake my head, "Was never a place I wanted to come."

She smiles. "You're missing out. There's something special about being here, it's sometimes overwhelming," she says as Casey puts the SUV in drive and we exit the garage.

We're only in the car for a few minutes when we pull up to the backside of what I'm guessing is a memorial of some type. It's lit up in the darkness. It's a rectangular building. "Lincoln?" I ask.

She smiles and nods. Why on earth would she bring me here? Casey drives past the monument and finds a place to park. It's still dark, so the only people who are really out and about are runners.

I climb out of the car quickly and I open her door for her. She smiles up at me. "Wow," she breathes, shocked.

I want to roll my eyes. "I am capable of being a gentleman, once in a while." I offer her my elbow and she takes it with a small giggle. It's chilly, though not as cold as New York was and I'm glad she had me bring a jacket.

"So sweet girl, what are we doing here?"

"I'd really like to show you some things."

"I gathered that, but what?" I ask her.

"That's the surprise." She smirks at me as we walk toward the Lincoln Memorial. From this side of the building, that's really all you can see.

I can feel Troy and Casey behind us, trailing some distance away. They're doing everything they can to make it less obvious that they're following us, maybe Rusty and Tori should have come instead, at least they could possibly see the romantic aspect of what I have a feeling she's about to bring to this.

"Okay, close your eyes and stop. Stop here," she says and we stop. I raise an eyebrow at her. "Just face that way," she says, pointing me toward my right. "Okay, back up like three steps." I laugh but obey her command. Then she moves from my peripheral vision and the next thing I know, she's climbing onto my back.

I laugh. "What are you doing?"

She laughs too. "Covering your eyes." She puts one leg around me and I hold it, then the other. She really weighs nothing so I don't have a problem carrying her. What I do have problems with is when her dainty fingers cover my eyes. "Do you trust me?" she asks softly.

"Yes," I admit.

"You're on very flat, even ground. I want you to take five steps forward and then go ahead and turn to your right."

I do as she asks on shaky legs. I don't want to fall with her on my back, ironically it's not me I'm worried about getting hurt. It's her I'm worried about.

"Keep walking."

"How many steps?" I ask.

She giggles. "Until I tell you to stop." I shift her, adjusting her on my back and she squeaks when my fingers brush along her ass.

I walk forward for a couple minutes before she finally tells me to stop. "Turn to your right, but don't walk anywhere." I do as she's asked and turn. "Ready?"

I can hear the excitement in her voice. "Yes," I say softly and her hands come away from my eyes. But I keep them closed. "Can I open my eyes?"

She giggles and I can feel her kiss the back of my head. "Yes."

I do and standing before me is a mountain of stairs that lead up and into the Lincoln Memorial. The lights are still on but I am noticing now that the columns are a little bit lighter. It's pretty, don't get me wrong. "I figured you'd want to be able to see the stairs." She giggles again. "Climb, drummer boy," she teases and I pretend to drop her and she squeaks. I start to climb with her on my back. "You can let me down, you know?"

"I know, but princesses don't walk," I say and she laughs again. Where the hell that came from, I have no clue.

"I'm no princess," she says softly.

"To me, you are, and that's all that matters," I say and I'm about three-fourths of the way up.

"This should be good," she says. So I stop. "Now that I'm sure you're thoroughly convinced that this is what I brought you here for, and we've arrived just in time, turn around," she says and I do just as the sun crests the horizon behind the Washington Monument. The sky lights up in magnificent yellows, oranges and blues on the cloudless morning.

The sight in front of me steals my breath away from me for a moment. She kisses the back of my head again. "Put me down, please?"

I nod and kneel down so that she can climb off of me. She does and comes to stand next to me. I notice now that we're not the only ones on the stairs.

"Sit," she orders and we do.

"You're too far away," I tease her and go to grab her arm but I stop myself and grab her around her waist, pulling her toward me and she leans into me as she wraps her arms around her legs.

We sit like that for some time as the sun continues to rise over the Capital, the Mall and then finally the sunrise is reflected back in the pool.

chapter
43
raine

"Thank you for my surprise," he tells me before kissing my forehead.

Sitting here, watching the sun rise over DC is fulfilling one of my deepest fantasies and one of the many bucket list items I'd come up with a long time ago. A list of things to do with someone who means something special to me and that someone special is Dex. I didn't know it until I'd brought up the surprise. I'd have done this in New York, but what happened after that last show was proof enough, not only to him but also to myself, about where this might be going. So I moved Central Park down my list, to save it for another day and time.

"You're welcome. Though I'm pretty sure this means more to me," I tell him.

He looks at me then. "I doubt that." I give him a sad smile. "Care to explain?" he asks and I shake my head.

"Let's make a rule," he says and I raise an eyebrow at him in question. "Actually, a couple of rules."

'Okay?" I say skeptically.

"That we always be honest with each other, no matter what. We never hesitate to tell…" His words fall flat on his lips.

"Dex, I vow to always tell you everything and answer your questions honestly, but the reason I brought you here is pretty personal for me. I'm more afraid of how you'll take it, so right now, I'd rather not tell you," I tell him quietly and I squeeze my legs a little harder.

He doesn't say anything for a few moments. "Well, I will tell you this," he says softly, kissing my forehead again. "This has been the best night of my life."

My breathing stops all together as I look at him. "You mean that?" I say breathless.

He smiles. "Absolutely."

I lean over, wrap my hand around his neck and pull his lips to mine and he grants my tongue entrance on the first attempt. I moan softly into his mouth as I taste his sweet Dex taste and my hands slide up higher into his hair, holding him more firmly as our tongues slide against each other. My nipples harden and my clit explodes with desire. What I wouldn't give to be able to take him right here and now.

His hands cup my cheeks and he pushes me back slightly, pulling his lips from mine and I begin breathing again. My head is spinning. Then his lips land on mine, harder, firmer and more insistent. He starts to push me back and I let go of my legs. He has me laid down on the steps of the Lincoln Memorial just after sunrise. His lips slow their intensity but the passion and desire that is coursing through my veins is too intense. I want him and I would love to take him right here and now…but yeah, not gonna happen. I pull back slightly.

"I want to take you back to the hotel, like right now," he growls.

"Sorry slick," I say with a mischievous grin.

"You are not. You dirty, naughty girl." He smirks.

"Come on, let's walk," I tell him.

He scoffs. "Like I can walk in this condition." I cannot help but laugh.

"I'm sorry," I say through giggles.

"You are not," he grumbles but he's still smiling and his eyes are light with humor. He seems happy. It's a sight I'd like to see more often from him. "Fine," he relents and sits ups, pulling me with him as he stands. "Let's walk, princess. Where are we going?" I get the impression he wants me to say the truck, but instead I point to our left, where we were when we came in. "Lead on." He smiles and holds his elbow out for me to take and I do.

We spend the next several hours wandering around the Vietnam Memorial, the Gardens, and the WWII Memorial and then finally walking around the Washington Monument. After a full rotation, we walked along the opposite side of the reflecting pool and wrapped up with the Korean War Memorial. Dex is pretty quiet, somber even, throughout our journey and as we're walking toward the truck, I finally manage to build up the courage that I need to ask him why he's so sad.

"What's the matter?" I ask softly.

His eyes shoot to me and then back on the ground in front of him. He doesn't answer me. All throughout the morning we've chatted about different things, like where we're from, where we grew up, high school, silly insignificant stuff if you want the truth, but in the whole of who Dex is, it's helping me to better understand him and furthermore, bringing up those feelings I never thought I'd have again, but this time it's different, so much more intense.

"I have a bucket list," I tell him, hoping that if I open up to him, maybe he will do the same for me. "But it's not...jeez, how do I explain this?" I mutter. "I have a list of places in my head that I've always considered romantic, places that I vowed to one day return to when I had someone in my life that I really, truly cared about."

He looks at me. His eyes are weary, concerned, but yet there is an element of intrigue hiding there too.

"This..." I twirl my finger around, indicating our surroundings, "was number two," I tell him softly.

He frowns as he comes to a stop, standing in front of me. We're back in front of the Lincoln Memorial, but we're on the edge of the reflecting pool. His hands come up to cup my cheeks, cradling my head in his hands. He gently rubs his thumbs along my cheeks, searching my eyes for what, I don't know, but I try to convey what I'm feeling through my eyes. "What," he says hoarsely, "is number one?" "Central Park," I tell him, and he leans his forehead against mine.

"Number three?" he asks, a little less hoarsely but full of emotion.

I smile. "The Eiffel Tower." His breath hitches.

"Four?"

"Venice, Italy. Outside the Colosseum in Rome, In front of the Castle at Walt Disney World, The Outer Banks in North Carolina and Venice Beach at sunset," I say softly.

"Edinburgh Castle..." My breath hitches as he continues with his own list, a list that is matching mine, "The Louvre, Piccadilly Circus..."

"Dex...how?"

His eyes meet mine. "We have the same list." Tears stream from my eyes. "Though maybe not in that order and this, this one wasn't on my list. I once played in Central Park and I noticed all the couples that would come into the fields and have a picnic. It's so quiet and peaceful in that part of the park. If it weren't for the huge sky rises surrounding the park, you'd think that it was the middle of nowhere. Despite the constant flow of traffic and sounds of the city, it's so quiet there." He's whispering by the end of his little speech.

I kiss him. Softly, affectionately, desperately.

When we break from this kiss, my stomach growls. "Shall we feed you?" he says and I smile.

"I'd love that."

dex

Casey and Troy switch places with Beck and Rusty to join us downstairs. Raine and I sat alone with the two of them closely watching from a distance at their own table. We enjoyed breakfast together. We talked more about Bold and about her job, what her job here would be and finally what it would be after she got back to California.

She'd told me, but I'd completely forgotten that she wasn't sticking around this party forever and I dread saying good-bye, and though I knew it wouldn't be permanent, the idea is already bothering me.

"So, because I'm pretty sure I won't be able to spend a single minute without you while we're here, are we officially... you know?" I say with hesitation.

"No," she says so straight-faced that I can't tell if she's serious or kidding.

"No?" I raise an eyebrow at her.

"I will spend as much time with you as humanly possible while we're here, but…" She takes a deep breath, "but I need to know that this," she gestures between the two of us, "is what you really want."

"It is what I want."

"Sure, you say that today, but what about tonight, Dex? What about after your show and you've got an entire hoard of chicks throwing themselves at you, offering themselves to you?"

"That won't happen," I growl at her.

"Really, because I've seen it, Dex. It does happen."

I put my silverware down. "No, it won't happen because I will be with you, you will be the one throwing herself at me."

She raises an eyebrow questioningly at me. "Okay, that's tonight, but what if I have to go back to California and you're off god knows where and I'm not there to occupy your time and attention?" She takes a drink of water. "Look, I'm not punishing you or making assumptions that this thing between us will last longer than my stay here on the road and you shouldn't either. We need to just take this one day at a time. I need to know that I can trust you, you need to show me that I can trust you."

She's absolutely right of course. "There are three things here. First, after last night and this morning, no one, and I mean no one, will ever compare to you. I meant what I said, tonight has been the best night of my life, and that includes you. Second of all, you're right. I do need to show you that you can trust me, but I don't need to start off in the negative here. Give me some credit. I've been and can be a decent man when I need to be and I intend to be that way with you, no matter what. And lastly, who burned you?" It's obvious that the lack of trust is from scars of past bad relationships.

"Who didn't might be a better question," she tells me. "The most recent one, I found in my house, in my bed, fucking some chick. The one before that, I heard about through friends and the one before that basically just said that he'd been sleeping with someone else who was far better in bed than I am and that was pretty much the end of that."

I'm speechless for a few minutes. I take a few sips of orange juice wishing it had some vodka in it.

"Your looseness scares me," she breathes out.

"What do you mean?"

"In New York you were itching to take me to dinner, I turn you down because I honestly needed some time to just chill and be by myself. Think through some things. Then I come back, see you and some bimbo making out on the couch in the bar, then less than an hour later, you've brought her to your room. So, as you can imagine, that was a little harsh and confusing."

I frown at her then scrub my face. "I've really fucked up, but I'd really like the chance to redeem myself."

She smiles then says, "And I'm willing to give you that chance."

"Thank you," I say in relief.

chapter
44
raine

Dex and I parted ways after our breakfast. He needed to run off and handle something with his equipment. Kyle and Talon were joining him to help. I tried to convince him that it could wait and that he needed to get some sleep but he refused.

After a couple of hours of doing work in my room, I got this from him.

Dex: Will you do something with me tomorrow?

I look at my phone…puzzled.

Raine: Anything…what are we doing?
Dex: I need a new piece.
Raine: I have a better idea than ink.

Dex: You're not mad?

Raine: Mad because you fought your addiction? Never. Gave in? That's another story.

Dex: Fought, didn't give in.

Raine: When? You've been gone ten minutes.

Dex: The day I rescued Kyle.

Raine: No new piece to the puzzle. Have other idea. How do you feel about clothes pins?

Dex: On you- fucking gorgeous.

Raine: :-) Promise? And no, on you?

Dex: Depends - can I tie you up afterward?

Raine: Yes.

Dex: Deal. I'm coming back over.

Raine: No you're not. We agreed we needed sleep. You have to get all sweaty on stage tonight.

Dex: I'd rather get sweaty with you.

Raine: Me too, Sir.

I smile at my phone. I know that last text is going to bait him, then chew him up.

Reading Dex's texts sends a shiver of anticipation through me. No, I am not a "you do drugs you're gone" type of person. I understand addiction as a non-addict far better than most people can. I've seen it way too many times and I can completely understand the appeal of drug, alcohol and gambling to excess but the idea of being addicted to something scares me so much that I think that's what has kept me away from things.

Despite being 'good Catholics' my parents were far from innocent. My father drank way too much, way too often, and my mother was highly addicted to my father. Unable to function without him, despite the fact that he'd beat the crap out of her. It was unhealthy for anyone and it was unhealthy to grow up in.

Looking back on it now, I can almost say that their disowning me was a blessing. It forced me to move on, be independent and it pulled me away from them. But I also spent a lot of time trying to recoup myself. Spending a lot of time in semi-abusive relationships. Though never physical, but certainly emotionally abusive. The man I lost my virginity to is a shining example of emotionally abusive. He was very good at putting me down and bringing me down on more than a few occasions. Finally, I'd just had enough. Though if you were to ask him, he broke up with me.

I fight to shrug off all thoughts of past lives and move back into the moment, this moment.

Dex's addiction is very real. And while I would love to see him finish his piece, and there is a good likelihood that he will add a piece for that day at some point, I want to see him finish it because it is unfinished. Not because he continues to fight with his addiction. Somewhere in the back of my mind, I wonder if I can become his new addiction. Become his new source of pain therapy. But then that nagging little voice in the back of my head is screaming at me that I'm stupid for even considering the idea of any type of future with Dex. I'm here; I'm in the moment, but what about when Cami calls me back to Los Angeles? Or when the tour breaks in a couple weeks, and I don't get to get back on board.

I'm afraid it's too soon for me to be able to fully commit to him. But it's not going to stop me from having a good time while I'm here. I wonder idly if I can tell Cami, who needs an answer by tomorrow, yes and then back out later. What would those consequences be?

I look over at the bedside clock and fifteen minutes have passed since Dex's last message. I expected him to be pounding down my door by now.

My phone chimes.

Dex: Open your door before I get a key.
Raine: Can't, sorry. Naked.
Pound, knock, growl. "Open up, princess."

I hop up out of bed and unlatch the door, then swing it open, holding on to it and stretching my arm out to brace against the frame and I hang onto the door's edge.

"Fuck me," Dex growls as he charges into the room, wrapping his arms around me and picking me up. I wasn't kidding, I'm completely naked.

His lips land on mine and his knees run into the bed. I pull back. "You're supposed to be sleeping," I playfully scold him.

"I'd rather be sleeping with you." His lips come back to mine and desire ignites full force. I wrap my legs around his hips and hold him to me. I can't help but grind my pussy against his nylon shorts covered cock. He moans and I grind again. "You naughty fucking girl," he growls and he lays me down on the bed.

I feel him searching, fishing for something. "What are you doing?"

Then his hand comes out with a condom in it. I grab it from him and throw it on the floor. "We've breached that barrier, so to speak, no going back." I smile sweetly.

The next thing I know, his shorts are coming down, his cock is slapping against my pussy, and he lines himself up and slams into me.

"Ahh, fuck," I cry out. He stills. "Jesus, don't stop," I whine and he smiles wickedly at me. "Fuck me, Dex," I growl; ready to just let it all go. "Take me," I moan as he thrusts in and pulls out. In and out. The head of his cock rubbing along that special spot, my legs tremble.

His head dips, taking a tender nipple into his mouth, the pain quickly melts into pleasure and I moan. He doesn't let up, sucking and flicking his tongue against the tight pebble. He lets that nipple go, and licks along my chest until he pulls the other one into his mouth. I put my hands into his hair, holding him to me, but that's not what he wants. He rears up, off my nipple, and he steadies himself quickly and grabs my wrists. He pulls them from his hair and pins them over my head. I wrap my legs around his waist as he continues sliding his hard cock deeper into my pussy. His hands are hard and heavy over my head and his lips land on mine, soft and passionate.

I moan into his mouth as he swallows my cries of pleasure. I pull my head back, gasping for air. "Fuck," I cry out and he slams into me harder. There's a stab of pain that is quickly washed away when he withdraws and slams in again. "Dex!" I cry out. "I'm...fuck...I'm coming." My legs tighten around his hips, the orgasm he started with the look in his eyes the minute I opened the door is boiling now. Ready to unleash, to explode. I bite my lips and he grunts.

"Give it to me, Raine," he growls, and I release my lip as my orgasm explodes all over his cock and he thrusts harder into me. Pushing past the tight squeezes of my entrance, milking him, sucking him in deeper, he explodes inside me as he calls out my name.

dex

"Come on, sweet girl. Let's go to bed," I say quietly as we break from a kiss.

"It's like eight o'clock." She giggles.

"Well, I didn't say we had to sleep." I smirk at her and wiggle my eyebrows.

'Horny bastard." She laughs.

"I resemble that remark." I kiss her again and reach down, behind her, pulling back the covers. Then I set her back on her feet. Fuck, there is nothing in this world more gorgeous than when she is completely naked. "Climb in, princess." She smiles and lies down. I lean down and kiss her forehead. "I'll be back in ten minutes."

"Where are you going?"

"Just going to run to my room, grab some clean clothes. I too have to be up early tomorrow. We have a show."

"Stay, we'll get clothes tomorrow." I kneel down. "I really want to fall asleep with you," she says and yawns. "I won't make it until you get back."

I smile, stand up and strip off my shorts. He's wide awake of course and it doesn't go unnoticed by Raine. I watch as she licks her lips. "You're a dirty girl."

"Horny bastard," she mumbles as she reaches out for my cock. I don't stop her. She's been begging to suck my cock and frankly, I'm tired of rejecting her. Her hand wraps around the base of my cock and she pulls, pulling me closer to her. I step closer and watch as she wraps her lips around the crown.

"Ahh, fuck," I moan out as her tongue strokes along the underside, tickling that super sensitive, sweet spot. Then she strokes up and sucks me down her throat. I wrap my hand in her hair and she moans, sending vibrations along my cock and straight into my balls. My knees wobble and I fight the urge to call out. I add my other hand to her hair, holding her head to me. When my fingers slide along her scalp, I can feel three raised scars. One is very long. The other two are shorter. I pull my hand back.

She releases my cock. "It's okay." She looks up at me. "It doesn't hurt. I like it when you put your hands in my hair." I smile at her and she strokes upward. My eyes roll up, what I wanted to say dies on my lips and I can't remember when her tongue strokes along my shaft once more. She begins licking and sucking, the mission clear. She wants to make me come.

I step back, out of reach. She pouts at me. "I have a better idea," I tell her and she smiles, throwing the covers off of her. I shake my head. "Cover yourself back up," I say with a smile. She smiles back and covers up. I walk around the bed and climb in on the other side and I spoon behind her. My cock presses along the crack of her ass and she grinds her hips into me. "You've got to be sore," I whisper.

"I am," she says softly. "But I enjoy it too much when you're inside me. "

"Good," I say into her hair and kiss her head. "Relax for me, princess," I tell her quietly and she settles in. I push her right leg, the one on top, forward. "Bend it for me." She does and she's half on her stomach and I run my hand up the seam of her cunt. She's wet already and I love it. "Is this for me?" I ask her.

"Yes," she moans as I find her clit with my finger. She squirms and pushes her pussy back into my hand.

"So eager."

"It feels so good." I continue playing with her clit until I know she's close and I can feel her pussy get warmer and wetter. I pull my hand away and she groans.

I grab my cock and run it along the same seam and she moans, relaxing further into the mattress, giving me more access as I start to push inside her from behind. She adjusts, allowing herself to slide down further on me and I keep pushing forward until I'm buried as far as I can go. It's like heaven, steel wrapped in silk and I won't be able to sit still for long. I wrap my arm around her, snuggling into her and holding her to me as I find the leverage I need to slide slowly in and out of her.

Her pussy is so tight, I have to fight the need to come the minute I'm inside. Skin to skin is something that's so amazing, so perfect, I'm so glad she's my first.

The thought occurs to me that maybe, just maybe, this woman may be that last notch.

"Oh god," she cries out, and her pussy tightens around my shaft, but she's not quite there. Not yet.

"Close your eyes, and just feel it," I whisper into her ear. I slide my hand under her arm and find a perfect nipple. Thick, long and hard. I play with it gently and she relaxes a little more, giving me more room and more access to tug and twist.

"Fuck!" she mewls and I'm so fucking close. I need her to join me. I can't come without her. I need to feel her orgasm.

"There's no place I'd rather be than right here," I tell her. "Buried in you, claiming you."

"Fuck, Dex!"

"I love it when you scream my name."

I slam into her. "Dex," she cries out as I slide out and slide home again. I start to tug on the nipple between my fingers. Her arm comes up, wrapping around my head, her fingers slide into my hair and she tightens her fist. Pulling hard.

"Argh." I slam into her, pulling on her nipple harder, and her hand pulls harder.

I adjust myself by getting my left arm under me, and lifting myself up so that I am over her. Her hip hits my pelvic bone and she rolls her shoulders back, exposing her nipples to be licked and sucked. My hands are on her hip and thigh, pushing down as I slam harder into her. Her eyes roll up. "Don't. Stop," she moans and I take her nipple into my mouth. Her hand comes back into my hair and I can't resist the nip and pull of her nipple in my mouth. Her pussy spasms, her hand tightens, her legs lock down and my cock explodes, tipping us both over the edge and into oblivion.

chapter
45
raine

Once our breathing returned to normal, Dex wrapped himself around me from behind. His cock is soft and my eyelids will no longer open. He's holding me tightly to his body, like he needs me to breathe, to survive, and it comforts me as I fall asleep wrapped in his arms and his warmth.

When the alarm fires off at six thirty, my eyes barely want to open. But I manage to see the alarm clock enough to turn it off, or hit the snooze, not sure which. Dex is no longer wrapped around me but the soft snoring coming from behind me tells me that he didn't hear it. Taking my chance, I roll over softly and watch him sleep.

He looks ten years younger, so peaceful in sleep. I can see how vulnerable this man really is and my heart melts a little more for him.

He scared the hell out of me last night when he said something about me going back to California. I was so afraid that's what he would want and it was stupid of me to think that he would really want me to stick around. It was rather selfish of me to think that my climbing on board would be anything but professional. I just assumed that my climbing on board would mean that we could possibly further our relationship. If that's what this is.

The sex is off the fucking charts amazing. I've never felt so whole and complete when sleeping with someone and ironically enough, being with Dex is the first time I don't feel dirty or like I'm doing something scandalous while having sex. I know it probably sounds ridiculously stupid, but it's the truth. Yes, I've only slept with a handful of men, but none of them have ever treated me the way Dex does, has.

He's conscious of my body, what I'm feeling, making sure I'm not hurting and even more importantly, it's very important to him that I come first or with him and I adore that about him.

I said yesterday that we weren't a couple, that I needed him to prove to me that he really wanted this before I could make that kind of commitment, but in reality, it almost feels like I need that commitment to know that he's going to be with me and me alone. Sure, I'm fresh, I'm new, but what's going to stop him from turning on the assholian switch and finding someone else to sleep with?

"What are you thinking about so hard?" I start a little. I hadn't realized he'd woken up.

"Good morning." He rolls toward me and kisses me sweetly on the nose, and then he settles back, with his elbow bent and his head on his hand. He looks so young and sexy like that.

"Good morning, beautiful," he says back with a smile.

"Did you sleep well?" I ask him, deflecting his question.

"Stop deflecting, answer my question, please."

"I was wondering how long this was going to last."

He raises an eyebrow at me. "Elaborate, please?"

"I'm worried about the assholian returning. Finding something better, greener, and then what?"

He reaches over and tucks a stray strand of hair behind my ear. "No one compares to you." He smiles.

"Now, sure. This is new, fun, fresh, it's easy, but what happens if we fight? Or I do something you don't like?"

'What do you want, Raine?" he asks questioningly.

"I think I'm starting to rethink the whole boyfriend - girlfriend thing."

"Okay now you have no choice, explain please," he says slightly exasperated and I don't blame him, I'm being unintentionally vague with him and I'd be getting pissed too.

"Remember yesterday, when I told you that I needed a chance to see, to know, to feel that this between us is real?" He nods. "And I said that I needed to be able trust that you won't run off with the next piece of ass that captures your attention? Sure, it's easy to look the other way now, but I realize that this will only get stronger. What I'm feeling is only going to get stronger and I need to decide whether to cut it off now, or jump in with both feet and see if I can swim." By the time I'm done, I'm whispering.

He doesn't say anything right away but his hand comes to rest on mine. "I don't have a clue how to do this, a relationship. Aside from the guys, and maybe even Addison, I don't have relationships with people, friendships or sexual. The guys are not my friends, they are my family. They put up with my shit. They deal with my being an assholian." I snort at my name for him and he smiles. "They don't judge, and I would do anything for any of them, without hesitation. In fact, I have. But had it not been for me, 69 Bottles would have died before we even got started. Talon, Eric, Calvin, and Kyle are the reason I stayed sober. They're the reason I was able to get up every day and function. They are the reason I am able to do the one thing in the world that I love more than anything, play music. I kept the band afloat. When we were out of money, needed new equipment, needed a new van to travel around to the bars, I paid for all of it. Minus the money we'd made at different gigs. It's the reason I'm the primary payee of the band, at least until I'm paid back, but that's moot." He takes a deep breath. "My point is this, if I bring you into this circle, my circle, my family, it will be impossible for me to let you go. The idea of another woman makes me sick. There is no woman out there that makes me feel the way you do, that makes me wish I was a better person, or that makes me feel worthy of being in her presence like you do. I've told you already that I will find a way to fuck this up. Without a doubt, I am going to hurt you along the way, but I can tell you this, no woman holds a candle to you, so finding another woman that will turn my head is impossible. I also know that I need to prove that to you. Whether we're 'officially' a couple or not, the rules remain the same. I respect you too much to ruin this when it's only just beginning."

He wipes a tear away from my cheek. "I'm sorry, I don't mean to cry," I mumble and wipe the rest of them away.

dex

I left Raine shortly after our relationship talk. I'm not entirely sure what to make of it anymore. I am so fucking confused about how I feel about this girl. I mean, come on, for the first time in my life, I don't want anyone else. For the first time in my life, I feel like...like I've found my equal.

When I return to the hotel after beating away like an idiot on my set, or a giddy school boy with new toys, depending on how you want to look at it, I'm standing in the hallway talking to the guys about our plans for the rest of our stay in DC, though there does not seem to be too many at this point. When I'm asked about going out, I decline, but not fast enough. Raine opens her door and joins in the conversation.

I watch as she steps back, toward her door, holding it open for me.

"Are you coming or what?" she says softly and I can't help sauntering toward her.

"Not yet, but I plan to be," I tell her with an evil smirk on my face.

"Does that fucking line ever work?" Peacock says and he laughs. I'm too distracted to really care.

I watch as she looks around me, finding the guys. "I'll let you know later tonight," she giggles.

"No way," someone says.

"Why is it always the fucked up drummer that gets the girl?" Mouse says, jokingly.

"Tell me about it," Beck says and the rest of them just laugh. She grabs my hand, pulling me into the room.

Just as the door closes someone says, "Lucky bastard."

chapter 46
raine

"He's right. I am one lucky bastard. Though I'm disappointed."

My smile falls.

He laughs.

"Why?" I say sheepishly.

"Because you're not waiting, naked, in bed for me." His expression is hard, but his eyes speak another language altogether.

"I'm sorry. You said ten minutes. I haven't slept, so I either needed to get up or you would have found me asleep. When I heard the commotion in the hall, I... I'm sorry."

He runs a finger down my cheek. I look up to him and the little crinkles in his eyes are there and I know that he's happy to see me, regardless of my disobeying his request. "Sweet girl. You should probably sleep."

I shake my head. "I've been waiting all day to see you." My candor surprises him and even me.

"You really meant it when you said you missed me?"

"Didn't you?" I ask.

"I did, very much miss you today," he tells me with a smile.

"Well, I did too. It sucked being here, in this room without you." I give him a small smile.

His hands cup my cheeks and he tilts my head up. "Well, I'm here now," he says as he lays a firm kiss against my lips. My body ignites with need and all sense of tiredness is gone in a flash. I would stay awake for days if it meant him kissing me like this. My hands go to his shirt and I tug on the hem, trying to tell him that I want it off of him and he shakes his head against my lips. "Not yet," he whispers and goes back to kissing me. I deflate and he smiles before kissing me harder. Running his tongue along my bottom lip, tasting and teasing me. I do the same, but he still won't let me in.

"You're mean," I whisper and he chuckles. Then, he takes advantage of my position. Defenseless, I feel his thumbs graze across my cheek and I let out a rushed breath and he steals his chance. Sliding his tongue lightning fast into my mouth and my heart starts beating faster sending blood rushing through my ears. My inability to breathe causes me to sway as his tongue dances with mine.

My body heats, my pussy warms and my clit throbs, remembering just how wonderful that same tongue feels against my clit. Finally his hands come away from my face but he doesn't stop kissing me. I whimper at the loss of the warmth in his hands, and then shiver when I feel his hands skim across my breasts. My nipples harden fast and he quickly finds them through the shirt. I quiver with excitement and moan into his mouth.

He pulls back from his kiss and lifts my shirt. "I need to see you," he breathes as I lift my arms. Giving him what he wants. A view of my body. Once my shirt is tossed aside, he pushes down on the waist of my pajama bottoms and they quickly fall to the floor. I'd thrown them on in my haste to get to the door, so I'm wearing nothing underneath. His breathing stutters as his eyes rake over my body and he takes a step back. His eyes are hooded and dark. Something about them has me desperate to be on my knees. To please him.

I step out of my pajamas while maintaining eye contact with him. I lower myself to the floor. Tucking my feet up underneath me, I spread my knees wide and lower my head.

He hisses through his teeth. "I told you I had other ideas about how to handle what happened today. On the night stand you will find a few things that may or may not interest you. Everything there is something I am comfortable with at this stage. My safe word is kit kat. Your safe word is sunshine. Tonight, I am at your service, Sir."

He brings his hand to my cheek, gently stroking it and I lean into it. "Look at me, sweet girl." I do as he's asked and I raise my eyes to him. "Do you have any idea what you're offering me here?" I nod. "Say it."

"Yes, Sir."

"Do you have any idea how hard it is for me to accept your offer?"

Learning from his last request, I say, "No, Sir."

He smiles then he kneels down in front of me. "You, sweet, gorgeous girl, are more than I could ever ask for. But I do not trust myself enough to not hurt you. Not yet. While I don't mind the idea of what may be on that table, and while I don't mind the idea of using something from that table on you tonight, I want for us both to have good solid discussions about what we want, what we like, what we don't want, or don't like before we travel down this path together."

"It is a path I know I want to take with you," I say softly.

"And I with you, but there is so much more to this than me taking advantage of your willingness to submit to me. And right now, I feel that is what I would be doing if we did this tonight." I nod. Sadness creeps in. "But I do want you to do something for me tonight."

"Anything," I say without thinking. Dex smiles at me.

"Do to me what you will."

I gasp. "Why is it okay for me to..."

"Because, I don't trust myself to not hurt you but I know that at least for tonight, that I don't need pain to cure what happened. That I just need you." He rears up, grabs my cheeks in his hands. "I need to be buried in you. That will be enough for my penance for now." His lips slam hard and fast in to mine and I take his hands in mine as he holds my head in his. Holding him to me, I kiss him back.

What I'd planned to be the perfect gift for him, ends up being a better gift for me. I pull back. "I have one request," I say to him.

"What's that?"

I get to my feet and as I do, he reluctantly lets me go. I walk over to the table and I grab the one thing I bought today that I was truly hoping he'd use on me tonight and return to him with it behind my back. "Close your eyes," I say, a little command in my voice and he smiles, closing his eyes. I bring it around to the front and hold it so that he can see it when he opens his eyes. "Open," I say as the fur lined leather cuffs hang off my finger.

His eyes go wide with fear and he swallows hard. I vow to examine that reaction later, but for now, I let it go.

"They're not for you," I tell him and he immediately relaxes. "Please?" I beg him.

He stands up. His demeanor has changed slightly, but not in a bad way. His eyes go dark again. "On the bed. Now," he orders and I give him a wicked smile as I climb up onto the bed. At the same time, he pulls his shirt up over his head.

Once I'm on the bed, I lie down and look at him as he loses his jeans, but keeps his boxer briefs in place. I lick my lips. "Enjoying the scenery?"

"Best scenery in DC," I tease him.

He gives me a wicked smirk and climbs onto the bed near my head. I cannot resist the urge and I reach up and run my hand along his rock hard, well-defined erection lying across his pelvis, touching his hipbone. My mouth waters and he shivers. He grabs my wrist, pulling it up over my head.

The headboard is made of iron bars and before I know it, one wrist is wrapped up in a cuff that he's tightening, but it's not too tight that it will hurt me. I roll toward him, taking my other hand and tugging on the waistband of his underwear and watch as his cock falls out, protruding from his body at full mast. He's so long that I don't have to move very far to lick the bead of cum off of the tip. He twitches. "Ah fuck," he groans and I pull down on his boxer briefs so that he's fully free and I grab his cock with my free hand. Stroking upward, I lick again and suck him into my mouth. "Jesus, fuck," he growls and I keep licking and sucking, pumping my fist up and down, hoping to push him beyond his control so that he has no choice but to let me finish him off with my mouth.

I look up into his eyes. They're dark, hooded and the most exquisite pleasure is radiating off of him. I moan around his cock. He makes no move to stop me, but he also makes no advance on me either. He's holding my cuffed wrist at the headboard so I can't get both hands into the action. I tug and he smirks.

I pout.

He laughs and goes for my free wrist with his free hand. I still have his cock in my face so I lick it again and manage to suck it into my mouth before he's pulling my arm back to the point of forcing me to roll onto my back once again. He makes quick work of the cuff and I am effectively immobilized.

"Now that is one beautiful sight to see," he groans as he climbs back off of the bed, shedding his shorts at the same time. I moan as I watch his cock move and bounce as he walks from the bed over to the counter.

I watch as he leans down into the mini-bar fridge and his ass is on full display for me to see. I groan. I can see his shoulders shaking with silent laughter as he does a few somethings in the fridge before standing. I watch him grab a glass off of the counter and I hear the clinking of ice as it falls into the tumbler.

As he turns, I watch his cock as it moves and twitches then when he's totally facing me, my eyes travel up his abs, up his naked chest and finally to meet his bright, excited eyes.

With his free hand, he grabs his cock and begins to stroke it. My nipples harden and my clit throbs. I do my best to scissor my legs together, seeking the relief I so desperately need and it isn't there and it isn't coming for me.

He keeps stroking his cock as he watches me being tortured on the bed. "What a gorgeous princess you are," he says and I shiver. He slowly starts to walk toward the bed, bringing with him his glass of ice.

"What's that for?"

He gives me a wicked grin. "You," he says as he pops an ice cube into his mouth. He walks around the bed, setting the glass gently on the table and he kneels up onto the bed. The ice is still in his mouth, and he works it around with his tongue. When he's satisfied, he adds the ice back to the glass and he leans over and sucks my left nipple into his mouth. I cry out. The searing flash of hot and cold make my body come alive and my back arch. "More?" he asks as my breast falls from his mouth.

"Yes!" I cry out.

chapter
47
raine

Dex quickly captures my mouth with his. Still cold from the ice he had there a moment ago. I moan again and fight to find some relief from the overwhelming sensations in my clit. It's almost painful.

He pulls back and reaches for his glass. "Please," I beg.

"What do you want, princess?" he asks huskily and I groan.

"I don't want. I need."

He smiles wide. "And just what is it that you think you need?"

"You. I need you." My eyes dart to the clinking glass and I shiver knowing that he's absolutely not done torturing me. I watch as he pulls out a fresh cube. "No. No, no." I whine and he laughs.

"Yes," he grins.

I watch as he sets the glass back down, but he doesn't put the cube in his mouth. "Oh god," I groan. He situates himself, straddling my legs, forcing me to sit still and I try in vain to buck him off which only makes his cock bounce against my mound.

"Am I hurting you?" he asks, concerned.

"No. You're torturing me."

"Good."

"You're a little too excited about this you know," I tease him and he wiggles his eyebrows as he holds the cube over my stomach and it starts to drip down. I flinch with each cold drop that lands and starts to pool in the hollow of my stomach. My nipples are hard as diamonds and could easily cut glass, but he sees the effect the dripping water is having on me so he moves his hand around, up over my breasts and the moment the first drop hits my nipple, I arch, crying out and his mouth quickly seals around it. Cold and hot mix in a delicious concoction of pleasure and pain.

He hasn't moved his hand so the ice continues to drip. He sits back up and puts the cube in his mouth. I groan and he smiles. Holding the cube between his lips, he leans down and circles a nipple then trails the ice across my chest to the other nipple. Then he moves higher, bringing it to my neck and up to my jaw and finally over my mouth. The air in the room moves across the icy trail he's just left on my body and I shiver again as he brushes the ice across my lips. I open my mouth slightly and take the cube from him and quickly chew it up.

"Uh," he says with a laugh. He's shocked and I want to laugh but I'm afraid I'll choke. "You stole my ice cube." He's so cute when he's happily playing with me. He reaches over for the glass again and I squirm.

"I don't know how much..."

He brings a finger to my lips, shushing me. "You know your safe word."

I pucker my lips and kiss the calloused pad. "Never," I smirk. I've just issued a challenge and I see the recognition in his eyes, but I know he'd never push me to that.

In order for him to reach the glass he has to climb off of me. One flick of his tongue against my clit or a thrust into my dripping pussy will send me over the edge. I've never been as turned on as I am right now. My clit feels like it has swollen to massive proportions.

I watch as he quickly pops a cube into his mouth and he slides down the bed. He lifts my leg and I moan as he takes up residence right where I need him the most. I feel his cool finger running up and down the seam of my sex and I squirm. He presses in a little further, teasing my entrance and ignoring my clit. "Please," I beg.

That's when it happens. His mouth lands on my clit. I'd forgotten about the ice in his mouth and the extreme cold against my warmth is nearly painful, but I explode around him. Coming hard and fast. My eyes slam closed, my hands tug at my bindings, my back arches and he quickly slides a finger inside me, milking my orgasm for everything it's worth. I can't breathe. My orgasm is so intense that it's stolen all ability to function. His tongue doesn't stop, causing my legs to twitch and he presses with great force and almost immediately pushing me toward another orgasm. Then he presses the ice to my clit. The little that is left in his mouth quickly dissolves. Ice-cold water runs down to his hand and the entrance of my pussy.

The sensation is so overwhelming and I try in vain to pull away from him, but his other hand holds me steady. I try to grind my sex against his mouth silently begging him to suck and lick faster. "Please," I cry out.

"What do you need, princess?"

"You, please, I need you inside me, fucking me."

He hisses through his teeth and pulls his hands away from me as he rears up. He positions himself and lifts my legs higher, allowing him easier access to my dripping pussy. He's watching me, looking at my pussy. I can feel the remains of my orgasm in my muscles as they spasm. "So fucking gorgeous," he says reverently and I feel the head of his cock at the very entrance of my sex, but he has my legs pushed up toward my chest and I have no leverage to move.

"God, Dex, Please. Take. Me. Fuck me."

His eyes meet mine. There is an unspoken question in his eyes with a hint of concern.

"Please, take me," I whisper and he slides in hard and fast. I cry out and my eyes close. "Fuck," I scream.

He pulls back slowly and I open my eyes, trying to convey to him that I'm okay and he needs to continue. "Don't. Stop," I say between ragged breaths.

He smiles and slides in again. Then out and back in. He leans forward, placing my legs on his shoulders as he starts to really slide in and out of me. I fight my bindings because the need to touch him is too much, but he ignores the noise as he leans down further, pushing my knees to my chest and lifting my pussy to the perfect angle, allowing him to slide deeper inside of me and I can feel him rubbing along my g-spot. My walls tighten around him.

"So fucking tight. So. Fucking. Good," he says between thrusts. His breathing is ragged like mine. He reaches up and moves my legs off of his shoulders, but his thighs keep me held higher. His cock drives harder and deeper inside me. He reaches up over my head and I can feel him messing with the cuffs. His motions slow. "I need you to touch me," he breathes and as soon as my hands are free, I wrap my legs around him and he moves down so that I can wrap my arms around his neck. Holding him to me. I run a hand into his hair, making a fist and his eyes roll up. "Harder," he growls.

I pull on his hair harder and he pulls his head back, roaring. With my other hand, I run it along his chest, over his nipples and his breathing becomes shorter, raspier, and I realize I've found a sweet spot with him. I release his hair and lift myself up. I run a wet fat tongue over his nipple and he trembles. I repeat the process, making his nipple pebble as I suck and nibble. When there is a flash of pain, his cock twitches inside me. "More," he demands and I move to the other nipple. Repeating the process but this time I bite harder. "God, Jesus. Fuck!" he continues with a string of expletives and I can no longer hold my head up. Falling back to the mattress, he pounds into me harder and I can feel it. My orgasm building, threatening to ruin the moment, but I know he has to be close.

He sits up straighter. His back arches as he pounds into me. The muscles of my sex clamp down hard, my legs start to shake and he knows I'm close. "Fuck," I cry out. My back arches and the angle changes so that his cock rubs me just right. Just right to cause me pain and just right that my orgasm explodes, literally. I shatter. Lost in bliss.

chapter
48
dex

I've been beating away on the new heads of my drums for the last little while. Trying to wrap my head around what happened with Raine this afternoon.

I can't quite seem to understand. She was so open, willing and...Jesus, I'm turning into a fucking sap.

The show tonight has a little bit different line up, which isn't uncommon for Sunday shows, but tonight is definitely different than a Friday night. We have two opening acts, the girl group that joined us after the Dallas incident with Addison, Tender Souls, and another band of dicks. I don't bother to learn their names. The show is still starting at eight, the one hit wonder group will get twenty minutes and Tender Souls gets their usual thirty-five minutes, so we won't take the stage until almost nine.

While walking back, after running a final check on the set I bought in New York, I walk past the dressing room that has the one night band in it. I freeze. *Damn it. No, no fuck no! Keep moving, you idiot, keep fucking walking.*

That all too familiar ache returns, the drive, the desire, the...fuck!

"Dex." I don't look up to see who's calling my name. I can't fucking look away.

That's when something stronger fights through the fog, something familiar, something like home. It touches my arm, it radiates into my heart and throughout my body. I look into ice blue eyes. There's fear in hers, concern. Without even really knowing what I'm doing, I cup her face in my hands and slant my lips over hers. Savoring her sweet cherry taste, the chocolate scent of her skin, and the softness of her flesh as her lips move to kiss me back. With the warm wetness of her tongue against mine, the burn of addiction dies within me. Washed away by this gorgeous woman.

This woman who's unraveling everything I know about myself, the woman who I want desperately to have in my arms, to hold her, to caress her, to adore her. To worship the ground she walks on. The princess that she is. I no longer feel the desperate need to find a spot for new ink, to find..."Fuck," I growl as I pull back from her lips. "Take my face," I tell her. She obeys, cupping my cheeks in her soft warm palms. "Hold me tight and back the fuck up," I growl. She starts to look into the room. "No. Don't. Please, just back up. Pull me with you. Look into my eyes, Raine." I plead and her eyes lock hard on mine. She takes one step back, followed by another, and then finally I manage to get my feet walking, to get my feet going forward.

"You're all right, bubba. Come on. You got this. I got you," she says, but I'm too distracted by her eyes, the way they aren't judging me. They aren't angry or scared, she's simply seeing me, seeing into me and seeing a part of me that I'd hoped she'd never see in person, but I'm also seeing the one thing in life that means more to me than drugs.

Her.

She's claimed me. I'm addicted to her.

I crave her.

She redeems me.

She's taming me.

Did you enjoy Taming Dex?
Please consider leaving a review on your retailer of
choice (Amazon, Barnes & Noble, iTunes, Kobo, etcetera)

Thank you for purchasing and reading Taming Dex. I
truly hope you enjoyed reading their story as much as I
enjoyed writing it.

Their saga continues in ***Devouring Raine, releasing July
2015.***

Find Zoey on Social Media or sign up for her newsletter
for all the latest news. (Turn the page for all those details)

Zoey's Bio:

Zoey Derrick is a Best Selling Author of Contemporary, Erotic, Erotic Romance and Paranormal Romance from Glendale Arizona. She was once a mortgage underwriter and she now writes full time.

She writes stories as hot as the desert sun itself. It is this passion that drips off of her work, bringing excitement to anyone who enjoys a good and sensual love story.

Not only does she aim to take her readers on an erotic dance that lasts the night, it allows her to empty her mind of stories we all wish were true.

Her stories are hopeful yet true to life, skillfully avoiding melodrama and the unrealistic, bringing her gripping Erotica only closer to the heart of those that dare dipping into it.

The intimacy of her fantasies that she shares with her readers is thrilling and encouraging, climactic yet full of suspense. She is a loving mistress, up for anything, of which any reader is doomed to return to again and again.

Stalk Zoey on Social Media:

Facebook
Twitter

Website:
www.zoeyderrick.com

www.ingramcontent.com/pod-product-compliance
Lightning Source LLC
Chambersburg PA
CBHW020244200626

46816CB00001BA/126